firegold

firegold

Dia Calhoun

Pictures by Hervé Blondon

WINSLOW PRESS

I would like to thank my family, friends,
editor, and all those who helped with this book.
Special thanks to Anna, Joan, and
Chuck Hommel for the Loft.

Text copyright © 1999 by Dia Calhoun
Illustrations copyright © 1999 by Hervé Blondon
All rights reserved
Library of Congress catalog card number: 98-89830
Printed in the United States of America
Designed by Bretton Clark
First edition, 1999

For Shawn,
and the farm.

part one

The colt

chapter one

W hen Jonathon cast his line toward the boulder that split the river, he didn't see the girl crouched in its shadow, peering around the edge. The line whisked through the air and unfurled across the current until the fly dimpled the eddy behind the boulder. The water exploded as a fish struck.

Jonathon's arm snapped high, setting the hook. He had it! Suddenly, the line slackened and the fish vanished.

"Blast," he said, then frowned at the October sun splintering through the cottonwood leaves. If he didn't leave soon, he would be late for lunch, and he was already in enough trouble.

He raised the rod one last time, lifting the line of braided horsehair off the water. As it sailed behind him, he saw the girl climb around the boulder and perch on a ledge only inches above the swirling water. She leaned in, holding an out-cropping of rock; it looked as if the boulder were a mountain and she were holding it up. She wore a hat, which rose into points high above each ear, and a white deerskin tunic over brown leggings. A small bow hung over her shoulder.

But girls always wear dresses, Jonathon thought, letting the line fly back toward the water. The girl reached up as though trying to catch it and stepped out of the shade and into the light. The sun flamed her red hair—red striped with gold. No one in the South Valley had such hair, no one. All at once, Jonathon knew who she was. Fear filled his throat until he couldn't swallow or even breathe—the girl was a barbarian, a Dalriada from the Red Mountains.

His line puddled onto the water. I'm a boy and bigger, too, he argued with his fear. But she was a Dalriada. He had never seen one before, only heard the terrible whispered tales.

Another fish grabbed the fly. Again Jonathon's arm jerked up, and the rod arched like a fighting cat. The huge, speckled fish jumped, tracing silver arcs against the boulder. Fascinated, the girl leaned farther out, not twelve yards away. Jonathon gripped the rod so hard it seemed to press through his skin and into the bone. What if she nocked an arrow to her bow?...

Then he saw the color of her eyes, and the line slipped from his fingers. Her eyes were blue, as blue as a lupine—as blue as his.

The fish dashed down river. Jonathon snapped the tension back in the line as the fish tried to circle a sunken log. Struggling to keep the rod tip up, Jonathon eased the fish out of the fast water where the river roiled silver and white.

With one eye on the girl, he heaved the fish, an elger, into the air and backed away from the river's edge. The knobheaded elger gasped, pulled into a strange world where it could not breathe, where its thrashing tail could not propel it to safety.

Jonathon grabbed a rock and hit the fish's head. Wincing, he hit it again, a hard, fast mercy. The elger flopped once more and died. Although his stomach tightened, Jonathon's chest lifted with pride: the fish measured longer than his arm.

Out on the boulder, the girl kicked her leg in the water, splashing it into spires of light.

Blondon

"Eir-a! Eir-a!" someone called, half obscured in the shadows across the river.

The girl turned. On the far bank, through the sweeping willows, Jonathon saw the glint of horses, magnificent horses: bays, browns, chestnuts, and silver roans. The roar of the current had covered their sound. Only the water of the Mirandin River flowed between the Dalriadas and him, but Jonathon knew they could not cross, not here where the water ran deep and swift, though their arrows could.

His legs longed to run. Every tale he had ever heard about the Dalriadas flashed through his mind. They were barbarians who worshipped the sky and scorned the ways of the Valley. Flaming horns spiked from their heads. With their dark, magical powers, they sent nightmares and cursed crops, bringing verblight and barrenness to the land. Worst of all, they ate raw human flesh.

"Eir-a!" the voice called again.

The girl clambered back around the boulder and looked at a smaller rock poking out of the river some six feet away. It was the first in a series of stepping stones leading to the far shore, stones so far apart that Jonathon imagined only a deer could leap from one to another.

The girl jumped. She bounded from stone to stone, her feet hardly pausing on one before she was soaring through the air again, her strange red hair streaming behind her. When she reached the shore, she turned and looked back at him.

Magic, Jonathon thought, his hands trembling as he wound his line and hefted the fish. With his eyes on the girl, he walked toward her, toward the river's edge and the thicket of wild-rose bushes that led home.

Then she smiled at him. She pressed both palms together, wiggling them through the air like a fish swimming. Her face was the color of a peach. Where were her horns? he wondered. Were they hidden beneath the points on her hat?

He crashed into the thicket, braced to feel an arrow pierce his back. Thorns scratched his arms. His mind filled with the image of a glacier-hewn mountain, with the scent of a dry hunt, with the splendor of horses who might have sprung from his dreams. What was happening to him?

On the far side of the thicket, he faced the Mirandin again, but here it churned through a gorge. He had been fishing on the tip of a peninsula that connected to the western shore a quarter of a mile south. Now, with the Dalriadas near, a quarter of a mile seemed like a hundred.

Jonathon saw a shortcut—a log spanned the foam-flecked water. If he crossed it, he could escape to the western shore in less than a minute. He hesitated, watching the spray rake over the slick log. Cross, he told himself. Hurry. He stepped up, but instantly slipped on the wood and pitched backwards. By twisting in midair, he managed to land on his feet. The log was too dangerous.

He backed away from it, turned, and raced down the peninsula. One by one, the red-winged blackbirds stopped spinning out their songs and scattered from the brush. The elger slapped against his thigh.

Beyond the gorge, the river widened, slowed, then spilled in a shallow stream over the neck of the peninsula. Jonathon plunged through the knee-deep water, fighting the current. He slogged up the bank, burst into a run, then tripped, his rod flying one way, the elger another.

Half-dazed, Jonathon sprawled on the ground. His forehead throbbed where a rock dug into his eyebrow. He sat up and blinked. Red as blood, the rock stood out from all the others on the stony bank. Sometimes the Mirandin carried rocks down from the Red Mountains, pounding them to pebbles by the time they washed ashore this far south.

Jonathon had seen maps and knew the Mirandin's source lay north, high in the snowmelt of the Red Mountains, where the elgers spawned. From there, the river twined through the North Valley, then the arid South Valley, for almost two hundred miles. After that, the land blanched into desert hills. The river threaded those for another hundred miles before it surged into the sea. The elgers traveled all that way and back again.

Jonathon picked up the rock, the size of a grouse egg. Chiseled marks curved around it. As he turned it, the image of a horse took shape—an image that captured the spirit of the Dalriada horses. Jonathon whistled.

"A barbarian must have carved this," he said, marveling at the mane streaming in long, exuberant swirls. He shoved the rock in his pocket.

Suddenly he heard drums beating all around him: slow, then fast, high tones against low tones. He sprang up, but no one moved along the riverbank. His head throbbed. He grabbed his rod and the elger, then sprinted toward home. "Dalriadas!" he tried to shout. "There are Dalriadas in the Valley!" But he had no voice.

The drums pounded on—mad, hypnotic—like a thousand beating hooves until, in the space of a breath, they merged into a single rhythm, the rhythm of his heart.

chapter two

Jonathon ran down Guther's Way and scrambled up the hill into his family's orchard. He dodged branches, leaped irrigation ditches, and burst out onto the road that divided the lower orchard from the upper. He froze. Then he tore across, running two, three, then four rows into the cover of the trees. His side ached, but the drums had stopped pounding.

He tried to think. If the Dalriadas wanted to follow him, they would need to ride a half mile upriver to the ford, cross, and ride back down. Even then they would not know where he had gone, unless…he glanced at the blood seeping from the fish, unless they tracked the blood trail.

Suddenly, he heard the thump of hoofbeats—had the Dalriadas used their magic to leap the river? Jonathon threw himself down in the tall grass and felt the vibrations roll through the earth. Cautiously, he raised his head.

The horse, three rows over, was screened by leaves, but he saw the brown legs bending up and down. A familiar white stocking on the left foreleg flashed—the marking on Sammy, his father's pinto stallion. Jonathon let out a long breath, bending the blades of grass that prickled the scrape on his forehead.

"Jonathon?" his father called as Sammy slowed to a walk.

Torn between his fear of the Dalriadas and his fear of his father's anger, Jonathon hesitated. He should have had a fighting lesson that morning, but he hated them—hated seeing his father's face under the shadow of the twisted oak and hated hearing his father's voice urging him to be strong. To avoid the lesson, he had gone fishing.

"Hey, Jonathon?" his father called again. The silence stretched between them like an invisible string. Jonathon caught a glimpse of his father, still three rows over, as he passed between two apple trees.

Brian Brae's face was eclipsed in the shade of his hat brim. His brown boot gleamed, the black sole at the toe turned up by the stirrup. A sheathed knife hung like a rudder from his hip. He sat straight, holding the reins short in his clamped fists. Then the orchard hid him again, and Sammy's tail swished. Soon even the horse's legs would be out of sight.

Jonathon jumped up to shout the news about the Dalriadas, but his eyes blurred as though fog surrounded him. He blinked hard. Had he hurt his head worse than he thought? That would explain those wild drums. He picked up the elger and his rod, then jogged through the orchard. Five minutes later, he reached his house.

The two-storied white house seemed rooted in the land. Four massive chimneys climbed, river rock by river rock, up the sides. Beneath the roof peak, a round window in the attic stared like an ancient eye. Jonathon's ancestors had built the house over four hundred years ago. The Braes had lived on Greengard Orchards for too many years to count, almost back to the Golden Age, Jonathon's father said.

Outside the kitchen door, Jonathon stopped. He had to tell his parents about the Dalriadas, but how? No one talked openly about them; no one he knew had ever seen them. Until today the Dalriadas had been only a vague fear in his mind, like death or the whirling wind that struck the Valley every thirty years. But now they had a face, the face of a blue-eyed girl.

The fish's gills clamped down on his fingers. Blood, grass, and fish smeared his hands; he couldn't go inside like this. He glanced at the road, expecting to see a charging band of Dalriadas, but only a flurry of dust whizzed along the edge.

Jonathon walked to the vegetable garden, opened his knife, and, with his hands shaking, cleaned the fish faster than he had ever cleaned a fish before. The red rock dug into his thigh. He couldn't wait to show it to Timothy Dakken at the Harvest Supper tomorrow. Not only would Timothy be envious but he might be so impressed that he would stop making wisecracks about Jonathon's blue eyes.

After the fish was clean, Jonathon laid it under the wash-stand beside the kitchen door, then scrubbed his hands and wiped them dry against his hair. He hopped over the daisies that poked between the porch stairs and opened the door.

"But, Karena," his father said, stacking wood into the wood box, "Jonathon has got to be strong. This will toughen him up."

"He is still too young," Jonathon's mother said from the stove. "There are greater dangers, and greater strengths, than those of the body."

The news about the Dalriadas faded on Jonathon's lips. His father straightened and saw him standing by the door.

"Just where have you been?" his father asked, frowning. His eyes flicked from the cupboard to the window to the wrought-iron rack where the copper pots hung, never resting anywhere long. "I told you to meet me under the oak at ten."

Jonathon looked down. "Guess I lost track of time."

"That's three Saturdays running," his father said. "Starting today, boy, you'll muck out Sammy's stall every time you forget."

Karena turned, her hands full of rosemary for the stew bubbling on the stove. Her hair, the color of polished chest-nuts, was tied behind her neck with a red ribbon, then curled to her waist.

"My son," she said. Her eyes, nutmeg brown, looked straight at him. The sun shining through the window touched her face, making one side light, the other dark. When she turned back to the stove, her long skirt swayed. She crushed the rosemary, releasing its pine-wood fragrance, and then dropped the leaves into the stew.

"What am I too young for?" Jonathon asked.

"Hunting in the southern Red Mountains," his father said. "I want to take you this year. I'm leaving at dawn on Monday."

Jonathon couldn't speak. For as long as he could remember he had wanted to join his father on this hunting trip. And after today—his hand curled around the rock in his pocket— he wanted to go more than ever. He wanted to know more about the blue-eyed girl and the Dalriada horses.

"But," his father added, "your ma thinks you're too young."

Jonathon's mother, now chopping carrots, whirled with the knife in her hand. "We've had an agreement about this for years, Brian. Jonathon may go when he turns fourteen. Not before."

"But he's not tough enough for his age," his father said. "When I was twelve, I did a man's work stacking props in the orchard. He's only done a half section of Appelunes."

"Daydreaming slows him," his mother said, "not lack of strength."

Brian sat down at the table. "I don't care about the reason. This trip will make a man of him."

Jonathon rose on the balls of his feet. He imagined himself riding beside his father in the Red Mountains, sharing the silent companionship of men. Maybe then his father wouldn't be ashamed of him.

"I'd sure like to go, Ma," he said. "I'll make up the schoolwork."

"Oh, Jonathon, it isn't that." She wiped her hands on her apron, spattered, like the table, with the applesauce she had been canning. A fabulous cook, his mother never used recipes, but everything tasted wonderful and nothing ever tasted the same twice.

"You don't…shoot your bow well enough yet," she said, putting her hand on his shoulder. "The Red Mountains are full of danger, dangers you can't even imagine. Your pa can't watch you every minute."

"But, Ma," Jonathon said, shrugging off her hand.

"I can protect the boy," his father said.

"That's a great comfort," she said, her shoulders suddenly stiff. "Even in the hills?"

"Yes." The scar over Brian's eyebrow whitened. "And in the mountains too."

"Brian, there are some dangers you can't protect him from."

Jonathon looked from one of his parents to the other and felt a tight, hot ache under his ribs.

"I want him to come," his father said.

"No. He's not ready!" She slammed a jar of applesauce on the table, then put both hands on her hips. "Unless?" Her question hung in the air.

Unless what, Jonathon wondered. His father looked at him, looked straight into his eyes, something he rarely did. Then his head jerked sideways: a short, sharp, "no." At that moment, the sun flashed across the brass lid on the jar.

No.

The word and the brightness fused in Jonathon's mind, and he remembered the first time he had learned he was different.

He had stood here in the kitchen; his eyes came just above the table. On it sat a silver bowl filled with red, green, and yellow apples. Jonathon looked into the silver brightness and saw a face looking back, distorted by the metal. The face had blue eyes. Astonished, he blinked; so did the face. When he raised one hand to touch his eye, a hand entered the reflection and did the same. His heart raced; it was his hand and his eye. Slowly, he looked over the silver bowl and saw his father staring at him across the table, his brown eyes wet. Jonathon opened his mouth to ask…but his father shook his head no, a short, angry jerk, then leaned forward and slapped his forefinger against Jonathon's lips. As his father walked away,

Jonathon's gaze dropped back to the silver bowl, to the dreadful eyes. Then his breath clouded the surface, and his face was lost. Something was wrong with him, terribly wrong, yet he must never ask his father about it.

"No?" His mother's voice broke the memory. Jonathon found himself blinking down at the brass lid on the jar of applesauce. "No?" she was saying to his father. "Then our agreement stands."

"All right," he said. "You're wrong, but I won't break my word."

She turned to Jonathon. "I'm sorry, son. I know how much you want to go."

"But—" Jonathon said.

"You're not a man yet," she added, then looked at him for a long moment. "Though I believe you're becoming a fine one." Suddenly, her face turned pale.

"What's that, there on your forehead?" She bent close and brushed his hair aside.

"Nothing." Jonathon dodged away. "I scraped it."

"Oh," she said, glancing at Jonathon's father, who had sat up, rigid, in his chair. "Oh. It doesn't look—serious. No, not serious." She took four bowls out of the dish cupboard and put them into the flour bin. She walked to the pantry door, then back to the counter, where she picked up a potato, put it down, then picked up an onion and put that down too.

"Oh yes," she said. "I'd better ring the bell. Call Uncle Wilford for lunch." And she hurried out the kitchen door.

Jonathon took a step after her, his mouth opening to say: but I must go to the Red Mountains; I must see those horses. We're already in danger. There are Dalriadas by the river and a girl with...but he was afraid to say it.

"There's a fish under the washstand," he muttered instead and ran into the hall. Two at a time, against the rhythm of the bell, he climbed the stairs to his room, one hand skipping along the picture frames that lined the stairwell. Portraits of his father's ancestors looked down on him across the past four hundred years, looked down on him with brown eyes.

Later that night, when the grandfather clock chimed a quarter past midnight, a man, whose face was hidden inside a hood, bent over Jonathon's bed. He stretched out his white hand, palm up. One minute dragged by, then another, until at last he straightened, limped past the cedar chest, and slipped out the bedroom door. It clicked shut.

Jonathon woke sweating, his heart slicing through his chest, and pulled the quilt over his head. Would this nightmare never stop troubling him? It was always the same and had bothered him for as long as he could remember. Lately, though, the man had seemed more frightening.

Jonathon got up, found his pants draped on the cedar chest, and pulled out the red rock. He took it back to bed, where he closed his eyes and ran his finger along the carving, trying to picture a horse instead of the hooded man, trying to lull himself to sleep. Even though he imagined himself galloping all over the Red Mountains, an hour passed before he slept again.

chapter three

The next evening, Jonathon followed his parents into the Village Hall, which blazed with lantern light for the Harvest Supper.

"Good Harvest, Kenneth. How are those grafts doing, Stephen?" Jonathon's father nodded curt greetings left and right. Most of the farmers around Stonewater Vale were orchardists; they took advantage of the rich soil and moderate climate to grow the Valley's best fruit. After walking around a shock of corn ringed with pumpkins, the Braes stopped beside a table covered with a yellow checked cloth.

"Sorry," said Dan Tiller, "but those places beside me and Margaret—they're saved."

"Is that so?" said Jonathon's father, looking him up and down. "For who?"

"For, well, that is...." A nervous smile worked under Mr. Tiller's straggly mustache. He glanced at Jonathon.

Jonathon's mother touched his father's arm.

"We'll find better places," Jonathon's father said, striding across the room. He slapped their cloaks down on a bench beside another table. Jonathon followed, his cheeks hot, and rubbed the sore spot on his forehead. Why hadn't Mr. Tiller wanted to sit beside him? His mother carried a tall basket toward the kitchen, while his father walked beside her, swinging a bottle of wine like a club. Jonathon looked around, hoping no one from school had seen the dispute.

The smell of roast pheasant lured him over to the serving table. He saw steam coiling from dishes of stewed rabbit, sugary, brown sweet potatoes, and scalloped potatoes baked with ham. Creamed peas, corn, and cabbage floated in chafing dishes. In the middle of the table were platters heaped with Jonathon's favorite bread—three-seed harvest rolls.

"Hey, loony-blue," someone said, jabbing Jonathon in the ribs. Jonathon spun around and faced Timothy Dakken, whose black hair bunched in curls.

"Don't call me that," Jonathon said.

Timothy laughed. "Come on. Everybody knows blue-eyed kids go loony when they grow up. You're going to turn into one any day now."

"That's just an old wives' tale," Jonathon said. He should have been used to this teasing by now, but the older he grew, the more afraid he became. "My ma says Old Man Craven didn't go crazy," he added, "and they say he has blue eyes."

"Yeah, but there's been no other loony-blues in years, except you and him. That's not enough to judge."

Jonathon bit his lip.

"I've never seen a crazy person before." Timothy's eyes darted, crow-like, over a side of venison wrapped in bacon. "Bet your folks will chain you to a post. You're just lucky they didn't dump you in the hills when you were born—folks used to, you know. Used to be a law."

"Not anymore," Jonathon said.

"Pop says the old ways are still best."

A knot of anger burned in Jonathon's chest. He fumbled for the rock in his pocket, itching to scare Timothy with news of the Dalriadas, when his mother came out of the kitchen with a bowl in her hands.

"Did your ma make something strange again this year?" Timothy asked.

Jonathon glared at him. "What do you mean, strange?"

"Don't get me wrong—her food tastes really good." Timothy cocked his head and eyed her. "But, she's...I mean, it tastes kind of different. That's all. Kind of different."

Jonathon's mother set the dish on the serving table, then stepped toward the stone fireplace where a fire roared around a log the length of a man. Flames curved like teeth against the soot-blackened stones. A knot of women clustered around Mrs. Tiller, heavy with child, who was sitting on a chair near the hearth. Although they nodded to Jonathon's mother, they tightened their circle, raising a hand on a hip here, turning a flame-lit skirt there. Jonathon's mother stood alone, a wistful look in her eyes.

Jonathon frowned. His mother was different, and that, he knew, was a terrible thing. She wore a red dress made of finely woven cloth, finer than any the other women wore, without a single bow or ruffle. Did that make her different? Or perhaps the proud way she held her head?

"Ma's from up North Valley," Jonathon said, turning toward Timothy. "And Uncle Wilford says the food's different there. Besides, she made mushroom puffs and a chocolate cake. What's so strange about that?"

Timothy shrugged. "Maybe nothing. Let's go look—you can show me her cake."

Jonathon hesitated, then trailed behind. They reached the dessert table, which was loaded with pastries; cakes; cherry, apple, and sweet potato pies; and dozens of cookies.

"That one." Jonathon pointed to a towering, six-layer chocolate cake. Timothy's hand darted out, gouged off a hunk, and popped it into his mouth.

"Why, it's yellow inside," Timothy said with his mouth full. "What a fake." Suddenly a hand gripped his shoulder.

"Timothy," said Mrs. Dakken, "stay out of that! Go outside and help Pop turn the spit. Now get!"

"Sure, Ma," said Timothy, licking his fingers. "Come on, Brae."

Outside, smoke drifted on the cold, night air. Jonathon and Timothy clattered down the steps as the Landers family from Sunny Hollow Orchard spilled out of their wagon. The Landers owned the biggest orchard and had the biggest family in all of Stonewater Vale. Rosamund Landers stepped out last, holding her baby sister in her arms.

Folks said that Rosamund Landers was born into the Valley when the sweet corn stood high under the sun and the meadowlarks sang of bountiful harvest. Jonathon believed it. She glanced over her shoulder at him, and her golden hair swung, shimmering in the lantern light.

Timothy sighed. He looked at Rosamund the same way he had looked at the cake.

"You stay out here," he told Jonathon and followed Rosamund inside. Jonathon walked toward the smoke spiraling from the back of the hall, turned a corner, and stopped.

Twenty yards away, a wild boar revolved on a spit over glowing embers. The belly slid into the orange light, turned, and faded into the darkness as the flank gleamed, turned, and also faded into the darkness; the back rolled round, then the other flank, until at last the belly shone again.

Three men watched Mr. Dakken work the handle. The orange light from the coals lit the underside of his chin, touched his nostrils, and flooded the white of his one eye. A black patch covered the other.

"Brian's leaving tomorrow for another trip to the southern Red Mountains," Kenneth Landers was saying.

Jonathon froze, hidden by the darkness.

"Why can't he hunt up in the Ptarmigan Hills like everybody else?" asked Stephen Stoddard.

"Does he ever do anything like anyone else?" Mr. Tiller said, grinding a clump of dirt with his heel. "I swear he almost hit me, just because I didn't want his wife or that—boy—to sit by Margaret in her condition."

Ma? Jonathon thought. He didn't want Ma either?

"Brian's edgy all right," Mr. Stoddard said.

"If you had his worries," Mr. Landers said, "you'd be edgy too."

As fat dripped down the boar and sizzled onto the coals, blots of smoke rose into the sky.

"But even before the boy," Mr. Tiller said. "Brian was always restless, always after something new."

Mr. Stoddard nodded. "Who else would waste money looking for magic apples from some old legend?"

"Firegolds," Mr. Dakken scoffed.

"It's a harmless enough hobby," said Mr. Landers.

"Hobby!" Mr. Tiller threw a stick on the coals. "Try obsession. And now he's growing pears on some new-fangled trellis wires. Why can't he just follow the old ways?"

"Brian's made Greengard ten times more productive than his father ever did," Mr. Landers said.

"Greengard's tainted," Mr. Dakken said. "Always has been, going back years."

"Maybe." Mr. Lander's silver coat buttons gleamed red in the light from the coals. "But nobody can remember why, Bill, so what does it matter?"

"Matters to me," Mr. Dakken said. "I don't know why every man in the Vale tiptoes around Brae."

Mr. Stoddard sighed. "Money. Most everybody owes him for something or other."

Mr. Dakken spit into the coals; they hissed.

"And Brae's a fighter," Mr. Stoddard added. "No one could best him when we were boys, and no one can now."

"But he scorns Valley ways," Mr. Dakken said. "I mean that boy, how can he bear to look at that...boy?"

"He doesn't," Mr. Landers said, softly. "Haven't you ever noticed? It's a sad case. I hope...the worst doesn't happen."

The worst? Jonathon strained to see their faces better, but

the light from the coals didn't reach far into the darkness. Did they mean going mad?

"Brian will pay for it all, one day," Mr. Dakken said. "You mark my words."

"I hear strange northern traders been seen at his place," said Mr. Tiller.

Mr. Dakken grunted. "Likes northern things, doesn't he?" The men laughed.

"Well, there's no denying his wife's the prettiest woman in Stonewater," said Mr. Stoddard. "I'm hoping for a dance with her myself."

"Karena Brae is a good woman," Mr. Landers said.

"Think so?" asked Mr. Dakken. "Then why is there a blue-eyed Brae when there's never been one before? There are only two possible reasons; both point to her. One of them means she's not a good woman. But," he added, leering, "maybe a lot of fun." Again, the men laughed, except Mr. Landers.

Jonathon backed away, feeling as though he had swallowed coals from the fire pit. He slipped around the corner of the Hall, then ran down its length through the buggies and wagons until he finally found Sammy. He threw his arms around the horse.

"Sammy, Sammy," he said. How he hated those men! If only the Dalriadas would ride in this instant and attack them. Jonathon pressed his face against Sammy's warm neck until he stopped shaking.

"Supper!" shouted a voice from the porch.

Jonathon trudged toward the hall and saw a yo-yo some child had lost; he kicked it across the ground until it split in two. When he slipped into his seat beside his mother and touched her hand, she smiled at him. The four men from the fire pit carried in a plank bearing the boar and placed it on saw-horses. A red apple shone between the curving tusks. Jonathon looked away, sickened by the sweet-fat smell of pork and the *shu-shu* sound of Mr. Dakken sharpening the carving knife.

After supper, the men stacked the tables along the walls

while two harpers warmed up. People began to dance, and soon the Hall filled with skirts billowing out like poppies. Brian held his wife in his arms. She danced like flowing water, smiling her best smile up into her husband's eyes.

With a rush of shame, Jonathon wondered about what the men had said. If he had a "crazy" strain, could it have come from his mother? Did Mr. Tiller fear his wife's baby might get blue eyes simply by sitting near them?

Kenneth Landers tapped Brian's shoulder and began dancing with Jonathon's mother.

"Loony-blue." Timothy elbowed Jonathon. "Let's see if there's any of your ma's fake chocolate cake left." They passed the plank where the bones of the boar lay, picked clean, with the apple withered in its teeth. Part of the skull gleamed.

"Hello, Jonathon," Rosamund said, smiling, holding a cookie in her hand. Her cream-colored dress fell to her calves.

Jonathon nodded, thinking how different she was from the fiery Dalriada girl he'd seen the day before: one was like a flash of lightning, the other, a steadily burning candle. Timothy elbowed in front of him, grabbed a piece of cake, and crammed it into his mouth. He sucked his fingers with long, loud slurps.

"Hey, Rosy-mud," he said, brandishing his sticky hands. "Wanna dance?"

She wrinkled her nose and turned away.

Timothy grinned.

Mr. Tiller's oldest son, Howard, walked up and asked Rosamund to dance. When Howard slipped one arm around her waist, Jonathon twisted his thumb until it hurt.

"In a few more years," said Timothy, his black eyes glittering, "Rosamund won't dance with anyone but me. You mark my words."

Jonathon's mother was now dancing with Mr. Stoddard. So he got his old dance, Jonathon thought. The music froze in his ears as Mr. Dakken elbowed through the couples and dropped one hand on Mr. Stoddard's shoulder. Mr. Stoddard stepped back, and Jonathon's mother hesitated before Mr. Dakken.

Jonathon rushed onto the dance floor. "Ma! Ma!" he shouted, darting between them. "You promised to dance with me!"

"Jonathon," she said, half laughing at his urgency and rudeness. He grabbed her arm and tried to pull her away.

"You need to learn some manners, boy?" Mr. Dakken said. "I've a mind to take you out back and lay my belt where you'll remember it."

Karena Brae's eyes flashed. "Don't you dare touch my son," she said. "Don't you ever, ever touch him."

Startled, Mr. Dakken stepped back.

"Come, Jonathon," she said, holding out her hands. "Excuse us, Mr. Dakken," she added coldly. Then Jonathon and his mother began to dance. Now she was smiling her best smile at him.

"Ma?" Jonathon asked.

"Yes?"

"Did I get my blue eyes from you?"

"Hush." She glanced around, her smile fading. "Of course not. What nonsense you talk. Did someone give you wine?"

He stared up at her and stumbled. She was the only person he could count on to look straight into his blue eyes, but she wouldn't meet them now. She must be lying—why else wouldn't she look at him? But what was terrible enough to make her lie? Was he really going to go mad?

Something nameless, something terrible sang on the strings of the fiddles; it went whispering through the skull of the boar, whipped along by the women's whirling skirts; gleaming, red, it quivered in the air between Jonathon and his mother.

He leaned away from her, dancing as if his boots were full of stones.

chapter four

After school on Monday, Jonathon slammed the kitchen door behind him and waited for his mother's voice to scold, an angry answer ready on his lips. He had been angry since dawn when his father had left for the Red Mountains without him. He banged his books on the table. Again, he listened. Again, the house remained silent.

"Ma," he called, walking into the hall. "I'm home." The old grandfather clock ticked in the parlor. Jonathon climbed the stairs two at a time beneath the watchful eyes in the portraits and searched the two main wings, poking his head into rooms, some long unused, with furniture shrouded in dust covers.

"Ma?" he called again.

At the end of the hall, Jonathon passed his own room and came to the narrow flight of stairs leading to the attic. He stopped. Six steps led up to a landing, then the stairwell turned, ascending beyond his line of sight to the attic.

The last time he had gone up there, a year ago, he had found a carved cedar chest and dragged it down to his room.

He had not been back since. The brooding stillness in the attic always made him uneasy.

A faint scratching came from above.

"Is that you, Ma?" he called. Slowly, he climbed the stairs. Dust coated the steps, mixing in the air with another smell he couldn't name, something sharp yet sweet, something that did not belong in an old Valley house. When he reached the landing, he saw the portrait that had always hung there, the portrait of a young man with an angular chin and a broad, thrusting brow. It hung alone on the wall in the dim light. The man's eyes were a dull, flat brown, crudely painted, without even a black pupil. His fingers held a five-petaled white flower.

Jonathon looked up the stairs that led from the landing to the attic door. Although the door was ajar, no footprints smeared the dust on the steps. How could his mother be up there?

The scratching, like fingernails on wood, grew louder.

"Ma?" he called "...Ma...Ma...Ma..." The sound echoed in the stairwell. The house listened. The man in the portrait listened, and the strange sweet smell seemed to call, come up! come up!

His heart pounding, Jonathon remembered the hooded man in the nightmare. Where did he go after he limped out of the bedroom? Jonathon blinked up at the vertical shaft of light edging the door. The light must be coming from the round window under the roof peak. He sensed a warmth in his pocket and pulled out the rock. It felt hot.

Then footsteps creaked on wood, one, then another, coming closer and closer in slow, stuttering squeals. Jonathon froze. The flat brown eyes of the man in the portrait loomed out. Ma, where was Ma? Suddenly Jonathon knew that something terrible had happened to her. The rock burned in his palm, and the carved horse seemed to leap off the rock, dragging a scream up and out of him.

"Jonathon?" said a familiar voice. Uncle Wilford, his head tipped back, was staring at him from the bottom of the stairs. "What are you screeching at?"

"You startled me." Swallowing hard, Jonathon thrust the

rock back in his pocket and clattered down the stairs, hurrying away from the attic, away from the portrait.

"I've been looking all over for you," said Uncle Wilford, who looked as thin and dry and wrinkled as an ancient daddy longlegs. "I'm too old to be climbing all the stairs in this house."

Wilford was not really Jonathon's uncle. When Jonathon's mother had been a girl in the North Valley, he had worked for her family. Here at Greengard, he lived in a cottage near the barn—though Jonathon's mother often shook her head in exasperation saying, "There are so many empty rooms in this house, why doesn't that ornery man use one?"

"Why didn't you put Nellie into the barn after school?" Uncle Wilford asked now.

"I don't know. Where's Ma?"

"She's waiting for you up on the sagebrush flat. And she's been waiting for almost an hour."

"Is she all right?"

"Of course she's all right," Uncle Wilford said. "What ails you, son? You look peculiar—white as a ghost."

"Nothing," Jonathon said, trying to stop panting. "Why is Ma up on the flat?"

"Just you ride on up there and see."

Outside, after Jonathon untied Nellie from the hitching post, Uncle Wilford gave him a leg up on the old piebald's back. Jonathon glanced up at the window in the attic; flat, opaque, it reflected the blue sky. He shuddered and looked away.

Nellie neighed at the barn as they passed. Caleb, one of the crew, opened the gate in the deer fence that separated Greengard from the canyon, and Jonathon rode up Coyote Road. The brush along the creek sheltered grouse and quail. Aspens shivered with gold. On one side of the road, the tracks from Sammy and the pack horse overlapped, still fresh.

Jonathon scowled. Two years must pass before he could go with his father to the Red Mountains, two years before he could learn more about the Dalriada horses, the blue-eyed girl, and the red rock.

"I can't wait that long," he said aloud. Nellie twitched

back one ear. There had to be a way to go sooner.

The rock felt cool again. Was its heat some type of magic? But why should the magic awaken on the attic stairs? He remembered how the carved horse had suddenly pulsed with life and tried to recapture that feeling. He imagined that Nellie was a Dalriada horse, a golden bay with a black mane and tail, imagined that they were riding through the Red Mountains. Up they climbed, up to the sagebrush flat where the sky widened, freed from the Valley walls.

Across the flat, his mother stood beside four stacked bales of straw, her purple cloak billowing around her. She waved, but he didn't wave back. He walked Nellie slowly to avoid kicking up the dust. Then, when he saw his bow leaning against the bales, Jonathon clenched his teeth. His mother must have snooped through the private things in his cedar chest to get it. But why bring it up here?

He tied Nellie to a sagebrush well away from his mother's horse, Windborn, then scuffled toward her through the dry grass. She sang one of the old songs about the Firegolds while she pushed apples into the straw.

Cattle grazed on the slope behind her. Beyond them, were low hills scattered with pines. Higher up, to the north and west, beyond ever-rising foothills, the Red Mountains scraped the sky. Far, far distant, one snow-covered peak glittered, towering above all the others. And somewhere, even farther away, were the Beyondlands—a vast gray plain without joy or terror, or so the legends said.

His mother held out his bow.

"Practice, Jonathon," she said. "Learn. And next year, if you're shooting well enough, you may go with your pa even though you'll only be thirteen."

Jonathon's crossed arms fell open, and his anger ebbed into the dust. His mother was fair.

"But," she warned, "I will give you a test next fall. You'll need to work hard to pass it. And you must pass in order to go." She paused. "Do we have an agreement?"

Jonathon thought it over; he knew how firm his mother was

about agreements. He looked at the red peaks rising up like a dream, a place where he could become a man. Longing twisted inside him. This was his chance to get there a little sooner.

"Yes." He took the bow. "We have an agreement. But who's going to teach me?"

"I will," she said. "Your father is better with wrestling and a knife than a bow."

"You can shoot?" Jonathon's eyes widened.

She bent down, her face hidden, and rearranged the arrows in his quiver. In the silence, grasshoppers whirred, bird wings swished, and somewhere, a coyote yipped. The sun arced toward sunset, lengthening the shadows of the bitterbrush.

"I learned when I was a girl, up North Valley," she said at last. "Women hunt up there."

"Pa says the bow is a coward's weapon."

"Does he?" She raised one eyebrow. "I would like to see him catch a deer with his bare hands. Now, let me watch you shoot."

Jonathon's first arrow wobbled wide and right of the bales; the second and third arrows zoomed high; the fourth, fifth, and sixth sank into the straw a foot above the ground; and the seventh flew left. Not one came close to the apples. Jonathon kicked a Barnaby's Thistle, then retrieved his arrows.

"It makes me nervous having you watch," he said when he returned. "I usually shoot a lot better."

"Of course I make you nervous," she said. "And a charging bear or wolf will make you even more nervous." Her eyes sparkled.

Sheepishly, Jonathon grinned.

"Now, don't grip the bow, son, hold it lightly. Draw back the string with your fingertips only. And don't strike your forearm. If you don't get in the way, the bow will work for you."

"Show me," he dared her, unable to believe that she knew about archery.

She smiled and took the bow. With one smooth motion, she nocked the arrow, pulled the bowstring back to her chin with her first three fingers, held, and then shot cleanly, holding the position of release. The arrow struck the apple in the center of the bales.

Jonathon blinked. His mother laughed and a breeze lifted her purple cloak, rippling the cobalt-blue lining.

"Try again," she said.

Jonathon did. This time four of the arrows hit the bales.

"Better," she said. "One day you will shoot well, though you have much to learn about aiming. But that's enough for now. It will soon grow dark." They tied canvas around the bales to keep out the deer and cattle, then rode side by side back across the flat.

"Why up here, Ma?" Jonathon asked. "We could practice in the North Pasture."

"I like the wide open space here," she said, avoiding his eyes.

His jaw tightened. Was she evading the truth again as she had last night?

"You just don't want anybody to know you can shoot," he said.

Her shoulders rose, then fell. "I—yes."

Jonathon could guess what Timothy would say, what the men by the fire pit would say, if they ever found out his mother could shoot. Why did she have to make things worse? Make him even more different from everyone else?

"Does Pa know?" he asked.

"Oh yes," she said, softly.

As they left the flat and started down Coyote Road, Jonathon glanced back at the Red Mountains. The setting sun edged the tallest peak with a shaft of light. Beautiful, ominous, it seemed to call him, to fill him with a hunger so immense that his hands trembled in fear of it. For the Dalriadas were murdering barbarians, and no sane person would want to be anywhere near them. No sane person.

Maybe he was not sane.

Then, as the peak glowed crimson, he knew why, in spite of all the dangers, he had to go to the Red Mountains. He wanted to learn about the red rock, the Dalriada horses, and the drums, but most of all, he wanted to ask the blue-eyed girl if she, too, was afraid of going mad.

chapter five

One Saturday afternoon, when October had darkened into late November, Jonathon twirled his bow and scuffled through the snow toward the house. After six archery lessons his mother had left him alone with this advice: "When you have shot as many arrows as there are stars in the sky, you will be good. Practice." And he had practiced nearly every day. Sometimes he concentrated on the target, sometimes on the Red Mountains, until the two blurred into one.

Now, Jonathon looked at the smooth snow on the back porch stairs and sighed; his father still had not come home from his hunting trip. Jonathon slipped off his boots and opened the kitchen door. His mother stood dipping bayberry candles for Sunturn, the festival of light, held on the eve of the winter solstice in December. She turned toward him.

"Jonathon!" she said. "Your face is white. Come and get warm."

Jonathon leaned his bow against the wall, then rubbed his hands in the glow of warmth around the stove. The smell of bayberries and beeswax from the hives in the orchard filled the room.

"I'll make tea," his mother said. She jumped up and reached for a tin on a high shelf, her yellow sleeve fluttering to her elbow. Her dress floated out as she landed without a sound, tin in hand. "Mr. Craven gave me some of his peppermint leaves yesterday," she added.

Jonathon frowned. Even though Old Man Craven lived miles away in the Wildcat Hills, his mother took him gifts of food every month.

"Why do you always have to visit him?" Jonathon asked. "I suppose you wanted to see if he'd gone crazy yet. Can it happen when you're old too?"

She slammed the kettle down on the stove. "How many times do I have to tell you? Don't listen to those old wives' tales!"

"I can't help it."

"You must trust me. Believe me, I…." She stopped, and they stood staring at each other until her face softened. She reached out one hand, then drew it back. "Your hair needs cutting," she said and turned to the stove.

Jonathon sat down, rubbing an itch on his forehead. "Don't listen" and "trust me" were the only answers she ever gave to his questions about going mad, but that was no longer enough, not when he had found four dark hairs on his chest this morning.

"What's for supper?" he asked, eyeing the table. For days now, both the table and her apron had been spotless, without a single splash or spatter.

"How about your favorite?" she asked.

Neatness certainly took the zip out of her cooking, he thought later, as they ate the bland chicken pie silently in the lantern light. He missed Uncle Wilford, who was eating with Caleb's family. After supper, Karena lifted a small crate onto the table.

"This came today," she said. "More linens from…from that famous weaver in the North Valley." Jonathon pried off the lid with a hammer, and she reached inside.

"How beautiful," she said, pressing a length of white damask to her cheek. Her eyes turned sad, then angry.

Suddenly she dropped the cloth back into the box and spun toward the dark window.

"Blighted Earth!" she swore.

"Ma?" Jonathon dropped the hammer.

"Where's your pa? He's been gone too long. He should have been home by now."

"You don't think that—the Dalriadas got him?"

"Hush." She took a deep breath while the grandfather clock chimed. "If he's not back by morning, I will go look for him. Something's wrong. Why doesn't he come home? Oh, why doesn't he come home!" Her cry sounded small and young, like a bleating fawn.

A vein throbbed in Jonathon's neck. With his knees pressed tight together, he watched his mother jam the lid back on the crate. Then she pulled bowls and spoons from the cupboard and thumped canisters of sugar, flour, and salt down on the table.

"But Ma," he asked. "How can you go look for Pa?" He didn't want them both to be gone.

"What do you mean, how can I?" The sifter clanged in her hand, sending clouds of flour across the table. She separated eggs into bowls and threw down the shells. "I pack my saddlebags, take my bow and Windborn, and go find him. That's how."

"But how will you know where to look?" Jonathon asked. "The Red Mountains go on for miles."

"I will know," she said and whipped the egg whites into stiff peaks.

"But you told me the Red Mountains are dangerous."

"They are."

"Then…" He sat straight up. "Then I better go with you." The image of the jagged mountains rose up inside him, stirring the longing again, and his head felt light. Would he actually be riding toward them tomorrow?

"No," his mother said. "You will stay here."

Jonathon's fist clenched around the red rock in his pocket— he carried it all the time now. How could he persuade her?

"Pa wouldn't like it if I let you go alone," he said. "You're a woman."

She stopped beating the eggs and looked at him. "Yes, I am. And I can go alone wherever I choose, because in ways you don't yet understand, I can defend myself. You cannot." She folded the egg whites into the batter. "Besides, we have an agreement."

Jonathon sighed. Footsteps clomped on the back porch.

He jumped up. "Is it Pa?"

His mother shook her head. "Uncle Wilford. You can tell by the way every other step lags. Besides, that old man can smell a cake baking before it's even in the oven."

Uncle Wilford knocked, then came in with his gray felt hat in his hands.

"Evening, Karena," he said, spying the flour dusting her dress; she had forgotten to tie on an apron. A smudge of cinnamon daubed her cheek. He glanced at the litter of eggshells, at the canisters with their lids scattered everywhere, and then winked at Jonathon. "Looks to be a mighty good-tasting cake. Mind if I stay for some?"

"Sit," she said. Turning her back on them both, she poured the batter into the pan and banged it into the oven.

Uncle Wilford raised one scraggly eyebrow. He took off his jacket, folded it in thirds, and hung it over the back of a chair. When he sat down, his long legs didn't seem to fit under the table.

Karena poured coffee into Uncle Wilford's special crystal cup, added cream until the coffee turned the color of biscuits, and put in exactly four teaspoons of sugar.

"Why, thank you," Uncle Wilford said. "So, Karena, just what have you decided to do?"

Surprised, Jonathon blinked.

"You know what I'm going to do," she said.

"I'd hoped I was wrong." Uncle Wilford sipped his coffee.

"She's going to go look for Pa," Jonathon said. "I think I should go along to protect her. I'm shooting lots better now."

Uncle Wilford looked him up and down. "And I suppose

you expect me to keep this fireball tied up so he won't ride after you?"

"That's right." Karena started scrubbing the table.

Jonathon's mouth opened.

"Well now," Uncle Wilford said. "That won't be easy, will it? Especially since he's so much like someone else I knew when she was little—someone I was always chasing after. I may just have to ask for a raise." He grinned.

She shot him a dark glance over her shoulder.

"You chased after Ma?" Jonathon asked, sniffing the sweet smell of cake that began to fill the room.

"That's right." Uncle Wilford nodded. "She used to sneak off, up into the...ah, the woods, going hunting. I had to find her. Got an arrow through my hat once, for my trouble."

"You were bobbing behind a thicket, old man," Karena said. "Wearing a brown hat with a white feather. What did you expect?"

"Ma?" Jonathon asked, incredulous.

"Your ma." Uncle Wilford said. "The very same. That woman there with a smudge of cinnamon on her cheek."

She lifted one hand to her cheek, then reached for a cloth.

"As a matter of fact," Uncle Wilford added, "she was stalking a deer in the woods, first time she met your pa. Or so she said. But I always wondered if it wasn't your pa she was stalking."

Jonathon's mother whirled around.

Uncle Wilford looked her in the eye. "It was sure lucky for your pa, Jonathon, that he was wearing a red hat so she didn't shoot at him too. At least, he never mentioned it to me if she did." Uncle Wilford leaned toward him. "But then your pa's a real gentleman."

Jonathon grinned. His mother threw down the cloth, clapped both hands on her hips, and tried not to smile. When Uncle Wilford finished laughing, he told another story, but Jonathon only half-listened. He fiddled with two halves of an eggshell, still trying to think of a way to persuade his mother to take him with her.

A half hour later, she took the cake out of the oven and served it. Jonathon took a big bite; the cake tasted like a piece of warm yellow sunlight.

"That's good," said Uncle Wilford, finishing the last of his third cup of coffee. "Now, Jonathon, don't you worry. I still have that brown hat, hole and all. I've cherished it as a sign that your ma would be all right in the world. She'll be fine if she goes looking for your pa. Mercy, he's gone looking for her often enough."

"Uncle Wilford," Karena warned, "you talk too much."

As he went up to his room, Jonathon felt a twinge of guilt for pretending he wanted to protect his mother. He kicked open his door, undressed, and climbed into bed.

It was not fair. First his father rode off to the Red Mountains, now his mother. He was the one who really needed to go. He might not have much time left before he went crazy, perhaps only weeks, days, or—he squeezed his eyes shut—even hours. He had to do whatever he could to stop it.

Then blackness tore through him. What if he could not stop it? He saw himself shackled to a post, wild-haired, slavering. As he lunged to break free, the chains clanked, and the iron band clamped around his waist jerked him back.

No. Jonathon took a long, shaky breath. No. The answer lay somewhere in the vastness of the Red Mountains. It did. It had to.

Suddenly he remembered what Uncle Wilford had said: I suppose you expect me to keep this fireball tied up so he won't ride after you.

Jonathon's eyes flew open. Could he? Did he dare ride to the Red Mountains alone? But the blackness gripped him again, unfurling like a banner until he floated, lost, and his mind wandered in uneasy dreams.

When he was sound asleep, the attic door opened.

chapter six

Each morning after his mother left, Jonathon thought about riding after her, and each morning he decided to wait until the next. The snow was too deep, the day too dark, or too many of the crew might see him riding away with packed saddlebags. He always found a reason to stay home.

One Sunday, after she had been gone for two weeks, Jonathon wandered from room to room, trying to shake off the loneliness that trailed him like a shadow. He paused outside his father's study, then turned the cold, bone-white doorknob and went inside. Brass locks shone on every drawer of his father's oak desk. Usually the desk top had stacks of account books, scattered papers, pens, and a bottle or two of ink, but now it was empty. The whole house felt empty, even though Uncle Wilford had moved in to keep him company.

Behind the desk was a brown leather chair with a shiny streak from his father's shoulders. Jonathon reached toward it, but the sight of his hand made him stop. Last night and every night since his mother had left, he had dreamed about the hooded man, dreamed about a white hand reaching toward him. The man seemed to want something, but neither spoke nor showed his face. Don't think about it, Jonathon told himself.

Instead, he looked at a framed poem hanging on the wall beside the desk. The sun glinted off the glass. The poem, *The Ballad of the Firegold*, claimed that the Firegold apples had been the first fruit ever grown in the Valley, though they grew here no longer. When Jonathon read it, he could almost hear his father whistling the tune:

> The maiden Spring flew down to the Valley
> From the heart of the Mountain's Hart;
> She planted her roots in the fertile soil
> And stretched her boughs to the stars.
>
> Alas, for the Firegolds bloom no more;
> The Firegolds bloom no more.
>
> She drank of the River long and deep,
> As water plunged from the Snake.
> Her song enchanted the bitterbrush
> And charmed the land awake.
>
> Alas, for the Firegolds bloom no more;
> The Firegolds bloom no more.
>
> With magic the First Tree bloomed:
> Firegolds! Now break the chains!
> Oh, apples sweet and red as wine
> And gold as a leaping flame.
>
> Alas, for the Firegolds bloom no more;
> The Firegolds bloom no more.
>
> The world was whole, a garden green;
> Tillers and Makers were one.

But the Makers looked up from the Valley soil
At the mountains under the sun.

Alas, for the Firegolds bloom no more;
The Firegolds bloom no more.

"There is our home!" the Makers cried,
"From there our powers flow."
But the Tillers feared the Makers' dreams
And refused to let them go.

Alas, for the Firegolds bloom no more;
The Firegolds bloom no more.

Horses came galloping fast and fleet,
The Makers heard them roar:
"Ride on our backs to follow the dream!"
The Tillers and Makers went to war.

Alas, for the Firegolds bloom no more;
The Firegolds bloom no more.

They ringed the Tree with arrow and bow;
Split the earth from the sky.
Stone by stone the wall was built,
And the Tree withered and died.

Someone tell me when—Oh, when?
Will the Firegolds ever bloom again?

Climb the mountain to the stars,
Fling wide the Darkened Door;
Follow, follow the flame-lit horse,
Through pain and tears and horror.

Someone tell me when—Oh, when?
Will the Firegolds ever bloom again?

The skull pulses with golden light.
The arrow's path is truth—
Aim for the Hart from the heart:
Seed, blossom, fruit.

Someone tell me when—Oh, when?
Will the Firegolds ever bloom again?

A promise from a drop of blood
Springs from death's maiden eye.
Eat of the Firegold from the Tree!
And earth rejoins the sky.

The Song in the World shall soar!
The Firegolds bloom forever more.

Jonathon knew that his father and many Braes before him had been searching for the Firegolds. "I don't know why or when it started," his father had said once while sawing a board in half. "And they might not even exist, but I think they do. So many of the old songs and stories mention them—there's got to be something to it. My ancestors have gathered a lot of evidence over the years."

"If the Firegolds are magic," said Jonathon, "and the Red Mountains are magic, why don't we look for them there?"

"We?" The saw stopped in mid-stroke.

"I want to look for them too."

His father began to saw again. "We'll see. When you're—grown. But the mountains are too cold for apple trees." The saw rasped in and out like the breath of a running man, faster and faster until the board split. "And there's no magic in the Red Mountains; that's only superstition."

Superstition? Jonathon wondered now, scratching his forehead and staring up at the poem. He had a rock from the Red Mountains that grew hot all by itself. Wasn't that magic? He hoped there was magic in the Red Mountains, magic to keep him from becoming a madman chained to a post.

As he scratched, Jonathon felt a faint bump or ridge over his left eyebrow and probed it with his fingers. He turned toward the glass doors on the bookcase beside him, lifted his bangs, and peered at his reflection in the glass. He saw his blue eyes and blonde, almost white, hair—a startling contrast against his dark eyebrows and tanned face.

Although he tilted his head from side to side, the leatherbound books with their golden titles hampered his vision: *Laws of the Valley, Highgate, The War of the Renegade King*. Finally, he saw a faint, freckle-colored streak where he had scraped his forehead on the riverbank. Because he avoided mirrors, he had never checked to see whether the scrape had left a scar. The streak began at the inner point of his eyebrow, curved up and out, then branched halfway between his brow and skull. The bump ran beneath it. Not a scar, he thought. A rash? But a rash would not leave a bump.

When he pressed it, he felt no pain, only the itching that had plagued him for weeks. He shrugged. Somehow he must have hit his head and forgotten. And yet, he must have hit it hard to leave such a bump. It seemed strange not to remember.

Suddenly, he grabbed the bookcase to steady himself. Was he losing his memory? Was that the first sign of the madness?

"Jonathon," Uncle Wilford called from the kitchen. "We could use a hand with the pruning."

Jonathon raked his bangs over his forehead, spitting on his hands to plaster them down, and left the study.

For two hours he pruned trees in the west block of the Greers. Each time he slid the wooden sleeve on the pole lopper, another branch thunked into the snow; it looked as though a trail of gigantic, scraggly antlers pursued him. Brown tinted glasses protected his eyes from the sun glaring on the snow.

He had stopped to feel the strange bump for the third time when he heard boots crunching toward him.

"Afternoon, Jonathon," called Mr. Landers, muffled in an overcoat with wide cuffs on the sleeves. His beard was clipped as neat and even as a hedge.

"Hello." Jonathon yanked his wool hat down over his eyebrows.

"I came by to see how you and your ma are doing, but nobody answered the door."

Jonathon hesitated. He knew that tongues would wag if folks learned his mother had ridden to the Red Mountains.

"She's around—somewhere." Jonathon waved one hand.

Mr. Landers rubbed his lips together. "I see. Any news of your pa?"

"None."

"I'd like to form a search party, but most of the men would be too afraid to go." Mr. Landers sighed.

"Pa's all right." Jonathon glanced up, brave behind the cover of his glasses; through them, the silver buttons on Mr. Landers' coat looked tarnished. "There's nobody as strong or smart as my pa. He can take care of himself just fine."

"Yes, yes, he can." Mr. Landers paused. "Rosamund mentioned you've been having trouble in school."

Jonathon's face flushed. He had been kept after school four times in the last two weeks: twice for hurling rocks at the fence and twice for not doing his homework.

"I know it's difficult having your pa gone," Mr. Landers said, "but he's not the only one who expects things from you. I do too. You remember that now, and behave."

"Yes, sir."

To Jonathon's surprise, Mr. Landers put one gloved hand on his shoulder.

"If you need anything, Jonathon, you come to me. If Dakk…if anyone's bothering you or your ma, come to me. I mean it now." Then Mr. Landers walked away. In the distance, a pack of coyotes howled.

Tears pressed in Jonathon's eyes, but he winked them back. He would even welcome a fighting lesson under the old oak if only his parents would come home. Why had they left him alone this long? Had the Dalriadas captured them? Had they fallen prey to those dangers he could not even imagine? The pole lopper shook in his hands. He began to prune again, and as each branch fell, he thought, gone, gone, gone....

An hour later, he finished the last tree in the row and glanced up at the low ridge to the west. A cleft rock nosed out of the snow. In the summer, rattlesnakes sunned there, but now they would be dreaming deep in their underground dens.

A whistle blasted the air and echoed off the rock.

Jonathon froze. It came again, a long, rising note that ended with two trills—his father's whistle! Jonathon dropped the pole lopper and ran through the orchard. When he reached the house, no one was there, so he raced on toward the barn, barging around the corner in time to see his father gallop out of the paddock.

"Now, Caleb!" Brian Brae shouted. "Close the gate!"

Jonathon hurled himself at Sammy. "Pa!" he yelled and grabbed his father's boot.

"Jonathon!" his father cried, his eyes sparkling. In his fur cap and coat, he looked like a bear.

"You're home," Jonathon said. "You're back!" But where was his mother?

"I am!" His father laughed and swung off Sammy. "And see what I brought you." He pointed toward the paddock. Jonathon tore his eyes from his father's face and looked.

A colt plunged in circles, first one way, then another, seeking to escape from the paddock. A blood bay, his coat shone like fire in the setting sun. Stripes of gold flashed in his black mane and tail, stripes of gold exactly like those in the Dalriada girl's hair.

This was a Dalriada horse; it had to be. Jonathon's throat ached with the wild, raw beauty of it. Never had he seen such a horse. Even the Dalriada horses he had glimpsed by the Mirandin could not equal this one.

"Did you say," Jonathon said, faintly, "Did you say, Pa, that you brought him...for me?"

"That's right."

"All the way from the Red Mountains?"

His father nodded.

Jonathon couldn't speak. All the wonder and mystery that

he had ever felt about the Red Mountains—about the blue-eyed girl, the rock, the tall, glowing peak—seemed embodied in this horse.

"Is that what the Red Mountains are like?" he asked finally. His hand tightened around the red rock in his pocket; it felt warm again.

"Yes," his father said. "That's why I brought him for you. To make up for...."

"Brian!" Uncle Wilford called, jogging up. He saw the colt and stopped dead. "Earth's Mercy," he panted.

"Wilford!" Jonathon's father slapped him on the back. "I made it!"

"We were beginning to wonder," Uncle Wilford gasped.

Jonathon frowned. "Is the colt why you were gone so long, Pa?"

His father nodded. "It wasn't easy catching him or dragging him back." He smiled one of his rare smiles. "But I wanted the challenge. I'd never seen anything like him. Look at those golden hairs, Wilford. Have you ever heard of a marking like that?"

Uncle Wilford mopped his forehead with his cap. "Not that I recall."

Jonathon said nothing but watched the horse scream and kick, demanding his freedom.

"He's completely wild," Uncle Wilford said. "What have you gone and done now, Brian?"

"Oh, he'll settle down. He can't be much more than a two-year-old." Brian Brae looked toward the house. "Where's Karena? I want her to see him. Is she in the village?"

Jonathon exchanged glances with Uncle Wilford.

"You know how she is," Uncle Wilford began. "You were way overdue, Brian...."

"Ma went looking for you, Pa," Jonathon finished softly and nodded toward the north.

There was a silence. As Brian Brae looked out across the orchard, where the bare branches pointed at the winter sky, the joy faded from his face. Suddenly Jonathon saw how lean his face was, how deep the shadows were beneath his eyes.

Again, the colt screamed. Jonathon's father turned toward the darkening north.

"How long ago?" he asked.

chapter seven

On a cold afternoon five days later, Jonathon and Timothy Dakken watched the colt run across the North Pasture while their fathers spoke in low voices behind them.

The news that Brian Brae had at last returned from the Red Mountains, bringing an uncanny horse, had flashed up and down Stonewater Vale. Many people had suddenly remembered urgent business they needed to discuss with him as an excuse to see the colt

The wind gusted. Jonathon glanced up at the gray clouds that gathered above and thought of his mother; she was still gone.

"I want him, Pop. I want that colt," Timothy Dakken said, jamming his hands into his back pockets. "Buy him for me, Pop. Please, please!"

"That thing?" Mr. Dakken spit into the snow. "You'll have nothing to do with that. It's from those cursed mountains."

"He's not for sale anyway," Jonathon said.

"You'll sell him to me if I say so," Timothy snapped.

"No, I won't." Jonathon looked at his father for reassurance, but his father's face was hard, with no trace of the joy that had brightened it when he had first come home. Beneath the shadow of his hat brim, Brian watched Mr. Dakken eye the colt.

Like a beacon of red gold, the bay dashed from one fence to the other, swerved, and raced back. Jonathon's father had put him in the North Pasture because the other horses balked at his wildness. In one corner of the pasture sat an old, listing barn, struggling to keep up appearances under a slap of red paint. If the colt could ever be coaxed inside, he would have it all to himself.

"The colt is not for sale," Jonathon repeated. Mr. Dakken stared at him, and Jonathon looked away.

"Sorry I missed paying my respects to your wife, Brian," Mr. Dakken said. "Again."

"I'll be sure to tell her you called," Jonathon's father answered.

"I was over at Sunny Hollow yesterday, talking to Landers. It seems that nobody's seen Mrs. Brae for a while." Mr. Dakken glanced at Jonathon again. "Off gathering wild honey in the hills, is she?"

Suddenly, everything seemed to stop: the pine trees, lashing a moment before, stood stiff and still; the clouds halted; the shadow cast by a flying bird caught on the ground, as though its flight had been arrested. Jonathon's father also seemed frozen, his face fixed as a stone.

Mr. Dakken's lips curled into a smile.

As Jonathon's breath rushed out, the trees lashed again; the clouds rolled; the bird flew off; and his father hunched one shoulder, tensing his arm to strike Mr. Dakken.

"Come on," Mr. Dakken said softly. "Do it."

Brian's arm poised, and his face clenched with rage. He struggled for control until gradually the rage swept back behind his eyes. His face became a mask, rigid, grim, with a muscle jerking at the corner of his mouth. His arm fell to his side.

"Say that again," he said, "ever, and I'll change my mind about that little business matter. Change it fast."

Mr. Dakken paled. He flicked his eye patch and looked back at the pasture. "That horse doesn't belong in the Valley. Everyone knows it's Dal—" he stopped. "You'll bring the blight down on us all."

"Buy him for me, Pop," Timothy begged, tugging on his father's arm, but Mr. Dakken cuffed him as though he were a stray dog.

"Hold your tongue!"

"Ouch!" Timothy yelled.

Jonathon's father laughed. "Yes, Bill, why don't you buy the horse for your boy?"

"Pa!" Jonathon gasped.

Mr. Dakken scowled. "Let's go, Timothy," he said. "Take care of your son, Brae." And he walked away.

"You, you…" Timothy said to Jonathon. "I'll get you at school." As he ran after his father, he shouted back over his shoulder, "Loony-blue! Your folks should of left you in the hills!" The Dakkens skirted the pasture and headed back toward Ironhill Orchard. An icy wind howled into the silence; a storm was rising.

"Pa?" Jonathon asked. "Would you really sell my colt?"

"No," his father said. "Dakken is in no position to buy so much as a wooden top for Sunturn." He wrapped his woolen muffler tighter around his neck. "In fact, Dakken owes me so much money that I could walk onto his land tomorrow and turn him out on Guther's Way. Or make him my tenant."

"Pa!" Jonathon's eyes widened.

"That's one reason he hates us, but he fears us more, which is exactly the way I want it." With his head tipped back, Jonathon's father scanned the clouds ramming forward from the north. "Where on Earth is your ma?"

He still looked grim, thinking, Jonathon guessed, of Mr. Dakken's crude remark about his mother; to say a woman gathered wild honey in the hills insulted her character.

"She ought to be home by now," his father added. The night before, Jonathon had overheard him arguing with Uncle Wilford.

"I've got to find her," his father had said.

"But this could go on forever," Uncle Wilford argued. "Each of you running off to look for the other. She'll be fine. Besides, Sunturn is the day after tomorrow. Jonathon needs one of you here."

Now, another blast of wind swept across the pasture. Jonathon shivered.

"Snow's coming," his father said. "Lots of it. We've got to get that horse inside before the storm hits. I'll be back in a while with Uncle Wilford and Caleb." He mounted Sammy and rode off.

Jonathon hopped up on the lower rail of the fence, rested his forearms on the top rail, and watched the colt paw the ground. Every day Jonathon had raced home from school, hurrying through his chores to spend more time with his colt. He longed to curry him, to bury his face in the silky, golden-striped mane. Most of all, he longed to ride him.

Jonathon pulled out an apple from inside his shirt. As he held it up, he wondered for the hundredth time what to name the red-gold bay. It had to be the right name, not something plain like Sammy or Nellie, but something grand—something as glorious as the Red Mountains themselves.

The Red Mountains. Now that he had seen the colt, seen another of the mountains' marvels, Jonathon longed to go there more than ever. Yet how could he leave his horse behind? The colt sniffed the air, looked toward the apple, then snorted, pawing the ground again. Jonathon tossed the apple into the pasture and sighed. Why does he always ignore me? he wondered.

A band of snow edged the fence railings, though the wind had ruffled it like the lopsided icing on the cakes he had frosted when he was little. Jonathon smiled, remembering icing all over his face and his mother's apron. Then his smile faded.

He pulled off his hat and gloves, scooped snow from the fence, and pressed it against his itching forehead, wishing his mother were home. She would know what to do about the bump; it was no better, perhaps worse. He had decided not to ask his father about it, reluctant to endure his scrutiny.

The snow numbed not only Jonathon's forehead, but his fingers too. Then the rock in his pocket grew warm—it often did when he was near the colt. Jonathon drew it out, held it up, and felt heat surge into his hand. Against the snow and the blue-black sky, the rock was a blaze of red. So was the colt.

"Will I get lost if I go to the Red Mountains?" Jonathon asked them both. "Will I find something to keep me from going mad? Can the blue-eyed girl help me?" First the rock grew hotter, then heavier and heavier until the horse carved upon it began to glow. Startled, Jonathon closed his eyes. He opened them again to see the carved lines gleaming like molten gold.

Out in the pasture the colt looked up, quivering. He started to gallop straight toward Jonathon, slowing to a trot, then a walk as he neared the fence. He stopped an arm's length away.

"Come closer," Jonathon whispered. The colt looked straight into his eyes.

The look pierced Jonathon's mind, burning, shooting through layer upon layer into a realm that was not dream or memory or vision, but a combination of them all. He was riding a stallion along high cliffs and meadows, riding lost through peaks with shapes almost familiar: a bear with wings; a deer with a man's head; a skull tipped on one side, listening. Drums echoed, pounding with his heart in fear and exhilaration. His stomach felt as though he had eaten well, and, then, there beside a waterfall stretched a trail he knew.

Suddenly the stallion reared beneath him. Jonathon blinked and found himself standing next to the fence while the colt's front legs churned in the air. After his feet struck the ground, he ran to the northeast corner of the pasture. Jonathon still held the rock, but it had stopped glowing.

He began to shake. Beyond all doubt, he knew he'd experienced a fit of madness. But before he could think further, hoofbeats came thudding down the lane: his father on Sammy.

Frantic, Jonathon stuffed the rock back into his pocket,

wondering how long had his father been riding toward him. The drums, the hoofbeats, Jonathon's own heart—they all sounded the same. Had his father seen him acting strangely?

Brian rode up and dismounted. "Uncle Wilford's on his way," he shouted to be heard over the wind. Above them, gigantic, bruised clouds knuckled the sky.

For the second time, Jonathon heard the hard thump of hooves on the crusted snow. He turned, but instead of Uncle Wilford galloping down the lane, he saw a woman.

"Karena!" Jonathon's father tossed his hat high into the air. She rode leaning forward, staring over their heads at the colt.

"Ma!" Jonathon cried, but she didn't seem to hear him. Her eyes glittering, she drew Windborn to a stop.

"Rhohar?" she cried, incredulous.

Jonathon smelled sage and leather on the wind and something else he could not name—fabulous scents, scents of danger, the secret scents of the Red Mountains. Was this woman in trousers really his mother? Hadn't she worn a riding skirt when she left? He didn't know whether to run toward her or away from her.

"Rhohar!" she cried again. "Are you mad, Brian?"

"It's all right, Karena. I'll see that the boy doesn't ride him until he's broken."

"Broken!" she exclaimed. "You will never break that horse; he is Rhohar. He belongs to the Dalriadas." Thunder cracked. Windborn reared, his eyes flashing white as he screamed at the colt; Karena slapped him down with the reins.

"We can talk about this inside," Jonathon's father urged.

"No." Her eyes blazed, sweeping the hills, the pasture, the colt, seeing everything at once. Everything but me, Jonathon thought. She hadn't even said hello, or I missed you, or I'm glad to see you. Didn't she care about him anymore? What had the Red Mountains done to her?

Again the drums began to pound, louder than before, and Jonathon clapped his hands to his head. Uncle Wilford ran up.

"You can't keep this horse, Brian!" Karena said. "He has

not consented. I must set him free while there is still time."

"No!" Jonathon cried.

"Then I will kill him. Choose." She reached for her bow.

Choose? Jonathon's thoughts turned black, black with the beating drums, black with thunder.

"Do you have any idea what it took to get him here?" his father shouted, the scar above his eye throbbing. "I brought him for the boy, Karena. No one will take him or kill him, not you, not them, not anyone. I won't allow it."

"And I won't allow you to destroy our family! Damn it, Brian!" she swore. "The Dalriadas will search for him, and they will find him. I have followed you for days, knowing you brought a wild, unwilling horse—though I didn't know what horse. Your trail leads straight to Greengard."

Jonathon turned his head back and forth, watching his parents clash above him.

"I can protect my own," his father roared over the wind.

"You cannot," she said. "The Dalriadas will come, and they will kill to get him back. Nothing can stop them." She turned Windborn toward the gate.

Jonathon ran in front of her, dangerously close to Windborn's hooves, and wrapped his arms around the gate and the post.

"He's not yours, Jonathon," she said. "Your father stole him. Stand aside."

But he didn't move; he couldn't move or bear to look at her, so bright, so fierce and strange above him.

"Then I must kill him." She grasped an arrow.

"No, Ma!" Jonathon screamed.

"Karena!" Brian shouted. "Don't!" But she had already nocked the arrow. Lightning flashed, edging the running colt with light.

With all his strength, Jonathon yanked on her leg as she released the arrow; it arced, speeding through the air. The beating drums became music, became the terrible song that plays in the moment before death.

chapter eight

The arrow pierced the ground. Jonathon, or perhaps the wind, had shaken his mother's aim: the colt ran on. When the drums snapped into silence, Jonathon's legs crumpled, and he slid slowly down the fence post onto the ground. His mother shuddered as Brian helped her off Windborn.

"It's all right, Karena," he said, wrapping his arms around her. "You're home now, at Greengard. We're safe here. Let's go up to the house where there's a good warm fire." The snow slanted down, falling fast, the flakes whirling so close together that even the barn was only a blurred shadow. With dull, flat eyes, Jonathon's mother stared across the pasture toward the colt.

"Nobody will be riding in this storm," his father said. "It can wait."

The cold from the ground reached up and crawled over Jonathon's bones.

Uncle Wilford stepped forward. "Glad you're back,

Karena," he said, his voice husky. "I was afraid I'd have to come after you and get another perfectly good hat ruined."

"Uncle Wilford," she said, sagging against Jonathon's father. "The world is too small here. Too dark."

"I know, child," Uncle Wilford said, "I know. But the fire burns brightly. Come inside now."

Hand over hand, as though climbing an endless ladder, Jonathon grasped each fence rail and pulled himself to his feet. How could his father and Uncle Wilford be kind to this strange, wild woman who had tried to kill the colt he loved? All the strain of the past weeks tightened in his chest until it seemed to explode.

"I hate you!" he shouted. "You went away, and that horse was all I had. You almost killed him!"

"Jonathon!" his father exclaimed. "That's enough."

"You're not my mother!" Jonathon hurled words as though they were arrows. "I hate you! I wish you were dead!" He ducked through the fence and ran blindly across the snow toward his colt.

* * *

The next day was the darkest day of the year—Sunturn—when the world spun at the uttermost reach of darkness, before beginning its journey back to the light.

In his room, burrowed half asleep in bed, Jonathon smelled bacon frying. His stomach growled and his eyes opened. He remembered he had not eaten the night before, and then, as the storm rattled his window, he remembered why. The terrible scene in the pasture flashed through his mind.

His knuckles white, he traced the green squares that crisscrossed the blue circles on his quilt, trying to see them instead of the arrow. He thought of how the colt had come to him at last, drawn by the rock's glowing magic. Or had the colt made the rock glow?

A deafening howl of wind shook the house, and something crashed in the attic. He stiffened, staring upward, thinking of the hooded man; last night the nightmare had been worse than ever before. With his white hand pressed to his heart, the hooded man had stood over the bed for what seemed like hours.

Someone knocked on the door. Jonathon jumped.

"Welcome Sunturn," his father said, coming in.

Jonathon took a deep breath and sat up. "Welcome Sunturn."

His father walked over to the window where snow curved like a sail against each pane. "Looks like the storm will go on for a while."

"How did I get here?" Jonathon asked. "Last I remember, I was in the barn, after Caleb and Spinney got the colt in."

"You fell asleep. Uncle Wilford carried you up to the house and put you in bed."

Jonathon twisted the quilt, bitter that Uncle Wilford had brought him inside instead of his father.

"There's something you need to know," his father said, still looking out. "I haven't decided whether to keep the colt."

Jonathon leaned forward. "Please don't let Ma kill him."

"She won't—not now. She was just, well—frightened. Confused."

Jonathon was silent.

His father turned. "Don't judge what you don't understand. Your ma was in the Red Mountains too long. That changes a person."

"It didn't change you."

"Yes, it did. Otherwise I'd have had sense enough not to bring you that colt—fine as he is."

Jonathon scowled. Then he remembered how happy his father had looked when he first came home, happier than Jonathon had ever seen him, his face bright and alive.

"I know your ma seems a little strange right now," his father said. "But she'll snap out of it. She always does."

"She's been like this before?"

"Yes." A brooding look settled on his father's face. "Get dressed. Uncle Wilford sent me to fetch you for breakfast."

Jonathon swung his legs over the side of the bed and stared

at his bow, which leaned in the corner beside the cedar chest. He shivered, remembering the vision of riding the stallion through the contorted peaks. If the Red Mountains could change his parents, he believed more than ever that they could change him too. They could stop this madness that was taking hold of him.

Although he had known for nearly a month that he must go to the Red Mountains, he had been too afraid of the "dangers he could not even imagine." But what danger could be worse than going mad?

On the faded blue wallpaper, golden lines intersected a pattern of birch trees. As Jonathon looked at them, the lines seemed to change into the golden hairs in the colt's mane. No matter what his father said, Jonathon couldn't risk the chance that his mother might harm the colt or set him free. As soon as the storm stopped, he would take him and run away to the Red Mountains.

* * *

Later that day, the fire crackled in the fireplace as Jonathon stood on a ladder in the parlor and fastened a pine bough onto a beam. His father lit the bayberry candles in sconces on each side of the mantle; between them hung a portrait of Karena holding Jonathon when he was a baby.

Lanterns glowed in every corner of the room. More candles—tall, thin, squat, and wide, placed on china saucers, wooden squares, or scraps of tin—burned on the tables and windowsills. The walls flickered like some quivering animal of light. Jonathon tied the last knot, then climbed down the ladder.

"Just smell Uncle Wilford's roast pheasant," his father said.

Jonathon eyed his awkward garlands and didn't answer. The house looked and smelled like any other Sunturn, except that usually his mother hung the garlands in graceful loops, cooked the festive supper, and whirled about, singing, instead of sitting in the rocker staring up at her portrait.

With her hair bound back and a black shawl draped over her shoulders, she looked old and tired, nothing like his joyful, dancing mother. She had neither spoken nor looked at him all day. Was this the same woman who had sat tall and furious upon Windborn yesterday?

Jonathon carried the ladder out to the pantry. There, as in all the other rooms, the curtains had been flung back to let the light inside the house encourage the sun to return. The snow still fell, spotting the darkness. He hoped it would stop soon; a packed bag already lay hidden under his bed.

How, though, would he handle the colt? He cringed at the thought of dragging him on a lead rope. Would he come willingly once he saw they were traveling north? Jonathon's heart beat fast—the colt might even guide him into the Red Mountains, guide him to the blue-eyed girl. He tried not to think of her as a barbarian. Jonathon pressed his forehead against the cold window, then left the pantry.

With his father and Uncle Wilford, Jonathon ate supper in the dining room, but the room seemed hollow without his mother; her empty plate shone bone-white on the green damask cloth. After supper, they carried their hot, frothy cregg—a Sunturn drink made of cream, eggs, and honey— into the parlor, passing beneath the mounted head of the eight-point buck above the archway. Jonathon's mother still sat in the rocker. Her eyes followed the pendulum on the old grandfather clock. Beside her, next to the hearth, gifts overflowed a wicker basket.

"Well." Uncle Wilford eased onto a straight-backed chair, his knees pressed in sharp points under his trousers. "I don't know about the rest of you, but I'm pretty interested in the contents of that basket." He set his crystal cup down. "Here's one for you, Jonathon," he said, giving him a flannel-wrapped bundle.

Jonathon tingled with some of the excitement of past years as he knelt beside Uncle Wilford and unwrapped the flannel. Tiny flies, made of feathers, fur, and bits of yarn wound on fishing hooks, spilled out. Jonathon smiled.

"Thanks," he said, knowing how many hours Uncle Wilford must have spent making the delicate flies with his big, shaky hands. "Your flies catch fish better than anything."

"Well, that's good then." Uncle Wilford said. "Now, here's one from your pa." Jonathon unwrapped a new bridle. The leather was soft and supple; the snaffle polished, cold to the touch.

"Thanks, Pa," he said, his eyes shining, thinking his father must have decided to let him keep the colt. His father avoided his eyes. Then Uncle Wilford lifted a package that Jonathon recognized.

"Here's one for you, Karena," he said and set it on her lap.

She looked at the gift, at the fire, at Uncle Wilford, then pulled the yellow yarn that held the flannel together; as it fell away, her eyes widened.

"It's a birdhouse for your garden," Jonathon muttered. The four sides of the little house fit together perfectly under a peaked roof. A hole made a doorway or window. He had sanded the wood smooth, then painted it white, three coats, with more sanding between each coat. He had built it when she was gone, missing her with every stroke of the brush, but now he didn't want to give her anything.

"I didn't know you could carve like that," his father said. Vines and stars and apples, copied from the cedar chest up in Jonathon's room, decorated the birdhouse walls.

His mother stroked the wood. "They can fly in and out," she said, "through the little round window." Her eyes filled with tears. "Thank you, son. It's beautiful." And then, for the first time since yesterday, she looked at him. Though her eyes had the soft warmth he knew and loved, lavender shadows ringed them.

"I have something for all of you," she said, "though I won't be giving it to you until summer." She paused, looking at her husband who stood leaning with one elbow on the mantle. "A daughter," she added softly. "I hope."

Brian's head jerked back, and he turned his face away from her. There was a silence.

"A sister for Jonathon," she added, her voice cold now. "And a niece for Uncle Wilford to chase after."

"Why that's wonderful news," Uncle Wilford said.

Jonathon said nothing. A sister? Would she have blue eyes too?

Karena still stared at her husband's back. "I have something else for Jonathon," she said abruptly and set the birdhouse down on the floor. She stepped over to the grandfather clock, took a brass key from her pocket, and turned it in the lock on the cabinet door. When the door swung open, she drew out a long, linen-wrapped bundle and cradled it in both hands, as though feeling its weight. Almost reverently, she held it out.

"For my son," she said.

When Jonathon took it, her fingers brushed his, and he knew that he still loved her. He hated himself for still loving her after what she had tried to do.

He pulled away the linen and his mouth opened. A bow made of a rich, tawny wood, with patterns of horn and gold inlaid on the grip and arrow plate, gleamed in his hands. The bow was very old—he could feel its age and the way it seemed almost alive.

"Karena!" his father said. "We have an agreement!" But she ignored him and sat down again.

"This bow is for your journey to the Red Mountains next year, Jonathon," she explained, as though certain he would pass her test.

"It's amazing," Jonathon said, afraid to look at her, fearing she might see he planned to run away. "Where did you get it?"

His father took two strides and stood over Karena.

"You broke our agreement when you stole that colt for him," she said, her chin high.

Jonathon's father stared down at her, the mass of his body like a wall. The scar whitened above his eyebrow. Karena's eyes shifted, and she looked past him at the portrait over the mantle.

"I..." she faltered, seemed to shrink, and leaned back in the rocker. "It's...it's from up North Valley, Jonathon." She reached out and traced the round window on the birdhouse.

Jonathon rubbed his hand from one end of the bow to the other; the polished wood felt as smooth as a cherry. All at once, heat sprang from the red rock in his pocket, and the drums began to pound—come, come, come—their rhythm clashing with the tick-tick of the grandfather clock. Jonathon dropped the bow and looked up. The night outside flattened against the windows, pressing close, as though to extinguish the light in the parlor.

Above the archway, the buck's glass eyes glittered red in the firelight. Flames danced on the points of the antlers; their branching shadows loomed upon the wall, flickering, growing bigger and bigger until they swallowed the ceiling.

Someone, something, called Jonathon's name. He looked at his father, then at Uncle Wilford, who were both staring at him, bewildered. With a shock, Jonathon realized that they heard no wild drums, saw no surging antlers. The madness had him again. His mother was watching him too—her head tilted as though listening to something far away—when a flash of understanding lit her face.

"Jonathon!" She stretched out her arms, but he leaned away, shaking with rage.

"You said it was an old wives' tale!" he cried.

She became still as a stone.

"Make it stop!" he pleaded.

A spasm of pain gripped her face. Then her eyes closed, her head bowed, and she drew her shawl close.

"Earth's Mercy," she whispered.

chapter nine

W hat's wrong, Karena?" Jonathon's father asked, bending over the rocking chair. "What's going on?"
"Can't you see what you have done?" she said, then sprang up and ran from the parlor, leaving the rocker swinging; it creaked, and waved a shadow on the wall.

Brian stood for a moment, his body rigid as a tree trunk, then followed her. Jonathon hunched into a ball, half blinded by the beating pain in his head.

"Come on, son," Uncle Wilford said. "Best place for you right now is bed. A sorry Sunturn this." And for the second night in a row, he helped Jonathon up to his room.

After midnight, the storm ceased and the drums stopped pounding in his ears. Jonathon lay exhausted on his bed, not asleep, not awake. He heard his parents arguing, but their voices seemed faint, removed from him, as though drifting from some other world. The night passed slowly.

Two hours before sunrise, when the dark loosened its grasp, Jonathon dressed, took the bag from beneath his bed, and crept down to the pantry. He filled another bag with food, careful to take nothing that might soon be missed.

As he rummaged, he checked through a list in his mind: bedroll, wax-treated canvas, rope, a pot, flint and tinder, hunting knife, wool clothes, hatchet, candles, arrows, and his old bow—though he hated to leave the new one behind. He had watched his father pack many times.

When all was ready, he glanced around the kitchen, wondering if he would ever see it again. He slipped his bow over his shoulder, tucked a bag beneath each arm, and stepped outside, where he took one look at the snow-shrouded hills and stopped. He sucked in his lower lip; snow or no snow, he would leave for the Red Mountains today. After ducking into the orchard to avoid the road, Jonathon trudged toward the old barn.

Except for occasional four-pronged bird tracks, the snow lay unbroken. The only sound was the swish-crunch-swish of his boots breaking trail. Near the end of one row of apple trees was a drift where a deer had foundered. Jonathon remembered the flame-lit antlers, and his head throbbed dully—either an ache left from last night or the drums playing faintly, he didn't know which.

Inside the old barn, the colt stamped in his stall, restless after being confined. Sighing, Jonathon let him out in the pasture; he would never be coaxed along on a lead rope until he released his pent-up fire. Then Jonathon found a dark corner, hid his gear behind a rusty plough, and went outside.

The sun had not yet risen into the clear, frosty dawn. The colt raced down the pasture, kicking up the new snow. Every few minutes he looked up at the low hills rising toward the sagebrush flat, then snorted and tossed his head.

As Jonathon watched, joy tingled from his fingers to his toes; it seized him, shook him, until he climbed the fence and ran into the pasture like a wild creature himself, his arms flung wide.

"Here, boy. Here, boy," Jonathon called, remembering how

the colt had come to him when the rock had glowed. Now though, the red-gold bay ignored him. As Jonathon panted, his white breath streamed into the air and vanished, taking his sudden joy with it. He came to a halt beside the open shed in the corner of the pasture and sat down to rest on one of the bales stacked beneath the roof. In a moment, he would sneak over to the upper barn to steal saddlebags and a horse. In an hour, if all went well, he would be riding away from Greengard.

He slipped one finger beneath his hat and scratched the bumpy ridge on his forehead. Would his father even miss him after what had happened in the parlor? His father had seen him act like a madman, seen the worst example yet of how different his son was from everyone else. A coppery taste filled Jonathon's mouth.

The colt whinnied. Jonathon turned and saw his mother climb the fence, her purple cloak whirling over the rail. He jumped to his feet, ready to protect the colt, but she didn't have her bow. She pulled off her glove, then held out her hand as she walked toward the bay, who stood watching. When she was two arm lengths away, she pressed her bare hand to her heart.

The colt nodded, tearing at the snow with his left foreleg, then backed up and bolted down the pasture like a flaming star. Smiling, Karena walked over to the shed. With her empty glove, she whisked snow off the bale beside Jonathon and sat down.

"I'm glad," she said.

"About what?" Jonathon muttered, still standing, not looking at her.

"I'm glad I didn't shoot him. It would have been wrong."

"I thought I threw off your aim."

"Perhaps," she said. "Maybe at the last moment, I couldn't bring myself to kill him. He means so...he's so beautiful." The bay ran to the west fence and pricked his ears toward the sagebrush flat. "He's restless," she added.

"Only because he was cooped up."

She shook her head. "He's restless because he hears what you heard last night—the drums beating, the Red Mountains calling."

Jonathon looked at her.

"What happened to you," she said, touching his arm, "was not madness. You are not going insane."

"How would you know?"

"Because I heard them too, faintly."

Jonathon said nothing. After all, if his blue eyes came through her, she might have a touch of madness as well, though not so strong as his.

"I think," his mother said, "that you saw something that I did not. Something—odd?"

He shrugged.

"You had a vision, a glimpse of a mystery. That doesn't mean you're insane." She slapped her glove against her knee. "Though most of the fools in Stonewater Vale would think otherwise."

Unconvinced, Jonathon dug his heel in the snow. These fits—or visions—were coming more often and with more power; soon they would consume him utterly. If that wasn't madness, what was?

His mother crossed her ankles, and her cloak fell open. Beneath it, she wore a long fur jacket, trousers, and high boots lashed to her thighs. His heart contracted in fear.

"Where are you going?" he asked.

She sighed. "I'm sorry, son. I know how you feel about the colt, but I have to take him back now—before it's too late."

"No! Pa won't let you."

"He has agreed—and I would do it even if he hadn't. We are in great danger. Besides, the horse doesn't belong to you."

Jonathon threw down his hat. This could not be happening, not when his bags were packed, his plans laid; he could not go alone. His heart was bound to the colt's; they belonged together.

"I won't give him to those barbarians," he said. "Why will they miss this one horse so much?"

"Why will you?" His mother stood up. "He is special. He is Rhohar."

"What's that supposed to mean?"

She hesitated. "I can't say anymore. Your father and I agreed that it's best not to discuss this. Now say good-bye to him."

"No. I won't let you take him. You'll kill him; I know you will."

Tears shone in her eyes. "I promise to set him free in the Ptarmigan Hills. He knows the way home. His people will be searching for him; they will find…" she stopped.

"Your forehead!" She grabbed his chin with one hand, swept back his matted bangs with the other, and tipped his face toward the light. "The mark!" she cried. "So soon? Why didn't you tell me?"

"Tell you?" he shouted, wrenching away. "I'll tell you something. The barbarians have lots of horses. Fine, beautiful horses! I saw them last fall, down by the river—and there was a girl with blue eyes like mine!"

"What!" Her face turned white.

Suddenly, a pounding like fists exploded inside Jonathon's skull; the red rock seemed to burn through his skin, and hoofbeats thrummed on the air. His mother spun around, looking toward the hills below the sagebrush flat, where a score of Dalriadas rode swiftly toward them.

"It is too late!" she cried. "Agreements be damned. Oh, Jonathon, Rhohar means King."

chapter ten

Jonathon's mother shoved him into a hollow between the bales. The hooves drummed louder.

"Get back," she said, dragging a bale over him.

"But...."

"Keep quiet!" Then she was gone.

Golden light filtered through the cracks between the bales. In his pocket, the rock seemed to come alive, beating with the same rhythm as his heart, the pounding hooves, and the drumming fists. Jonathon crouched down and felt straw prickle his cheek. Why hadn't his mother hidden too? He tried to call her, but no sound came from his throat.

The hoofbeats thundered, paused, then thundered again as the Dalriadas leaped the fence. Jonathon scooted forward and looked through a gap between the bales. The colt flashed by. King, his mother had said. King?

As the sun crested the hill and kindled the pasture into a glittering crystal of light, Jonathon saw the Dalriadas. They rode in a blur of spraying snow and churning hooves. Manes whipped out—brown, red, black—while the horses' legs gathered and stretched, gathered and stretched. A coppery braid swung sideways; a silver brooch gleamed on a shoulder; and a horse's golden tail, set high in the croup, streamed out like a banner. The Dalriadas wore leather hats pulled low that, combined with the dazzle of light and spray, concealed their faces.

Half of them veered off, herding the colt toward the gate; the others raised their bows and rode toward Jonathon's mother. The ground shook. She faced them, her purple cloak rippling behind her; the blue lining flashed like a jewel.

Run Ma, Jonathon tried to shout. He had to find her bow. No, his bow. No, the big one up at the house. But he didn't know how to shoot it....

Her lips moved; she was calling to the Dalriadas, but the bales muffled her words. Her bare hand rose toward them with the palm up, the wrist bent, as though in offering. Then an arrow whizzed through the air and knocked her backwards onto the snow.

Jonathon screamed. As the hoofbeats faded, he fought his way out of the bales. He climbed over them, jumped down, and ran toward his mother.

He slid to his knees beside her.

"I don't want the colt," he told her. "Take him back."

Her face ebbed white, and her eyelids fluttered. Thread by thread, her cloak turned red-brown around the arrow. Then Jonathon couldn't see: she seemed to be fading, the world reeling and melting. The arrow with its brown and white feathers twisted like a snake in her chest. He grabbed her hand; it felt cold. Her glove, where was her glove?

The rock, he remembered, the magic rock. He held it against her cheek. He surrounded her with his arms, pressed his ear against the wet, brown stain on her chest, and listened. The gate creaked on the wind; the Mirandin roared in the distance, but he heard no beat of drum or hoof—or heart.

He screamed and flung the rock away. On her cheek was an impression of the horse.

Then hands grabbed him; hands pulled him away from her.

part two

The valley

chapter eleven

our months later, spring crept out of winter. As Jonathon dug in the ruins of last year's vegetable garden, he heard a meadowlark call and looked up at the hills. The snow had melted. Yellow sun-daisies rioted among the sagebrush and bitterbrush. In a few months the sun would bake the hills brown, but now, at the end of April, all the land was green and waking.

Jonathon shrugged, then stabbed his shovel against the old pumpkin vines, which split against the metal edge. The impact from the blow shuddered up the wooden handle into his arms. He raised the shovel and hurled it down again and again. Metal rang. Plant carcasses, blackened by frost, flew everywhere. Usually the dead plants were mixed into the ground to enrich the soil in November, but last fall the work had not been done. Last fall, Jonathon thought, his mother had still been alive. It seemed like a long time ago.

He flung the shovel away, yanked down the pole beans, and tossed them into the wheelbarrow. Above it, perched on top of a fence post, sat the birdhouse he had made for his mother. It was empty. Jonathon looked at his own house. The round window in the attic flashed ice blue in the sun. Although spring had come to the land, the house still seemed locked in winter—just like his father.

The curtain at the kitchen window twitched, and Widow Grey, who lived down in the crew cottages, peered out. She had always done the heavy cleaning in the house, but now she did the cooking as well. The kitchen was always spotless; the food always bland, and Widow Grey was always spying on him. When Jonathon grabbed the shovel and shook it at her, the curtain fell.

Scowling, he attacked a clump of spiked dremweed. Keep working, he told himself. Everything will be fine if I just keep working. In a few days though, he would finish the garden. Then what would he do? His mouth felt dry, and, as it had all winter, his mind groped ahead for the next task, desperate to leave no void.

He threw a shovelful of weeds into the wheelbarrow and was lifting his foot to stomp everything down when he saw a smooth green leaf poking up. Mixed in with the spiked weeds was a tiny seedling, a rogue apple tree, which had taken root in an ill-fated spot. All at once, an idea sparked in his mind.

He looked over at the house again and saw Sammy standing at the hitching post. A minute later, Jonathon was searching through the house for his father. After checking the first floor and most of the second, he paused outside his parent's bedroom; the door stood halfway open.

"Pa?" he called softly, but the room was empty. Jonathon rolled his lower lip in his teeth, then glanced back at the hallway. Before he could change his mind, he stepped inside the bedroom and shut the door behind him. He had not been in this room since Sunturn.

The cornflower blue walls seemed to float, set off by white trim and the white quilt upon the bed. Between the two windows hung a tapestry of wild swans swimming on a lake. Jonathon walked over to his mother's walnut dresser. On it was her silver hairbrush, two agates, a seashell, and, in an oval frame, a sketch of a flaming, golden apple—his father's notion of a Firegold, painted years ago.

As Jonathon touched the brush's handle, light bounced off its silver back and flashed in the mirror above the dresser. Startled, he glanced up, but instantly turned away from his reflection. When he was halfway across the room, he stopped. Coward, he thought, look at it. He walked back to the mirror and pushed aside his bangs.

Ridges bulged across his forehead, as though something had tunneled beneath his skull and raised it up. Tinged reddish-brown, the ridges began at the corner of each eyebrow, near his nose, then swept up, curved, and branched into three forks, forming mirror images of each other. Although no one had noticed it yet, Jonathon knew that he couldn't hide it much longer.

"The mark," his mother had called it, but the mark of what? Madness? Jonathon laughed bitterly.

"Come on and get me," he said, staring at it. "What's taking you so long?" The sooner he went crazy, the sooner he could forget everything. As for seeking a cure in the Red Mountains, he would never set foot in the cursed Dalriadas' land now, not to keep from going mad, not even to save his worthless life.

Suddenly, reflected in the mirror, he saw the hooded man from his dreams standing behind him. Jonathon spun around, but no one was there; nothing moved except the tapestry stirring in the breeze from the window. When he looked into the mirror again, he saw only himself. His heart raced. Never before had he seen the man outside of his bedroom; it must mean the madness was growing. He stood quite still for a moment, then nodded. Good, he thought, good.

At that moment, he heard his father shouting outside. Jonathon ran to the bedroom door, left it exactly halfway open, and raced downstairs to the porch. His father and Widow Grey stood beside the hitching post.

"I told you to leave the flower beds alone!" Brian said.

"But they're so dreadfully untidy, sir," Widow Grey said, holding a pair of clippers; a trail of forget-me-nots littered the grass. "I'm just trimming them into nice, straight borders. The flowers are all jumbled together. Each kind should have its proper place."

"My wife liked them 'jumbled,' and that is how they'll stay. Understand?"

"Oh yes, sir." Widow Grey clutched her clippers, gathered up her skirt, and scampered toward the house, trying to shake a weed from her shoe even as she ran.

Brian, his eyes still angry, nodded at Jonathon and slammed his hat on his head. He looked thin, the skin around his eyes puckered and dry.

I don't care if he's angry, Jonathon thought. I don't care about anything.

"Pa," he said. "About those new apple trees—the Ruby Spice—the ones you're putting in the North Pasture...." He stopped, his tongue thickened like a sponge, stopping his throat; he had forgotten that it was the North Pasture.

"What about them?" his father asked, unlooping Sammy's reins from the hitching post.

"I want to plant them myself."

"What?" Surprised, his father looked at him. "If this is so you can get out of going back to school...."

"No. Besides, there's only a few weeks of school left. Can't I just start back in the fall?"

His father sighed. "I should have made you go back months ago."

Made him? Jonathon almost laughed. After his mother had died, his father had not cared about anything that Jonathon did. Brian had brooded for weeks: unshaven, drinking, raging at himself, raging at the Dalriadas. The snow had fallen on and on like a note crooned by a madman. Then, late in March, when Greengard had begun to creep alive again, he had too.

"I suppose you're right about school," his father said. "But why would you want to plant six hundred seedlings?"

"I...." Jonathon slid his jaw back and forth. "I want to work hard. Really hard."

His father bent his head and adjusted Sammy's stirrup. "All right," he said at last, seeming almost pleased. "It's time you had more responsibility around here. But the crew will dig the irrigation ditches. Let's ride down and see if the ploughing is done." He swung onto Sammy's back. Jonathon stretched up one arm, but his father shook his head.

"Go saddle Nellie," he ordered. "I'll wait."

His cheeks burning, Jonathon turned away and scuffled toward the barn. Pa blames me, he thought. He still blames me. Other than his ranting, his father had never discussed that terrible day: the Dalriadas, the colt, the killing. Jonathon had sat dry-eyed through his mother's funeral because weeping had seemed merely the tip of the mountain of his grief and guilt; he had sat silently, knowing he was responsible for her death. Even when they'd buried her, not in the Village graveyard but up the canyon beneath the pines, Jonathon had not wept.

Inside the barn, Jonathon leaned his forehead against Nellie's warm neck for a moment, then saddled and led her out.

* * *

On Tuesday morning, after Jonathon finished the garden, he began on the new orchard. Every morning after that, he gulped down two of Widow Grey's sour biscuits and rushed over to the North Pasture. First, he measured out the pasture with twine and stakes. His arms burned from swinging the sledge hammer, but he kept on, ignoring the blisters that covered his hands. After a week, six hundred stakes marked the pasture.

Then he began to dig. By the first stake in the first row, he stomped the shovel into the ground, scooped a load of soil, swung the shovel, and let the dirt slide hissing off. Then again, stomp, scoop, swing, hiss, again and again—lower, deeper— until a mound of soil rose beside the hole. He breathed the smell of the potent, almost black, Valley bottom soil, still moist from the spring rains. Sweat dripped down his back. Without raising his eyes from the ground, he walked to the second stake and began all over again.

Soon the shovel seemed an extension of his own arm. His muscles hardened. The days grew longer, and he worked longer, digging away until the very edge of nightfall. He grew so tired, so numb, that he hardly knew the difference between being awake and asleep; his whole life seemed one long dream of earth and digging.

When all the holes were ready, he transferred seedlings from the old barn to the wheelbarrow and, leaning forward into the weight, pushed the wheelbarrow out into the pasture.

Three more weeks passed. On a Saturday in the beginning of June, a few days after a hailstorm, the sun blazed on his head as he planted. He paused to wipe his neck and looked up; the sun shone bone-white on a boulder embedded in the hill. For a moment—through a hazy golden light—he saw again the wave of horses, riders, and bows that had poured down....

Stop it, he told himself. Stop it and work. He knelt and began to mix compost into the hole, when his hand felt a stone. He pulled the stone out and was about to toss it when something about its shape seemed familiar; he opened his hand. The red rock lay in his palm; he hadn't seen it since his mother had died.

"Rhohar," he whispered and heard beating hooves in his mind. A shadow arched over him. It must have happened here; his mother must have died here. He jumped up to fling the rock away, his face crumpled with rage, when he saw Rosamund Landers walking toward him.

chapter twelve

Rosamund waved. Her bare feet sank into the ground as she walked, her shoes swinging from two of her fingers. A wreath of sun-daisies circled her head like a crown; beneath it, her braid hung over her shoulder, gleaming as bright as corn tassels.

Jonathon froze; he didn't know what to do with the rock. He slipped it inside his pocket, dropped to his knees, and plunged his arms back into the hole.

"Hello, Jonathon," Rosamund said when she reached him.

"What are you doing here?" he asked, frantically mixing the compost.

"My pa's visiting at your house. I haven't seen you for a long, long time, so your Uncle Wilford brought me down here."

"Where is he?" Jonathon looked around, worried that Uncle Wilford might have seen him find the rock.

"He's chasing one of your milk cows that got out. I stopped by that hill to pick flowers." She pointed. "You have lots more sun-daisies than we do."

Jonathon relaxed, certain now that she had not seen the rock, and glanced up at her. Rosamund's dress shimmered the same pale pink as the blossoms on the Cheldy Apples across the lane. A white sock dangled from each of the two pockets on her skirt.

She touched one of the sun-daisies on her crown. "I'm glad that the late frost didn't hurt them. My pa's upset, cause we lost a lot of Appelunes. The buds were all opening, and they were so pretty." She paused. "When I was little, I used to cup the blossoms like this…" she lifted her hands "…and breathe on them to keep them warm." She bent her head and blew softly into her hands.

An ache welled inside him. Jonathon turned away, took half a fish from a bucket, and tossed it into the hole for fertilizer.

Rosamund dropped her shoes on the ground. "Did you catch those?"

"No, I've been too busy." He wished she would go away.

"I caught a fish on Saturday—about that big." She opened her hands as wide as her shoulders.

"You? What kind?"

"An elger."

"What did you catch him with?"

"A black leech."

He stared at her standing there in her starched pink dress, unable to imagine her impaling a leech on a hook.

"I didn't know you fished," was all he could think of to say.

"My brothers taught me. But my pa doesn't like me to, much. He said it was fine when I was little, but I'm getting too big now."

That made no sense to Jonathon. "But do you like fishing?"

"A lot." She coiled her fingers in the strands of her braid. "But not if it's wrong for girls to do it," she added quickly.

"Why would it be wrong?"

"Well, Pa always talks about the things women do, and the things men do, and the laws of the Valley and such." She frowned. "It's confusing. Do you think it's all right for girls to fish?"

"Sure." Jonathon pictured his mother fishing by the Mirandin, then saw her crumpled on the snow. He scowled and swept the soil back into the hole so fast that clouds of it drifted over everything, including Rosamund.

She didn't step back.

"I bet you didn't clean that fish yourself," Jonathon snapped.

"Nobody would ever show me how."

He felt sorry for her then, which made him angrier. "You have eyes, don't you?" he said and stalked to the next hole. Rosamund followed.

"How come you're planting trees?" she asked. "Why don't your hired folk do it?"

"Because I want to."

"Can I plant one? I've never done that either."

Jonathon shrugged. "If you want." He picked up a seedling. "Here," he gave her his knife. "I'll hold the tree. You cut the twine around the root ball."

She did.

"Now pull off the burlap," he said, "then spread the roots out a little."

Her small brown hands moved deftly. They knelt beside the hole, and she lowered the tree. She scooped the soil in, then patted it down, leaving her palm prints. Together they lifted a heavy bucket, and water fell like silver around the tree.

She spoke, but her voice was so quiet that he heard only the word, "blue."

"What did you say?" he asked, sloshing the bucket down. Had she called him loony-blue? He had never dreamed that she would tease him about the madness.

"I said," she whispered, "that I think the sky is beautiful today...so blue and clear. Blue's my very favorite color." And she looked straight into his eyes. The two of them still knelt side by side; a fold of her skirt draped across his knee. Her brown eyelashes had tips of gold. When Jonathon leaned closer, her head tilted.

"Oh," she said, "you've hurt your forehead!"

He froze, unable to breathe, unable to lean away.

"Rosamund!" a deep voice exclaimed. Jonathon started and looked up; Mr. Landers towered over them. "Rosamund! What are you doing?"

"Why, Jonathon was just letting me plant a tree, Pa."

"Letting you?" He yanked her up by the elbow. "Letting you squat in the dirt?"

Jonathon stood slowly as Uncle Wilford walked up.

"Look at your dress!" Mr. Landers said. "And your hands and feet are filthy!"

Rosamund looked, unperturbed, at the brown stains. "It'll wash off, Pa," she said, then blinked up at him, confused.

"We've got two more calls to make this afternoon and just look at you. And what's that nonsense on your head?" Mr. Landers stared. "You look like, like some, some…" and he plucked off the crown of flowers and threw it down. The corners of Rosamund's mouth quivered.

Mr. Landers turned to Uncle Wilford. "I thought you were with her."

"I had to go after a milk cow," Uncle Wilford explained. "What's the matter with you, Kenneth?"

"Get in the buggy, Rosamund," Mr. Landers ordered, glaring at Jonathon. Tears curved down Rosamund's face. She looked at the crown lying like rubbish in the dirt, then picked up her shoes. "Put those on!" Mr. Landers said. She slipped her dirty feet into her shoes and trudged away, the socks still dangling from her pockets.

Mr. Landers turned to Jonathon. "I know you and Rosamund are friends, but it will be best if you don't get too friendly." He looked immaculate in his black suit coat and white starched shirt; a silver slider held the cords on his tie. "Do you understand me?"

"No sir," Jonathon said, conscious of the dirt on his clothes and the fish stink on his hands.

"Then I'll explain it to you," Mr. Landers said. "The Landers family line is one of the oldest in the South Valley. It is pure and—how shall I put this?—it is sound. And I intend to see that it stays that way."

There was a silence.

"Now do you understand me, Jonathon?" Mr. Landers asked.

"Yes."

"Excellent." And Mr. Landers walked away.

"Earth's Mercy, Kenneth," Uncle Wilford swore, following him. "They were only planting trees...."

Jonathon spun and attacked the next hole with the shovel; dirt flew in every direction. After the Landers had driven off, Uncle Wilford came back.

"You're just going to have to fill that hole in again," he said.

"I thought he was supposed to be our friend," Jonathon said.

"He is. Your pa's best friend anyway. At least compared to some others I won't name."

"Some friend."

"You just surprised him. Parents don't like to think that their children are growing up."

"It wasn't that." Jonathon threw the shovel down and stalked toward the wheelbarrow. "You know it wasn't that." He ripped the twine off another seedling.

Uncle Wilford sighed. "You're right. But if you want to avoid trouble, you won't mention this to your pa."

"I know that."

"Good." Uncle Wilford glanced around the pasture and whistled. "I never thought you'd get them planted so fast. I better get the crew to finish up the irrigation ditches."

"What was all that about the cow?" Jonathon muttered.

"Bessie broke out of the south pasture and wandered up to the sagebrush flat. Looking for some wild garlic to flavor her milk, no doubt."

Jonathon snorted.

"Those bales you used for target practice are still up there," Uncle Wilford said. "Haven't been up this year, have you?"

Jonathon's hands trembled as they spread out the roots. "Been too busy here," he said.

"You're about done here. You can start practicing with your bow again—or better yet, the one your ma gave you."

Jonathon began filling in the hole.

Uncle Wilford sighed. "You've got to pick up your bow again sometime, son."

"No, I don't."

"Your ma loved shooting—and hunting too. It's probably the best gift she passed on to you."

"Gift?" Jonathon asked.

"Didn't she ever tell you how good she thought you were?"

"No." It seemed there were many things his mother had never told him.

"Well she told me. Probably thought it would swell up your young fool head too much."

"I don't need to hunt," Jonathon said, "I can get meat from the animals we raise."

"True. But shooting takes you down inside yourself. Helps you to find what's there, so you can hold on to it, use it to get stronger. Besides...." Uncle Wilford looked around the pasture, now an orchard, then down at a hole in the earth; the rims around his eyelids grew pink. "Besides, you've got to be able to defend yourself, or someone you love." Then he left.

Jonathon drove the shovel straight down and put both hands on top of the handle; his shoulders hunched. His head dropped forward onto his hands, and he stood, muscles taut. The bony ridges on his forehead pressed against his knuckles. Rosamund. His head jerked up; Rosamund had seen the mark. Would she tell her father? Jonathon fought down a sudden heaving in his stomach and told himself it didn't matter: Mr. Landers already thought of him as a freak. Jonathon lifted the shovel and went back to work.

Two hours later, he planted the last seedling, watered it, and stretched his arms above his head. As he looked over the work he had done, the magic of the Valley—planting and growing—surged in his blood, calling to him from all his ancestors who had worked this land, waking both joy and pain.

Jonathon pushed the empty wheelbarrow back toward the barn. Gold gleamed on the soil; he picked up the crown of wilted sun-daisies. He remembered the rock and wondered whether to throw it away. But how could he, when this very thing—his hand closed over it—had touched his mother's cheek? At the same instant, the wind blew gently on his face, and he pictured Rosamund breathing into her hands. Again, the pain swept over him, stronger than before.

He shook the dirt off the crown, then slipped it over the top of the tree he had planted with her; all around the trunk, boot prints trampled the impressions of small, bare feet. He bit his lip. You've got to pick up the bow again sometime. You've got to be able to defend yourself, or someone you love.

Jonathon thought about Mr. Landers' anger, thought about the Dalriadas riding toward his mother. Then he remembered what an arrow had done, and he hurried away from the tree so fast that the wheelbarrow rattled.

He didn't need to shoot; he didn't need to hunt. He already knew what was inside him.

chapter thirteen

Early the next morning, Jonathon walked through the Ruby Spice trees, checking his work and planning his next task—a better fence to keep out the deer. The world shone brighter and sharper than it had for months: the barn gleamed like a red geranium; water sparkled in an irrigation ditch; and the leaves on the cottonwoods winked in the light as they fluttered. The soil itself had a radiance, as though a song quivered above it. As the numbness inside him—which had begun to melt yesterday—melted even more, Jonathon stopped abruptly, staring at nothing.

At last he began to walk again, but he had taken only a few steps when he saw a strange mark on one of the trunks. He knelt down to look. A strip of bark had been cut off all around the trunk, exposing a yellow ring of bare wood; the tree had been girdled. Worse yet, it was not the work of tooth or claw; only a knife could have cut such a perfect ring. With the bark severed, the seedling would die.

Jonathon's hand closed around the wound. Who would

have done such a horrible thing? Deliberately destroyed life and livelihood? He ran to the next tree and found that it, too, bore the yellow ring, as did the one after, and the one after that. By the time he reached the end of the row, where Greengard ended and Ironhill began, he had counted thirty-six rings. Thirty-six dying trees.

He clutched a branch. Just when he had become attached again to something, more dying—first his mother and the baby she was carrying and now the trees. Was this field cursed? He felt as if his own skin had been stripped away, leaving him raw, exposed, bleeding.

He heard a sound like a muffled laugh and looked up. On the Dakken's side of the fence, two rotting wooden bins were piled on top of each other, with a black fringe rippling behind them. Jonathon squinted; was it an animal? Then Timothy stepped out; the fringe had been his black curls.

"Hey, loony-blue," Timothy said. "Looking for this?" He whirled the dried crown of sun-daisies around and around on his finger. "Or this?" And with his other hand, he held up a knife that glittered in the sun.

"You?" Jonathon asked. "But why?"

"Think hard and maybe you'll figure it out, though you're probably way too dumb."

"Tell me why!" Jonathon demanded.

"All right, dummy." Timothy laughed, flashing his perfect white teeth. "I'll spell it out for you." He set the crown on top of the bins, then jumped over the fence and swaggered toward Jonathon, who stepped back, fearing Timothy might see the mark.

"I saw you with Rosamund yesterday," Timothy said, scowling. "It was sickening—you practically kissed her. This," he held up the knife, "was a warning. You stay away from her. She's mine, and I don't want her polluted by some loony like you."

Jonathon glared. "You're going to be in big trouble when my pa finds out."

"You better make up a real good story, cause if you tell on me, this is what will happen to you." Timothy grasped one of the seedlings, worked it back and forth, and with a sudden yank pulled it out of the ground, uprooting it completely. He held the tree straight out, with its roots pointed toward the sky, then he threw it on the ground.

Jonathon stared down at the tree. That makes thirty-seven, he thought. Thirty-seven.

Laughing, Timothy hopped over the fence, grabbed the crown, and ran back to Ironhill.

* * *

"But what does it all mean, Pa?" Jonathon asked the following afternoon. He sat at the kitchen table reading the parchment his father had placed in his hands. Phrases about property, borders, and dates—beginning with words like 'wherefore' and 'thereunto'—jumbled across the page; in the center was his name, Jonathon A. Brae, decorated with curls and swashes.

"It means," said Brian, sitting down across from him, "that Timothy Dakken won't be girdling any more of your trees."

"I don't understand."

"It's a deed. The title to Ironhill Orchard, in your name."

"The Dakkens' land?" Jonathon asked, astounded. "In my name?" The parchment seemed to stick to his fingers. "But how—?"

"I called in the debt." His father crossed his left ankle over his right knee. "I'd been letting it slide because I thought the fear of losing his land would keep Bill from making more trouble over..." he stopped, glanced at Jonathon, then looked away. "But after what Timothy did yesterday...." He shook his head.

"It's all legal," he added. "Bill Dakken is your tenant: a tenant on his own land." Brian's eyes burned with land passion—an ancient passion, old as the Valley itself. "Timothy has no land to inherit now. You own it." He laughed and drummed his fingers against his boot.

Jonathon blinked; the lines on the paper wiggled like snakes, blurring before his eyes. He could almost feel his father's boot print in Dakken's soil, the sole ridged, the edges cut deep.

"Dakken will live on the place and work it," Brian said, "but it won't be his. And there won't be an hour in the day, not a minute in the day, that he won't think of that."

Jonathon stared at the paper. To lose your land…he couldn't imagine it. To be landless would be like being naked. The smell of blood came to him and the smell of smoke.

"Dakken's been a thorn in my side for years," his father said, holding out his hand for the deed. "He had this coming. As for Timothy, assuming he survives the beating Bill's giving him, he's not to set foot on Greengard. If there's any more trouble, I'll turn the whole family out on Guther's Way. I'll go lock up the deed now."

Jonathon didn't move. The kitchen seemed dark, close as a den in the earth. He rubbed his thumb on the table that Widow Grey had scrubbed and bleached until the wood looked beaten. His father had only made everything worse. Jonathon had always known that Mr. Dakken hated him because of his blue eyes, now Mr. Dakken would hate him even more.

But I own Timothy's land, he thought, a hard knot of triumph inside him. Me, a loony-blue. Timothy could never have Rosamund now, not without land. Jonathon smiled and fingered the bandage he had stuck on his forehead in the hope of concealing the mark.

All of a sudden, footsteps came pounding up the kitchen stairs.

"Mr. Brae, sir! Mr. Brae!" someone shouted, then beat on the door. Caleb burst in, panting, red in the face, his lone tuft of gray hair sticking straight up.

"What's wrong?" Jonathon sprang from his chair.

"Where's your pa? Get your pa."

Jonathon's father rushed into the kitchen. "Is the barn on fire?"

"No, no," Caleb said. "I don't know what's wrong. Wilford sent word to fetch you and quick—quicker than lightning. Hurry on sir, hurry on!"

"Calm down, Caleb," Brian said, walking out the door; Jonathon followed. "Fetch me where? Where's Wilford?"

"Spinney said that Wilford said the pears, sir."

Brian gritted his teeth. "Which pears, Caleb!"

"The Greentales. Mid section."

Jonathon wondered if Timothy had struck again. Girdling the seedlings would be nothing compared to destroying the Greentales, mature trees which produced the best crop on the orchard. His father ran down the porch stairs, jumped on Caleb's horse, and, shouting, "Yah!" rode away down Coyote Road. As fast as he could, Jonathon raced after him, the dust from the road flying into his face.

When he reached the middle section of the Greentales a few minutes later, he heard voices but couldn't see anyone; the leaves were too thick. He squatted, peering through the rows of trunks until he saw his father and Uncle Wilford. He ran another twenty yards and found them standing with their heads bent over a branch.

"What's happened?" Jonathon asked, breathless.

His father looked up. His eyes, nearly always bleak these days, were bleaker than usual.

"Verblight," he said.

"What!" Jonathon exclaimed. Verblight, a disease that attacked fruit trees, could devastate entire orchards. He saw the dead, brown leaves on the branches that framed his father's face. "Oh, Pa, are you sure?"

"Of course I'm sure," he snapped, then, as he looked at Jonathon, his thumb began to rub against the knuckle on his first finger.

"How bad is it?" Jonathon asked.

"Bad enough," Uncle Wilford said. "Forty-three trees showing signs so far. And that's just in this half of this section."

Jonathon's father sighed. "We'll have to search the entire orchard." The infected branches, even whole trees, would have to be cut out and burned to prevent the disease from spreading.

"Take a look here, Jonathon," Uncle Wilford said, "where we peeled off the bark."

Jonathon, who had never seen verblight before, examined the bright orange wood. The hailstorm that had struck a few days ago had gouged the leaves and bark, opening the way to disease. Timothy was not the culprit this time. Nobody knew what caused verblight; some folks said one thing, some another, and some—Jonathon's head snapped up—some said the Dalriadas. Had they befouled the land when they set their cursed feet on Greengard last winter?

His father was watching him, rolling one of the blighted leaves in his fingers.

Uncle Wilford wiped his forehead with his red plaid handkerchief. "I better ride over to the crew cottages and get everybody out looking."

"I'll check the Ruby Spice," Jonathon said.

His father still stared at him, frowning. "I'll keep searching this section," he said at last and walked away, dropping the tattered leaf.

Uncle Wilford shook his head. "Your pa didn't need this. Come on, son, I'll give you a ride."

They mounted Uncle Wilford's dappled horse, Steady, and rode back through the orchard. The threat of verblight hung over Jonathon like a menacing shadow. He wondered why his father had looked at him so strangely, then had a terrible thought: if the Dalriadas had befouled the land, then the blight was his fault too, as was his mother's death because he had stopped her from returning the colt.

"Here we are," Uncle Wilford said when they reached the fledgling orchard. "Let us know right away what you find."

After searching for an hour, Jonathon had found no sign of verblight. He paused beside the little stack of girdled seedlings that he had pulled out earlier and then looked out at the live trees instead. The sun, soon to set, spun a golden light through the clouds; they burned red gold and reminded him of...Rhohar.

On the south side of the orchard, a gray plume spurted up; the crew had already begun burning the contaminated trees. Jonathon watched the smoke curl up and point like a finger toward the sky.

How much more of his life would the Dalriadas ruin?

chapter fourteen

For three days and three nights, a smoky haze crept through Stonewater Vale, gathering, thickening, grinding like a heel into the hearts of the besieged. Greengard was not the only orchard struck by verblight; the weather had caused the same damage everywhere. All up and down the Vale, trees were burning.

At least, Jonathon thought, as he trudged through the Ambrosia Pears, the scope of the blight meant that the Dalriadas hadn't caused it and that he was not responsible. He spotted a telltale clump of brown leaves, climbed into the tree, and looped a yellow ribbon over the branch. Caleb, who was working behind him, would cut it off and haul it away. Limbs from hundreds of trees had been thrown on the fire, and still the crew searched.

Doggedly, Jonathon walked on. The smoke in the air stung his eyes. Each time he hung a ribbon, his hands moved more slowly. Sweat pooled along the top of the bandage on his forehead, making his skin itch; he wanted to peel it off but didn't dare. The image of a cool mountain peak towered up in his mind—the tallest, glimmering peak of the Red Mountains. For a moment he longed again to go there, until he thought of the Dalriada who had killed his mother. Then he wanted to take an enormous sledgehammer and with one powerful blow shatter the mountain to its roots.

When Jonathon came to the end of the row, he saw Timothy at the same instant that Timothy saw him; they stared at each other, separated only by a fence and twenty yards of air that seemed suddenly charged with lightning. Behind Timothy, two fourteen-year-old boys, Egan and Nick—part of Ironhill's crew—threw blighted branches into the back of a wagon.

Timothy walked stiffly toward Jonathon and didn't stop until his chest pressed against the fence at the very edge of Greengard. Timothy's hands hung loose, not jammed in his back pockets as usual. He said nothing but only stood, staring at Jonathon.

A dark, spidery bruise sprawled along Timothy's jaw and spread over his cheekbone, where it blended into another bruise—this one purple—around his eye. On the other side of his head, his ear was mangled and swollen. A gash in his lower lip had begun to heal crookedly. Even his curls seemed limp.

"You bastard," Timothy said, and Jonathon saw that two of his teeth had been knocked out, leaving gaps in his once-perfect, flashing smile. Timothy's good looks, like his land, were gone forever.

"You bloody bastard," he said again, louder.

Egan and Nick looked up from the wagon, saw Jonathon, and came running over to the fence.

"Want us to get him for you, Timothy?" asked Nick. One side of his ragged, green shirt flopped over his trousers.

"No," Timothy said. "This is between him and me. This is something you wouldn't understand."

Egan sniggered. "Oh. Listen to him. You're no better than us, now."

"Hold your tongue!" Timothy said. "You still take orders from me." Then he turned to Jonathon.

"You think you're so big, so important. But you'll never get my land. Pop's made a legal complaint to the Village Council; you're a bastard, and no bastard can own land."

Jonathon shrugged. "He can say whatever he wants. Nobody will believe it."

"Oh no? A lot of folks believe it," Timothy said. "Just like a lot of folks think your pa's gotten way too big for his britches. Pop has six people ready to testify against your ma. Everybody knew how much she liked to gather wild honey in the hills."

"You take that back, Timothy Dakken," Jonathon said.

Nick grinned. "Think about those trips your ma took alone, Jonathon. Your pa tried to hide it, but everybody knew."

"And she visited old Man Craven too," Egan added, pulling at the knobby mole on his chin. "Funny how much he looks like you, isn't it?"

"Two loony-blues," Timothy said. "Peas in a pod. I bet he's your real father."

"That's not true," Jonathon said.

"If you don't believe me, ask your pa." Timothy leaned over the fence, his eyes bright with malice. "Why, he told Mr. Landers that he thinks you're not his son."

"Liar!" Jonathon shouted.

"Poor little boy," Timothy cooed. "Poor little boy don't know who his pappy is."

"You're a landless liar! You're nothing but a dog-faced hired hand!"

Timothy grabbed the fence. "The barbarians should have shot you too. Then we'd be rid of you and your whoring mother!"

The world seemed to crack. The rage that had been buried for months in the pit of Jonathon's stomach flashed out, and his fist slammed into Timothy's nose. Timothy staggered back. Jonathon jumped over the fence, lunged, and dragged him to the ground. Punching and kicking, they rolled together.

"Go, Timothy!" Egan shouted

"Hit the bastard good!" yelled Nick.

Jonathon tasted dirt, then blood. His speed, strength, and the long lessons with his father under the oak made up for Timothy's greater size. Jonathon hit again, faster, harder. It felt good; it felt wonderful. Anger focused to a red point inside his mind, and his forehead began to ache. Then the drums, which had been silent since his mother had died, pounded wildly in his ears. He faltered.

Timothy seized the chance; he scrambled on top of Jonathon, scratching his face like a crazed cat. Timothy's fingers caught the edge of the bandage, dug beneath it, and tore it off. Pain exploded in Jonathon's eye as Timothy punched him. Then, his arm tensed for another blow, Timothy froze and stared down at Jonathon's forehead.

"What the...?" he said. A moment later, Timothy jumped to his feet.

Jonathon staggered up too, the pain in his forehead throbbing, burning fiercely; it far surpassed the sting in his eye.

"Look at that!" Egan pointed at Jonathon. "What is that? What is...he?"

"His forehead..." Nick shouted. "Those ridges—they're glowing."

Jonathon saw fear in their faces, even in Timothy's, crusted with dirt and blood, more battered than before. All three boys began to back away. Jonathon tried to look up at his forehead, but could see nothing. When he touched one of the ridges, it felt hot, searing hot, and his hand recoiled as though he had brushed an oven. And still the pain in his head throbbed on and on.

Timothy, Nick, and Egan turned and fled, leaving behind the wagon with its load of blighted trees.

* * *

"What are you doing, Jonathon?" his father asked, suddenly beside him. Jonathon blinked, and found that he was leaning head forward against the barn. Only inches from his eyes, a strip of peeling, red paint hung by its edge, exposing the gray wood beneath. How had he gotten here? How long had he been standing here? The peeling paint blurred; he felt dizzy and sick.

"I'm talking to you, boy," his father said sharply.

Boy, Jonathon thought, always boy. Never son. He took a deep breath, straightened, and looked his father in the face.

Brian frowned. "Earth's Mercy," he said, "look at that eye. What happened?"

"Fight."

"I never would have guessed. Who?"

"Timothy."

His father's lips pressed into a thin, hard line; he started to speak, then stopped: one of the crew was watching. "Get in the barn, Jonathon," he said.

Jonathon followed him around the corner and into the barn. Uncle Wilford was bending over a broken ladder, fitting a new rung between the sidepieces.

"Need more ribbons for the pears, Jonathon?" Uncle Wilford asked, looking up; then he saw the black eye and whistled. "Ouch," he said, his brow crinkling like a dried apple.

"Now," Brian said. "Tell me everything that happened. Was Timothy meddling with the Ambrosias?"

Jonathon shook his head. "He wasn't on Greengard, exactly. He was at the edge of the fence."

"By the look of you, I'd say you didn't fight on top of any fence."

"No. I...I went onto Ironhill."

His father sighed. "I thought you had better judgment than that."

"Why did Timothy hit you?" Uncle Wilford asked.

Jonathon dug one toe into a bit of straw on the dirt floor. "Because I punched him."

"You started the fight?" his father asked, startled. "Why?"

"Well, he called me a name."

"That's why you hit him?" his father exclaimed.

"No."

"Why then?"

"He..." Jonathon stopped, afraid to explain. Timothy's words shouted through his head. Bastard. Poor little boy don't know who his pappy is. The barbarians should have shot you too. Then we'd be rid of you and your whoring mother.... Jonathon squeezed his eyes shut, wincing at the pain, and tried to hold back the sound of that terrible word—and worse, the terrible thought that forced its way into his mind.

What if it was true? What if he was not his father's son?

Jonathon opened his eyes and looked at the two men; they seemed far away, as though they stood at the other end of a tunnel. Neither of them had a horrible mark on his forehead; neither of them had blue eyes. They didn't know what it meant to be different, to feel lost.

"Why did you hit Timothy?" his father demanded.

Jonathon shrugged. His father grabbed him and lifted him up.

"Answer me!" His father shook him.

"Put me down!" Jonathon cried, his feet swinging in the air. He squirmed to get away, but his father's fingers dug in harder. Jonathon glared into his father's angry eyes, only inches away.

"I hit him," Jonathon shouted, "because he called Ma a whore!"

Brian's head jerked back. He held Jonathon a second longer, then lowered him to the ground. Jonathon backed away, tears spilling down his cheeks; he brushed them off.

"It's all right, son," Uncle Wilford said, softly.

Son, Jonathon thought. The dizziness surged, and he knew that it was not all right; nothing had been right since he had looked into the silver bowl and seen his own blue eyes looking back. From that moment on, he had feared to speak of his strangeness to his father, feared his father might turn away from him again.

But now Jonathon knew he had nothing to lose; he couldn't be any more alone with this burden than he already was. He had carried it too long, and now, with the mark added, it was too heavy, too heavy to bear, and he could not live alone with it another day, another minute, even if that meant his father turned away from him forever.

"Pa," Jonathon said. "There's something wrong with me."

"What do you mean?" his father asked.

"I'm different. It's not just my eyes. I hear sounds—like drums beating. And look at this." Jonathon slid his hands up and smoothed back his bangs, exposing his ridged forehead.

His father stared. "No," he said. "Damn it, no." He stood silhouetted against the green orchard framed in the barn door. The barn was growing dark; only one lantern had been lit for evening chores.

"What is it, Pa?" Desperately, Jonathon looked at Uncle Wilford who still held the rung in his hands. His eyes full of love, Uncle Wilford nodded slightly, encouraging Jonathon to continue.

"Pa," Jonathon tried again. "During the fight, the boys said the mark—that's what Ma called it—they said it glowed."

His father turned his head away. His shadow, cast by the lantern, loomed upon the wall of the barn.

Uncle Wilford spoke. "You have to tell him, Brian. You can't put it off any longer."

The porch bell clanged; it was Widow Grey announcing supper. Before, Jonathon's mother had always rung the bell lightly, quickly, but now it tolled in a heavy, plodding rhythm.

chapter fifteen

Jonathon sat beside Uncle Wilford in the parlor and held a piece of beef against his black eye; the raw meat smelled good to him, pungent, almost vinegary. The fight had drained him so much that he thought he could eat an entire plateful of it. During the past hour, he had washed off the worst of the grime, and Uncle Wilford had dressed a cut on his cheek.

His father came in. "I sent the nosy Widow home early," he said and started closing windows. "Supper can wait."

"Aren't you being a little overcautious?" Uncle Wilford asked.

"You know what's at stake here," Brian said. After he slammed the last window shut, he sat down in the straight-backed chair—a chair which Jonathon had never seen him use before—and pulled off his boots. With the heel of his hand, he rubbed a smudge off the leather, then lined up the boots on the floor. The days spent battling the blight had left his eyes red-rimmed from smoke and lack of sleep.

As Jonathon watched, he wanted to scream with

impatience. What did his father have to tell him? And why didn't he start? His father peeled off one sock and began on the other, but stopped with it halfway over his heel.

"There's no good way to say this, Jonathon," he said, his voice low. "You're part Dalriada."

The meat slipped from Jonathon's fingers and fell with a splat onto his thigh. He must have heard wrong.

"Did you say...Dalriada?" he asked. He looked at Uncle Wilford, who nodded, and then at his father, who became busy with his socks. Dalriada? Jonathon stared down at the red slab of beef with its rind of fat, its stink of vinegar: a few moments ago he had wanted to eat a plateful, like...like some barbarian who craved raw human flesh. Suddenly he leaped off the sofa, and the meat went flying.

"Get it off me! Get if off!" he yelled, brushing his pants over and over even though the meat lay on the floor.

"Calm down!" Uncle Wilford said. "It's off. It's off."

But Jonathon kept brushing, his hands whisking all over his body as though a bee buzzed inside his clothes. "I can still feel it," he exclaimed. "I can smell it!"

Uncle Wilford picked up the beef. "I'll throw it away," he said, and carried it out. His face expressionless, Jonathon's father sat rigidly in the straight-backed chair, staring across the room at the dark window. Uncle Wilford came back with a damp towel. As though Jonathon were three years old, Uncle Wilford wiped his face, his hands, and then the spot on his pants where the meat had fallen.

"There," he said, in the voice he used with frightened horses. "There. Sit down—easy now. That's good." Then he turned to Jonathon's father. "You might have eased up to it, Brian."

Jonathon's mind floated in a haze. I am a Dalriada, he thought, but his mind could not grasp it.

"How?" he asked.

"Your grandma, Sephonie, was a North Valley woman," Brian said. "But your grandpa was a Dalriada. That made your ma a half-blood."

Jonathon blinked at the white shawl hanging over the back of the rocking chair; his mother, a barbarian, had crocheted it.

"The far northern part of the Valley is wild," his father said, "especially Highgate, where your grandma raised your ma. It's right next door to the Red Mountains." Uncle Wilford pushed his foot against the runner on the rocking chair until the shawl swung gently.

"The mountains used to call your ma," Uncle Wilford added, "that's why I was always chasing after her. She told me it was a longing, almost a thirst—"

"But I don't have horns," Jonathon interrupted. "Ma didn't either."

His father and Uncle Wilford glanced at each other.

"Neither do the Dalriadas," his father said. "Well, not in the way the Valley folk think. Not horns growing out of their head like a bull or a ram. But they've got that brownish ridging on the forehead, like you."

Jonathon touched his forehead, which now felt no warmer than his skin.

"The Dalriadas call it an antler-mark," Uncle Wilford said.

Instantly, although it had never occurred to him before, Jonathon realized that the mark did resemble antlers: in the way it branched and curved, in the way each side formed a mirror image of the other.

Uncle Wilford crossed his long legs. "We've had no dealings with the Dalriadas, not since the Encroachment Wars hundreds of years ago. Over time, the tales got twisted. They exaggerated the truth and turned the antler-mark into full-fledged horns."

"Why didn't Ma have it?" Jonathon asked.

"Because she had brown eyes," his father said. "Only half-bloods with blue eyes get the mark, and not even all of them—like Old Man Craven. He's a half-blood, though he doesn't know it."

"All full-blooded Dalriadas have blue eyes," Uncle Wilford said.

Shadows thickened in the corners of the room, crouched

behind the old grandfather clock, and lurked in the crevices between the hearth stones. Beside the sofa, on the round table covered with a damask cloth, the lantern burned low. Jonathon turned up the wick until the flame leapt.

"Last fall," he said, "I saw...a Dalriada girl down by the Mirandin."

Both men stared at him. Then Uncle Wilford raised his eyebrows. "Someone else has had secrets. I expect that'll be a story to hear."

"She was my age," Jonathon said, "maybe younger, and she didn't have any mark."

"It doesn't come out until thirteen or fourteen," his father said, "right on the brink of adulthood."

Jonathon tried to absorb all they had told him, but his mind still felt fuzzy; something seemed to be missing, some piece of the puzzle.

"If all the Dalriadas have blue eyes," he said slowly, "then don't lots of them go crazy?"

His father sighed. "There's no connection between blue eyes and madness."

"But everybody says there is. It's even happening to me. I get visions—that's what Ma called them. And they're getting worse."

"The Valley folk have twisted this too," Uncle Wilford said. "Once there were more half-blooded children with blue eyes. Some of them got the mark and turned into full-fledged Dalriadas, who are prone to visions."

Jonathon's father nodded. "The Valley folk think visions are a sign of madness. All they remember now is that a blue-eyed child can grow up to be insane."

"How could you let me think I was going to go crazy!" Jonathon shouted at his father. "How could you! How could Ma!"

"Hold your tongue!" his father said. "If anyone hears this, finds out what you are..." he stopped. "Your ma always told you it was an old wives' tale."

"If I'd known the truth, I might have believed her,"

Jonathon said. "I couldn't sleep. I had terrible dreams, was always afraid...."

His father slouched in his chair until his two bare feet, surprisingly pink and tender, stuck straight out in front of him.

"I thought the truth would be worse," he said. "Everyone would tell you that you were going to go mad anyway; I couldn't change that. Since you're supposedly only a quarter Dalriada, we believed, in spite of your blue eyes, that you wouldn't get the mark.

"I saw no need to tell you the truth at all," he added, "if you didn't get it. But your ma wanted to tell you everything when you were twelve. We compromised on fourteen."

"The agreement," Jonathon said.

His father nodded. "Your ma wouldn't let you go to the Red Mountains without knowing the truth. She believed they could overwhelm you somehow."

The Red Mountains are full of dangers, Jonathon remembered her saying; dangers you can't even imagine.

"But I disagreed," his father said. "Because most of you is Valley."

"But why did you marry a Dalriada in the first place?" Jonathon asked. "Didn't Ma tell you?"

"She didn't have to. I first saw her at the Highgate Lakes, while I was on another false lead to the Firegolds. One day I went hunting. Your ma and I were chasing that buck." He pointed at the magnificent deer head mounted over the dining room door. "I knew from the way she hunted and rode and dressed that she had to be part Dalriada."

"Weren't you scared?"

"Not for long. I'd never met anyone like her. So I hung around until she agreed to marry me. We didn't think anyone would guess she was half Dalriada. Folks blamed her 'unusual' behavior on her roots in the North Valley."

Jonathon's shirt clung to his back; with the windows shut, the room was stifling. "How come I have blue eyes and the antler-mark," he asked, "when I've got less Dalriada blood than Ma?"

In the sudden silence, the old grandfather clock ticked. Jonathon's father stood up, leaned against the mantle, and looked up at the portrait of Karena.

"I don't know," he said at last. "Your eyes were...quite a shock."

Uncle Wilford frowned. He set his foot on the rocker runner again and pushed up and down, his ankle flexing. The fringe on the shawl swung faster.

"Some folks thought," Jonathon's father said quietly, "that maybe you weren't my son."

Jonathon pressed back against the sofa, dread creeping over him. Was Timothy right? Was Old Man Craven really his father?

"Some folks will think anything," Uncle Wilford said. His foot pushed faster; the floor creaked, and the shawl shook and shook.

Jonathon stared up at his mother's portrait. She seemed to sail out from the canvas, her brown hair loose, blown by the wind. She clutched her baby, his face hidden against her shoulder. Eyes glittering, chin defiant, she looked into the distance, but her head tilted toward his; one strand of hair fell across his shoulder. A gold velvet dress buttoned tightly around her throat.

Ma, he thought, Ma.

When he looked at his father's broad back, still turned toward him, Jonathon remembered the weeks after his mother had died; he had wakened screaming night after night. His father had always come: sometimes he sat silently on the cedar chest; sometimes he stood looking out the window with his back to Jonathon until Jonathon slept again, his mind filled with the sight of that black bulk against the black night.

Now he knew why his father rarely looked at him. From the moment he was born, he had ruined his father's life.

* * *

A few hours later, Jonathon raised the lid of his cedar chest and leaned it back against the wall. The only light in his bedroom came from the crescent moon shining through the window. Inside the chest, he found the bow that his mother had given him on Sunturn. Somewhere, buried deeper, was a leather pouch with the red rock.

He pulled away the linen wrapping and the bow gleamed, oddly luminous, as though light burned from within it. He slid one hand along the polished wood; it felt cool. He traced the pattern of inlaid horn on the grip and touched the golden threads with his tongue. Then, bracing one end of the bow on the floor, he bore down hard, arched the bow, and tried to hook the bowstring. He held his breath. After struggling for half a minute, he eased up; his arms were shaking, his eye throbbing worse than before. He did not have the strength to string this bow. His father had told him that it once belonged to Jonathon's grandfather—a Dalriada.

So it was true: the horses that had run on the edge of his dreams for as long as he could remember…he was Dalriada, more different from the Valley folk than he had ever imagined. He couldn't hide it, not ever, not with the antler-mark, not with the blue eyes. No wonder the girl by the river had stared at him. He was like her.

"Everyone will know I'm a Dalriada now," Jonathon had said to his father earlier. "Because Timothy saw the mark, and glowing too."

"Haven't you been listening?" his father had asked. "The Valley folk don't remember anything about the mark. And it's not in any of the history books—I've checked. Unless you sprout real horns out of your head, you're safe."

Safe? Jonathon held the unstrung bow straight out, reached forward with his right hand and pulled slowly back, as though drawing the bowstring—which still dangled on the floor. He did not feel safe, not with barbarian forces inside him that he did not understand. His hand stopped beside his cheek, and he held the position of full draw.

A corner of the moon was caught in his bedroom window;

its loneliness curved in a long, slow slide through the night. The curve of the moon was like the curve of the bow. A bow like this had killed his mother. What good was it? He couldn't even string it. He wanted to throw it out the window just as he had once flung away the rock from the Red Mountains.

He was a Dalriada. One of the barbarians who had killed his mother.

"No!" he said. "I'm Valley. Only Valley."

Some folks thought that maybe you weren't my son.

His father had not said what he thought. Did he think Jonathon wasn't really his son?

"I am!" Jonathon cried. He wrapped the bow, put it back inside the chest, and slammed the lid; the sound echoed toward the attic. Carvings covered every inch of the lid: a running deer had antlers that curved into a tree with apples hanging from the branches; a snake twined through suns, stars and moons. Five-petaled flowers bordered the edge. Each petal, like each scale on the snake, was distinct, carefully made.

Then Jonathon burrowed under his quilts. His mind drifted. Part of him pruned trees in the sunlit orchard, and part of him galloped through the Red Mountains on a horse that was an arrow sent by the moonlight.

Why had his mother left him alone with this strange legacy? And if his father wasn't his father...who was?

chapter sixteen

Jonathon's eyes flew open; he lay on his bed, suddenly wide awake. The afternoon sunlight shone through the curtains and projected a triangle on the far wall. A moment ago, the hooded man had stood above him, pointing at the cedar chest; the nightmare had returned. As Jonathon rolled up on one elbow to look at the chest, pain tingled through his bruised ribs and spread over his body. Earlier that morning, his father had insisted he stay in bed to recover from yesterday's fight.

"But I want to help with the verblight," Jonathon had argued, although he was so tired that he could barely keep his eyes open.

"No need," his father said. "The crew's already finished the second check. It's bad, but not so bad as it might have been. Sunny Hollow's been hit far worse. Kenneth Landers is a much poorer man than he was four days ago. I hear he's lost over a third of his orchard."

Now, Jonathon eased himself back down on the pillows

and closed his eyes, but the image of the hooded man sprang into his mind. Never before had the man pointed to the chest. Moving slowly this time, Jonathon slipped out of bed and began to raise the lid; the hinges creaked. As the spicy scent of cedar filled the room, Jonathon froze, staring down with the lid only half open.

Taut, arched, the bow shimmered, freed from its linen covering; someone had strung it. But who? Jonathon wondered. His father, Uncle Wilford, or—the hooded man?

"Ghosts are the creations of superstitious minds," he said quickly, quoting his father. Jonathon decided he must have strung the bow during the night and then forgotten, like a sleepwalker who remembers nothing of his actions. He opened the lid wide. He touched the inlaid horn on the bow's grip, then jerked his hand away.

"It's not of the Valley," he whispered. It was Dalriada. And he hated the Dalriadas. It's for your journey to the Red Mountains, his mother had said, but he would never go there now. That was the last place in the world he wanted to go. Still, she had wished him to have this bow, had even defied his father to give it to him. Almost against his will, Jonathon found himself reaching toward it again. The sight of his trembling hand made him angry.

"I'm not afraid of any stupid barbarian bow," he said and seized it. Now that it was strung, the bow seemed more alive than ever. A breeze parted the curtains and enlarged the triangle of light on the wall. Jonathon dressed, slung on his quiver, and with the bow in his hand, crept outside.

Instead of opening the gate on Coyote Road, he climbed over the deer fence that separated Greengard from the canyon and dropped down into the brush. He didn't want his father to see him with the bow or to learn that he had disobeyed him. Jonathon walked up the canyon, the leaves from the wild-rose bushes crunching beneath his feet.

The aspens snaked up along the fold in the hills where the creek ran, then yielded to the sagebrush on the arid slopes. A few green pines swayed on the hills; there was wind higher, above the smoke-filled Valley. Somewhere, a grouse thumped.

A half mile up the trail, Jonathon dipped his fingers into a trough that cupped a spring where the cattle watered. A coyote had helped himself to water too, leaving only his tracks. The brush began to thin, and Jonathon climbed a rise that widened into a dry meadow.

A deer skeleton lay with its spine twisting across the trail, the bones brittle, bleached gray-white. He squatted, looking for antlers, but saw none. He touched the mark on his forehead and wondered why the Dalriadas had the antler-mark. What did it mean? As he stared into the black eye holes on the skull, his hand tightened around the bow, and he reached over his shoulder for an arrow.

Jonathon nocked it, began to draw the bowstring, then stopped, surprised by its resistance. No matter how hard he pulled, he couldn't draw the bow fully. He aimed at a snag on a pine tree forty yards away, only to discover that the bow had no sight line. The arrow flew wide.

He shifted his nocking point on the bowstring, checked his stance, shot, and missed again. And again. The sage-pocked hills looked back mutely. He frowned. He had expected his grandfather's bow to differ from his own, but he hadn't thought it would be this different. Although it measured four feet, like his, the wood was stronger, more flexible; it drove the arrow with greater force and subtlety.

He glanced at the deer skull and suddenly feared that the dark eyes might see, the dark mouth might speak. He turned away, wading through the Barnaby's Thistles to retrieve his arrows, when a startled grouse broke from the brush. Jonathon tried to aim at it, but his mouth went dry.

"I don't want to kill anything," he said and released the tension on the bowstring. Since the day his mother had died, he had killed nothing, not even a fish. At slaughtering time, he kept away from the spurting blood and terrified squeals of the animals.

Now Uncle Wilford's words echoed in his ears: You've got to be able to defend yourself, or someone you care for. Jonathon held up the arrow. The shaft was strong, the feathers bright, the metal arrowhead sharp. He knew what an arrow had done to his mother, what the Dalriadas had done—for a horse.

"Why did they kill one of their own people for a stupid horse?" Jonathon had asked last night.

"How would they have known she was part Dalriada?" his father answered. "She spent some time with them when she was a girl, but that was years ago."

"And it wasn't just any horse," Uncle Wilford added. "I asked Karena about that golden stripe. Rhohar is the king horse. That stripe in the mane marks them. He stands for the Dalriadas' freedom and way of life. That's why they killed to get him back. They're not barbarians."

Oh yes, they are, Jonathon thought now, kicking a rock. Even if he had not hidden beneath the bales, even if he had been armed, he could not have stopped the Dalriadas—not if they carried bows like this one; it shot faster and farther than the Valley bows. He could neither draw nor aim it; his old technique seemed useless. Besides, how could he defend anyone if he was too frightened to kill a grouse?

After collecting his arrows, he nocked one and crept toward the creek, where the grouse might be sheltering in the brush. Soon a hen came, bobbing her head as she walked. Jonathon drew the arrow, aimed, and shot. The grouse burst into flight, her wings thrumming; he had missed.

For twenty minutes he hunted, shot, and missed. Finally, his arms aching, disgusted with himself, he scuffled away from the creek until he came out onto Coyote Road. He hesitated. If he returned to the house, his father might make him go back to bed. Instead, Jonathon crossed the road and climbed a low hill. He exploded into a run, not caring where he went, only running as fast as he could to escape the word hammering in his brain: Dalriada, Dalriada, Dalriada.

When he stopped at last, he found himself on the sage-brush flat. A lone pine tree glowed like an emerald as the rays of the westering sun illuminated it from behind. The Red Mountains spread across the northern horizon, the tallest peak a cone of scarlet in the sunset. All at once, Jonathon understood why he had come here. The old longing for the mountains filled him again, but now he knew the true reason for it; his Dalriada blood was calling him. His mother had said it was a longing, almost a thirst.

I don't care, Jonathon thought. He was not an animal, some migrating elger that must blindly follow an inner urge. Neither the mark nor his blue eyes mattered, not to him. The Valley was his home; he belonged on the orchard, and here he would stay.

In the old days, Jonathon knew, he could not have stayed. Rather than hunting in these hills, he would have died in them—in fulfillment of the ancient law about blue-eyed babies. The law's purpose, his father had told him last night, had been to purge the Valley of half-blood Dalriadas. It had succeeded so well that over time, few remained. Now that blue-eyed children were extremely rare, and no one remembered they were Dalriadas, the law was not enforced.

Is Pa my real father? Jonathon wondered again. He looked eastward, toward the Wildcat Hills. Tomorrow he would sneak away and find out if Old Man Craven was his father. He had always looked to the hermit with hope, because he was not mad. Jonathon thought bitterly of all the times he had worried about going insane, all for nothing. Which was worse, though, being a madman or being a Dalriada?

Suddenly, from the corner of his eye, he saw a cinnamon-colored flash; a deer wandered out from behind a clump of sagebrush. Jonathon counted eight points on the antlers. The buck looked around, testing the air. Down wind, Jonathon stood still. Slowly, the buck walked closer, then turned toward the west and stopped, broadside, not thirty yards away. He nosed something on the ground.

Jonathon reached for an arrow and silently drew his bow. The buck's head snapped up. Jonathon knew he could kill the deer, but he felt black eyes looking at him and remembered the skeleton twisting across the trail. With a taste like rust in his mouth, he eased the tension on the bowstring.

Coward, he said to himself. Shoot it, shoot! We would eat it. But he thought of the bright stain of blood, the life going, the knife at the throat to finish it, and he stood frozen. A coyote called the first star.

The buck sprang away.

Now! the bow called out.

Jonathon drew it again and followed the springing leaps of the deer. The bow reached down inside him, aiming toward a voice, a faint, glorious, singing voice. As he struggled to find it, blackness towered up; he sensed terrible danger and instantly recoiled. The voice faded. His hand did not release the arrow. Already halfway up the hill that rose above the flat, the buck vanished into the sagebrush.

Jonathon stared down at his grandfather's bow, then over at the Red Mountains, now fading in the dusk. Had that been another vision inspired by his Dalriada blood and the Dalriada bow?

"No more," he said, shaken. He would put the bow back in his chest and never use it again.

He walked down the road and headed home through the canyon, listening to a pack of coyotes howl in the distance. Crickets whirred their singing spell. A moon as translucent as a thin paring of apple glimmered in the west.

When he dropped softly over the deer fence, back into the smell of smoke, he saw his father standing on the porch in a pool of light from a lantern; Mr. Dakken, Mr. Landers, and a group of angry-looking men crowded before him.

chapter seventeen

Y ou're drunk, Dakken!" said Jonathon's father.
"And I tell you that boy is a Dalriada!"
Keeping low, Jonathon crept toward the big oak by
the house and slipped into the darkness behind the trunk.

"That's ridiculous," his father said, his voice rising. "Don't
the rest of you have anything better to do than listen to a
drunk?"

Jonathon leaned around the oak. The men, about twelve
of them, shifted their feet and rattled the stones on the path.
Soot-dimmed lanterns hung from their hands. The low, sickly
light shone brightest on their boots, then slashed up across
their throats, leaving their faces shadowed and set.

"Timothy saw ridges on that…that boy's forehead," Mr.
Dakken said, tapping his own forehead.

"And Timothy drew a picture of them," Mr. Tiller added.
"They looked like horns—like antlers melded to the bone. He
swears they glowed, Brian. Glowed."

"The tales say the barbarians have flaming horns," Mr.
Dakken said. "Now I suspect they got blue eyes too."

"And there are two other witnesses besides Timothy," Mr. Stoddard said.

Mr. Dakken nodded. His eye patch dangled on a string around his neck, leaving the shriveled, red lids exposed. "You've been harboring Dalriadas, Brae. And you know it. That pretty wife of yours was a half-blood."

"I'm afraid it all adds up, Brian," Mr. Landers said. "All the puzzles, the legends, everything that's happened since your marriage." The cords on his usually immaculate tie had slipped through the silver slider; one side was only an inch long, the other dangled down to his belt. "And remember, I know you well. I can tell from your face that all this is true."

"So what if it's true?" Brian shrugged. "Jonathon's only a boy, three-quarters Valley. He's been raised here, with Valley ways. There's no harm in it."

"No harm!" A man spat on the ground.

"Everybody knows Dalriadas cause the blight," Mr. Dakken said.

"That's superstitious nonsense," Brian said.

"But Dalriada blood's a curse," Mr. Tiller insisted. "Your wife touched my Margaret at the Harvest Supper last fall. The very next day Margaret lost our baby."

"That's right," said another man.

"Yes! Yes!" others shouted agreement.

Jonathon pressed his cheek against the rough bark on the oak and watched his father stride down the porch steps; Uncle Wilford followed, holding the lantern higher. Half the men stepped back, squinting tiredly in the light; most looked as though they had not slept for days.

"That doesn't prove anything, Daniel," Jonathon's father said.

"Does to me."

"Does to us all," added Mr. Dakken.

"It's Dalriada magic," said Mr. Stoddard. "It's—"

"I'm surprised to see you here, Stephen," Uncle Wilford interrupted. "Didn't Mrs. Brae save your two young ones from the blackwater fever?"

"That's true."

"Don't listen to him," Mr. Dakken said.

"But she did save them," Mr. Stoddard admitted. "When no one else could."

"What are you, Stoddard," Mr. Dakken asked. "Some kind of barbarian lover? Or just a coward?"

Mr. Stoddard cleared his throat.

"Brian," Mr. Landers' voice sounded calm. Jonathon inched his head farther out around the trunk. Mr. Landers was his father's best friend; he would help them.

"I've lost half my orchard in three days," Mr. Landers said. "And the saws are still cutting. I can't stop it. I don't know what to do."

"I'm sorry for your loss, Kenneth," said Brian. "I've had losses too. We all have. But weather and hail caused it. You know it has nothing to do with Jonathon."

"Do I?" said Mr. Landers softly. "How can I know that? How can you, really?" In the yellow lantern light, the silver buttons on his coat looked brassy. "Isn't there some little doubt even in you, Brian?"

Jonathon's father watched him.

"There is, isn't there?" Mr. Landers went on. "Just as somewhere inside you there's always been a doubt that maybe, just maybe, the boy isn't your son."

Brian lunged forward, but Uncle Wilford grabbed his arm.

Mr. Landers held up one hand. "Hear me out," he said. "It's true, isn't it? Deep down, you've always wondered. All I'm saying, Brian, is let that doubt come forward. Acknowledge it at last. This is your chance. Forget you ever thought the boy might be your son. We all know what a burden, what a strain it's been for you all these years."

Jonathon felt tears starting in his eyes; certain his father would disown him. What would he do? Where would he go?

"You've got a silver tongue all right, Kenneth," Brian said. "You always have. But whatever I think or don't think, doubt or don't doubt, will not be dictated to me by you and a gathering like this."

Mr. Landers shook his head. "Why can't you make this easy on yourself? But then, you never could do anything the easy way." He sighed. "You knew what had to be done the day Jonathon was born. Blue-eyed babies are taken into the hills and left to die. That's the law. You should have gone through with it, hard as it would have been for Karena."

"I saw you, Brian," Mr. Landers added. "The boy must have been what, three days old? I saw you ride away with him up into the hills. Saw you come back without him. We all thought you'd done it."

Jonathon sagged against the oak and slid down the trunk to his knees.

"What happened?" asked Mr. Landers.

Jonathon's father rubbed the scar over his left eyebrow.

No, Jonathon thought, no. Tell him it's a lie, Pa. Tell him you never did that. But his father didn't speak.

"You should have seen it through then," Mr. Landers said.

In the silence, the night prowled around them.

"That law is obsolete," Brian said at last. "All that's needed now is a signed paper. I have one—most of you have seen it. A dispensation from the High Council at Middlefield, giving Jonathon the right to live."

"That was for a loony-blue," Mr. Dakken said. "They didn't know he was a Dalriada. Besides, we don't care about some scrap of paper. We follow the old ways here."

"The High Council doesn't know about the blight," said Mr. Tiller. "Middlefield's too far away. The boy's barbaric blood is defiling everything in Stonewater Vale. If we don't stop this there's no telling what might happen. We'll lose everything, our land, our homes."

"The boy could call his barbarian kin down on us," Mr. Dakken added. "They'd take our women. Kill us in our beds. We've got to stop it now."

As Uncle Wilford held his lantern higher, the round attic window flashed in the light.

"Hand over the boy," Mr. Dakken demanded.

Brian's back straightened. His right arm dropped toward the knife sheathed at his hip.

Jonathon looked over his shoulder and measured the distance back to the deer fence. He knew places to hide in the canyon where no one would ever find him.

"What do you want with my son?" his father asked.

"We want to stop the blight," Mr. Dakken said. "Same thing you should want. Don't you smell the smoke? That's our trees burning!"

"My trees." Brian's face filled with contempt. "You don't have any trees, Dakken. You're landless. You're nothing but Jonathon's tenant."

Mr. Landers laughed.

"You think that's funny, Kenneth?" Mr. Dakken asked. "Well, think about this. It could be your land the boy gets his hands on next, or that fine-looking daughter of yours. Timothy says that Rosamund's sweet on the little bastard."

Mr. Landers thrust his jaw sideways.

"I've got your grandson's name all picked out," Mr. Dakken said. "Jonathon Kenneth Brae. Just picture the little tike. He'd have your face—with his pa's blue eyes and horns."

"That..." Mr. Landers sputtered, "that half-blood will never touch my land. Nor anything else of mine."

"Purge the land of the Dalriada boy and the blight will stop!" cried Mr. Tiller.

"We should have killed him years ago," Mr. Dakken said.

Kill me? Jonathon clenched his grandfather's bow, and a bright, hot pain flared in his forehead.

"You want to kill my son?" his father said, shrugging off Uncle Wilford's hand. "A thirteen-year-old boy?" He stared incredulously at Mr. Landers. "You, Kenneth?"

"You betrayed me," Mr. Landers said harshly. "I trusted you, defended you, only to find out you've been risking our lives for years. Yes. I'll bloody my hands to save my land and family."

No one spoke. Son, Jonathon thought; Pa called me son.

As Jonathon put one hand on the oak and pulled himself up, power surged through the tree.

"Get off my land," his father roared. "Or by the bones of every Brae who's worked this land, I will curse you and yours."

All the men stepped back except Mr. Landers.

"Give us the boy, Brian," Mr. Landers said. "You have no choice."

Jonathon's father drew his knife. "You'll have to kill me first."

"No," Jonathon whispered. His grandfather's bow vibrated in his hand. Quietly, he pulled an arrow from his quiver.

His father drew up to his full height, his shoulders thrown back. The knife's shadow reared up, huge, grotesque, cast on the house behind him.

Even Mr. Landers stepped back. "Our quarrel isn't with you, Brian. It's with the boy."

"My son is part of me," said Jonathon's father. "Even the Dalriadas didn't kill a child. You are the barbarians."

Mr. Dakken flipped open his knife.

"My pleasure, Bill." Jonathon's father said, crouching.

They'll kill him, Jonathon thought, and then me. He wanted to run away to the canyon, but he had hidden once before and his mother had been killed. He took a long, ragged breath, nocked the arrow, and sprang out from behind the oak into the lantern light. He found himself aiming not at Mr. Dakken, but at Mr. Landers.

"The boy!" the men cried. "The Dalriada."

"Get him!"

"He's got a bow!"

"Look out!"

Jonathon's father turned. "Jonathon!" he cried. "Don't!"

Mr. Dakken threw his knife at Brian. Uncle Wilford swung the lantern, and the knife crashed against the glass dome, shattering it. The flame leapt.

Jonathon's arms trembled from the strain of holding his grandfather's bow at full draw. Drums pounded inside his

Blondin

head, and his forehead burned. Mr. Landers' mouth opened; stubble covered his chin. I could kill him, Jonathon thought. The inlaid golden threads on the bow's grip shone brightly.

"Look at that!" Mr. Stoddard said. "It's a Dalriada bow!"

"His forehead," Mr. Tiller cried. "The tales are true! His horns are on fire! It's Dalriada magic!" And he fled with all the other men, except Mr. Landers, who didn't move.

"Put that bow down, Jonathon," Mr. Landers said.

Traitor, Jonathon thought; I'll kill you. Suddenly he seemed to be dreaming: he was riding his anger like a bright, deadly horse; he was riding Rhohar across a ridge of dark mountains. He felt his power. Elated, he felt his strength. You've got to be able to defend yourself, or someone you care for.

He aimed at Mr. Landers' brown eyes, but suddenly they turned black, black as the eyes in the deer skull, growing bigger and bigger, until violet highlights gleamed in them. Jonathon cried out: they were his mother's eyes, and he remembered what an arrow had done, and at the last second the bow jerked his arms up, shooting the arrow high. It raced beyond him into the darkness. He galloped toward fantastic pinnacles of rock, toward a pass crowned by a towering ruin, toward a lake surrounded by ravens, where a deer drank. Then fear filled him. He was lost, in too deep, and didn't know the way back.

Then a light burned; Uncle Wilford held high the shattered lantern.

chapter eighteen

Early the next morning, Jonathon looked out the kitchen window while his father pushed another chunk of wood into the stove.

"How could I have been such a fool?" his father was saying. "I should have guessed they'd put two and two together. Where did I go wrong? What did I misjudge?"

Jonathon's breath fogged the window and concealed the two blue eyes reflected in the glass. He thought of Rosamund, how her breath warmed the blossoms.

"You stay inside today," his father said. "Lock all the downstairs windows. Keep your knife with you and keep that...bow strung."

Jonathon turned toward him. They wanted to kill me, he thought, dully; they still do. His arrow had hit the birdhouse in the garden, the one he had made for his mother. After that, Mr. Landers had run away.

"You and that bow frightened them plenty for now," his father added. "They really think you have some kind of magic power. But they'll be back, and with more men. Meanwhile, the crew's riding sentry; they know where their bread is buttered."

"I have to leave here," Jonathon said. But where could he go? The image of the tall mountain rose up in his mind. No. Not there.

His father nodded. "We'll get you to a safe place as soon as it's dark. But it's only temporary, while I go up to Middlefield and finagle a waiver from the High Council." He stepped into the pantry, grabbed some canvas bags off a hook, and brought them back.

"Start packing," he said, throwing them over a chair. "And another thing. Work on controlling your...urges. You were completely out of control last night, Jonathon. That glowing forehead. I would have sworn myself you were a full-blooded Dalriada."

"Don't ever say that again."

"You mind who you're talking to."

I am, Jonathon thought, I am. I'm talking to the man who took me to the hills to die. No real father would have done that. They stared at each other from opposite sides of the table, which seemed huge, growing leaf by leaf with the distance between them. On the table, was the broken lantern. Suddenly Jonathon felt confused, remembering how his father had risked his life to protect him, remembering how his father had at last called him son.

"I'm not Dalriada," Jonathon said. "I'm not like them. I didn't kill." But he knew the truth, and it terrified him: he had wanted to kill Mr. Landers; only the bow had stopped him.

"I'm not Dalriada," he repeated. "I'm..." he was about to say Valley, but stopped. He wasn't Valley. No matter how hard he worked in the orchard, no matter how many trees he planted, it wasn't enough. It would never be enough because he wasn't really Valley. Why pretend any longer?

"You shouldn't be like them!" His father hit the table. "Not if you are my son. Not if you're three-quarters Valley. Your Dalriada blood shouldn't be this strong."

Flames crackled faintly inside the black stove, but the heat seemed useless against the chill tightening around Jonathon. There's no place for me, he thought. I can't stay here. I can't go to the Red Mountains. He looked around the kitchen. It was so clean and empty; it was always so empty.

"I'm not going to lose you too," his father said abruptly, a flood of grief in his eyes. There was a silence while he turned and shut the damper on the stove. "You'll be safe."

"No. I can't stay."

"You don't really feel that way. Greengard is your home."

Jonathon turned back toward the window. "The Valley folk will never accept me."

"Oh yes, they will," his father said. "I'll get that waiver. And I'll have the Ironhill deed changed. When you turn sixty, Dakken—or his foul descendants—can have their land back. He'll want you alive all right. He'll be here every day asking about your health."

"What about Mr. Landers?"

"I almost wish you'd shot that..." he stopped. "Kenneth has his weak spots—I know them all. And after what he did last night, I plan to manipulate every one of them. Don't worry, I can handle him. Besides, one day, maybe one day soon, we'll have something that no one else has." His eyes gleamed. "I've had another lead on the Firegolds, a serious lead, from Endless Falls."

Jonathon sat down, his arms and legs heavy. "What difference will that make?"

"You'll be the richest farmer in the Valley, North and South. With money comes power. How do you think I'll get the waiver? Money. You'll be so rich you'll make Landers look like a dirty squatter." Jonathon's father laughed grimly. "He'll be begging you to plant trees with Rosamund—and marry her too."

"You know...?"

"Wilford told me last night all about that little incident. I only wish he'd told me sooner." Jonathon's father reached for his coat. "So Landers has a pure bloodline, does he? If it's anything like his friendship, it's pure as dross." He put on his hat and went out the kitchen door.

Jonathon sat at the spotless table, his mind overwhelmed with the question he'd been unable to ask. Had his father truly ridden up to the hills and left him to die? He looked up. No braids of garlic or onions, no bunches of rosemary or basil or peppers hung from the beams. The windows were bare too, ever since Widow Grey had shrunk the red curtains the first time she washed them. Nothing remained of his mother's presence.

He wandered into the dining room, then went into the parlor, passing beneath the deer's head mounted over the door. The fireplace looked cold. Thanks to the Widow, no speck of ash remained on the hearth to hint that a fire had ever burned there. The whole room bristled with cleanliness.

Jonathon plopped down in the rocker, hooked one foot over the rung, and pushed his other foot against the floor. He looked up at his mother's portrait. Her arms wrapped tightly around her baby, pressing his face to her shoulder. Had she betrayed his father? Was that why he had taken him to the hills to die? How had she saved him? She looked fierce, as though she feared that someone might snatch him away again. Jonathon rocked faster.

"What happened, Ma?" he asked, but only the grandfather clock ticked and ticked.

"I don't know how to shoot the bow, Ma," he said. "I don't know how to go where it…." He stopped, because for the first time he noticed the faint mountain painted in the background of the portrait.

Dangers you can't even imagine, her eyes warned.

But the Valley was dangerous too. Was there no safe place? What about his plan to go and ask Old Man Craven some questions? Maybe he should also ask Craven to hide him?

Jonathon's fingers, curving over the rocker's armrests, suddenly felt something soft and gritty; it was dust. A wild pain filled his throat. Dust! A spot Widow Grey had missed.

He jumped out of the rocker, leaving it swinging, and ran

to the kitchen. He slammed down a flour canister and wrenched off the lid. Scoop after scoop, he threw flour into the air, faster, higher, until fine white clouds swirled everywhere—drifting across the chairs, the black stove, the blue dishes on the shelves.

"Snow! Snow!" Jonathon cried, laughing, sobbing. Two at a time he threw eggs against the walls; yellow yolk spattered his father's best boots. Then he raised a jar of raspberry jam over his head and smashed it down on the table. Bright red blobs dripped onto the floor.

*　*　*

An hour later, Jonathon lay on his back in the Appelunes, trying to memorize a certain pattern of branches.

"Jonathon!" he heard his father shouting. "Jonathon, where are you?"

Jonathon didn't answer.

"What are you doing here?" his father asked a moment later. "Why didn't you answer when I called? I told you to stay inside. Earth's Mercy, I thought they'd taken you."

In spite of the June heat, Jonathon felt the cold from the ground reach through his shirt and surround him, settling in like a glacier.

"There's a mess in the kitchen that needs to be cleaned up," his father said. "Right now. Widow Grey about had a fit. We're lucky she even came in today, after what happened last night."

"Yes, Pa," Jonathon said, annoyed. He'd almost had the pattern of branches locked in his mind. "There are dangers, Pa," he sang softly. "Dangers you can't even imagine."

"What?" said his father. "Did you hear me, Jonathon? I said get up to the house now and clean up that mess."

"Whatever you say, Pa."

* * *

"I rode as fast as I could, sir," Spinney said, standing at the kitchen door, his clothes filthy with dust.

"Did you warn him?" Brian asked.

Spinney ran his tongue over his lips and avoided looking at Jonathon, who was rinsing jam off a rag. "It was too late, sir. I found him slumped over his table, with a knife in his back."

Jonathon's father nodded and shut the door.

"Who?" Jonathon whispered.

His father did not speak for a moment.

"Old Man Craven," he said at last.

* * *

Jonathon could not stop shivering. After the kitchen was clean, he went upstairs and got into bed, piling on the quilts, trying to stay warm. He stared at the carvings on the chest in his room and at his grandfather's bow in the corner. As darkness fell, he heard his father's steps coming down the hall—or was it the hooded man in the dream? He pulled the quilt over his head.

Then somewhere above him a voice spoke: "What are you doing in bed, Jonathon? Why aren't you packed? We're leaving in a few minutes." His father paused, then added, "I've changed the plans. You and me and Uncle Wilford are all going to Middlefield—I'm not leaving you. Then we'll head to the Highgate Lakes and spend some time fishing. You'll like that, won't you, Jonathon?"

He didn't answer.

"Jonathon...?"

He didn't move.

chapter nineteen

Three weeks later, they approached the south end of
Middlefield, and all that kept Jonathon riding
through the drizzling dusk was the thought of supper.
"Does the Inn have good food?" he asked.

"It used to," said Uncle Wilford, who was riding beside
him on Steady. He grinned. "But after traveling all day in this
weather, will you care?"

"No. I'd even eat a bowl of Widow Grey's soup," Jonathon
said. "I just hope they'll have room for us." Last night they had
camped in the rain six miles east of the Mirandin; their
bedrolls were soaked by morning. Now, water dripped down
Jonathon's hat and hair and drenched his clothes.

"The old Middlefield Inn's got a hundred rooms," said his
father, leading the three pack horses. "When the High
Council's in session, the members stay there. But they're not in
session now."

Jonathon yawned and patted Minna's neck. Although he
felt tired, at least the bleakness that had smothered every

thought and feeling had eased. The first few days of their journey, he had ridden without speaking, without sleeping at night, without noticing anything on the long, winding route his father had chosen to elude pursuit. That dull, dark blankness seemed more like madness than any of the wild visions. After five or six days of camping beneath the stars and sitting around the campfire at night, he had begun to come back—back from where he didn't know. His father constantly chatted, his eyes filled with relief, as if trying to prevent Jonathon from slipping into the bleakness again.

The horses' hooves clattered as the dirt road became a cobbled street. Houses with rambling porches soon gave way to prosperous-looking stores. Most of the buildings were fashioned of a dark stone, gray as the dusk, quarried from the eastern cliffs that rose above the river. In the center of town, throngs of people scurried through the streets.

"Carry your bundles!" shouted a scrawny boy. "Penny a bundle! Carry your bundles!"

Jonathon saw three men crowd into an alehouse. On one corner, a man used a pole to light a lamp over the chandler's door. A woman in a purple bonnet—with a purple bow wider than her face—stepped out of a baker's shop, and the smell of bread drifted through the air. Jonathon's stomach rumbled.

"I've never seen so many people," he said.

"This is the midway point in the Valley," his father explained, "so people from all over come to trade."

Jonathon kept his eyes lowered, but no one looked at him twice. People here seemed used to strangers, travelers, and traders. But what would they do if they learned a Dalriada was riding past them? Jonathon shuddered and pulled his hat lower. He knew what they would do.

"Easy, Minna," he said as three wagons loaded with crates lumbered by. He was riding Minna because Nellie was too old to travel more than three miles from her oat bin.

"The High Council meets there." His father pointed to a three-story building. "That's where they make the laws. And resolve disputes when the Village Councils are deadlocked."

Massive, ancient, the building sat heavily on the land. Huge blocks of the local gray stone—each taller than a man—pressed down on each other. Jonathon wondered if the law against blue-eyed babies had been made inside those walls. Thirteen years ago, someone there had signed a paper giving him the right to live. Tomorrow, his father would try to buy him the right to keep living.

They turned a corner and saw the Inn ablaze with light; it, too, was built of stone. The old Middlefield Inn had enough nooks and gables to hold all the secrets of its lodgers' hearts. Ten chimneys conspired in streams of smoke, while ten more stood dormant, unneeded in the July heat. Piano music streamed out from a gallery of windows on the main floor.

They rode to the hitching post near the stable and dismounted. Jonathon stretched his arms over his head.

"Stay with the horses," his father said, touching Jonathon's chin with his hand. "We'll see if they have room for us. We'll get you out of the rain in a minute."

Jonathon nodded and looked away. He knew it would be easier for his father to get rooms without a "loony-blue" standing beside him.

*   *   *

Jonathon woke in the middle of the night to the sound of music floating through the dark. He rolled up on his elbow. On the other side of the room, his father and Uncle Wilford slept in their beds. His grandfather's bow leaned against the wall; the inlaid gold on the grip shimmered, as though the bow, too, were awake. In spite of his hatred of everything Dalriada, Jonathon had felt compelled to bring it and the red rock because they were connected to his mother. He lay down again and stared at the ceiling. How many people had slept in this room over the past five hundred years? How many secrets had these walls witnessed?

The music, strange and yet familiar, wove into his mind: Find the place where the Firegolds bloom—the melody sounded like the old song his mother used to sing. He got out of bed; the floorboards felt cold against his feet. When he opened the door, the music grew louder. Who would be playing in the middle of the night?

Jonathon peered down the hall; only a lantern flickered on the table. He looked again at his grandfather's bow, which shimmered even brighter, then stepped out of the room and shut the door. He walked past the sleeping chambers toward the public rooms. The music, quite distinct now, had the percussive sound of rapidly plucked strings: each note was stately and crisp.

As he turned a corner, light billowed like a luminous cloud through an archway and glowed yellow on the oak floor. He stopped. Across the room, a woman sat playing the piano with her profile toward him. Candles burned in brackets on each side of the music rack; the light shone on her molasses-colored hair pinned high on her head. Behind her, a tall window was flung open. Her gown made a scarlet slash against the black night. Ornate scrolls swooped across the sides of the piano— some carved, some gilded in gold leaf. It didn't look like any piano Jonathon had ever seen.

A rush of wind blew through the room, and the candles wavered, then blazed up brighter than before. Jonathon felt a presence behind him, a presence so radiant with power that he was afraid to look.

"Amberly!" A man's voice rang out.

The woman lifted both hands from the keyboard, and the music ceased. She turned toward Jonathon, but did not seem to see him. Instead, she smiled at the man behind him. As she leaned forward and rose, a heart-shaped locket swung out on a blue ribbon around her neck. She stood with her brown eyes shining and held out her hands.

Jonathon stepped back, one step then another. Why did neither of them notice him? Then he saw the man, who was tall and broad shouldered with thick red hair falling to his waist. The antler-mark protruded from his forehead. Beneath it, his blue eyes looked back at the woman.

A Dalriada, Jonathon thought. A Dalriada here in the Inn! He fled back down the hall to alert his father.

* * *

The next morning, Jonathon woke with no memory of what, if anything, had happened after he saw the Dalriada. He lay in bed, listening, but heard only the usual sounds of an inn: the quick steps of serving folk carrying water, the creaking of doors, the murmur of voices, the clatter and bang of ovens from the kitchen. If he had raised an alarm and a Dalriada intruder had been found, wouldn't the place be in an uproar? Until he learned more, he decided to say nothing.

After his father left for the High Council building, Jonathon slipped into the public rooms to look for signs of last night's commotion. There weren't any, except someone had pushed the piano into the corner away from the window. Looking closer, he saw it wasn't the same piano at all; there were no carvings or gilding or swirls. He didn't test the sound because the innkeeper's wife was watching him. Where was the piano he had seen last night? Had it all been only a dream inspired by unfamiliar surroundings—or perhaps another vision? Yet everything had seemed real.

As the days passed—long days that he spent in his room because his father feared someone might see the mark— Jonathon waited for the dream to return. He wanted to know why a Valley woman would be overjoyed to see a barbarian. He also found himself wanting to learn more about the power he had sensed in the man.

Two weeks later, his father came back to their room one night and threw himself down in the green and yellow overstuffed chair.

"I can't get a waiver unless three-quarters of the High

Council votes yes," he said. "And they won't be back in session for another month."

Jonathon doubted that even his father had enough money to persuade so many people.

"We can't wait here that long," Uncle Wilford said. "It's too risky."

Jonathon's father nodded. "The innkeeper says having a "loony-blue" is scaring away trade—good thing he doesn't know the truth. He's demanding more money."

Jonathon stared at the brown timber dividing the plaster wall. The Valley folk will always think of me as a loony-blue, he thought, or worse. I'm not Valley. And I won't be a Dalriada. What am I?

"The Council will vote no," he said.

"Don't look so bleak," his father said. "If they do, I have a backup plan. I won't be caught off guard again. Meanwhile, we leave for Highgate tomorrow."

They reached the town of Alaire by sunset the following day. Jonathon's father led them along the Mirandin now, no longer fearing pursuit. Over the next four weeks, they passed through Lakewood, Meadows, and Shilaree as well as the smaller villages scattered between. They traveled slowly, taking time to fish and explore. Although Jonathon saw something new each day, he never forgot the angry mob at Stonewater, the knife in Old Man Craven's back, or that his father—who might not even be his father—had abandoned him in the hills. And he never forgot the part of himself he despised. The Red Mountains were a constant reminder; they appeared more often and grew bigger with every step the horses took.

Gradually, as they neared the town of Black Pine, the Mirandin began to narrow. The nights grew cold; they rode in the far north now, where fall and frost came early. At last, on the second day of September, they stopped on a vista overlooking the Highgate Lakes basin.

"There!" Brian exclaimed, pointing. Three lakes sparkled in the land below like blue diamonds on a gown of green.

High cliffs bordered the farthest. The pine trees grew taller and closer together than in the South Valley.

"The Highgate Lakes are holding places for the river," Jonathon's father told him. "Snowmelt from the Red Mountains flows here, gathers, and starts down to the sea. There are two more big lakes—not to mention hundreds of ponds and streams."

"And look at those tamarack trees, just as gold as can be," said Uncle Wilford.

"Where are we camping?" Jonathon asked.

His father and Uncle Wilford exchanged glances.

"We're not," his father said. "There's a house, up at the highest lake."

"Way out here?"

His father nodded. "We'll be staying there, I think."

"You hope," Uncle Wilford said.

They rode down the trail. After two miles they climbed a ridge, then dropped toward the last big lake where a pinewood house and barn stood near the shore. Grapevines tangled along a fence. The vegetables in the garden had suffered from frost, but a few straggled stubbornly on to confront the winter.

Uncle Wilford dismounted, looking around as though he couldn't take everything in fast enough. Jonathon and his father tied up the horses.

At first glance the house looked rough, with battered, unpainted boards, and shakes missing from the roof. One shutter leaned out, suspended from a single nail, threatening to crash to the ground at any moment. Then Jonathon saw the wreath of rose hips on the door and the yellow and white checked curtains rippling at the front windows. It looked like the kind of place that would always have a pie, piping hot, just out of the oven. Perhaps an apple pie, he thought, crusty on the outside and tart-sweet on the inside—not sour like Widow Grey's.

"Jonathon," his father said, "there's something I need to tell—"

"Who lives here, Pa?" Jonathon interrupted, watching the smoke snap in puffs from the chimney.

"Turn around and see, boy," a sharp voice commanded.

Jonathon spun toward the lake. A woman stared at him; her dark hair, peppered with white, was coiled in a braid on her head. She held a willow basket on her hip. She wore a blue-black dress the color of the sky when the evening star comes out. A piece of red yarn clung to her skirt.

No one spoke.

She glared at Jonathon.

"So," she said, "you've finally brought my grandson."

chapter twenty

Karena wrote me about the blue eyes, of course," the
woman said, still staring at Jonathon. "But she never
mentioned he was the spitting image of...." The
basket slipped from her hands—yarrow, foxglove, and olive-
green weeds tumbled onto the ground. She let them lie.

"He's got it, hasn't he?" she said. "Or you wouldn't have
brought him."

"Got what?" Jonathon said, although he knew she meant
the mark. "Don't talk about me like I wasn't here."

Her eyebrows rose. "Takes after his pa, I see."

"Hello, Sephonie." Uncle Wilford said, tipping his hat.
She looked the two men up and down as though they were
something unpleasant that had been swept out from under her
sofa.

"Why I should let the two of you in my house I'll never
know." She picked up the basket, walked into the house, and
slammed the door behind her.

"Uh-oh." Uncle Wilford sucked in his lips.

"Ma's...ma?" Jonathon asked.

His father nodded. "Your grandma. Sephonie Cassan."

"Why did you let me think she was dead?"

"It was part of the agreement. Your ma and I planned to tell you—once you knew you were part Dalriada."

"But I've known that for weeks," Jonathon said. "You could have told me she'd be here."

His father plucked a burr from Sammy's mane. "I wrote her about your ma, but never heard a word back. I thought maybe she'd died. You were already so—upset. I didn't want you to get your hopes up and be disappointed."

"Get my hopes up!" Jonathon exclaimed. Why would he ever hope to meet this woman? All his misfortunes had begun because she had married a barbarian.

"What else haven't you told me?" he asked his father. "Every day there's something new. What's next? Am I going to sprout wings? Turn into a squirrel? I don't know what to believe anymore."

Jonathon turned and ran toward the lake, following seven steps hewn in the bank down to a rock-covered beach. On the far shore, promontories of stone bulged out like knobby old toes testing the water.

He found a flat, shiny rock and skipped it three times. He thought of his grandmother with her long skirt and willow basket and then of the Dalriadas thundering down the hill at Greengard, but he couldn't reconcile the two pictures. Why hadn't she married a Valley man? As Jonathon hurled another rock, he faltered in mid-swing, and it sank. What if his Dalriada grandfather was alive too? Was that another secret they were keeping from him? Ripples of water circled out from the spot where the stone had vanished.

Maybe he should run away. But where would he go? He looked up. To the north, beyond the lake, rose a high ridge already freckled with snow. A massive ruin crumbled across a gap in the rock, stretching like a wall from one cliff to another. Who would build something that enormous out in the middle of nowhere?

The Red Mountains began only a few miles north of Highgate, probably over that ridge. For the first time, Jonathon realized how close the mountains were, how close the Dalriadas were, and he felt a stirring in his blood. On the other side of that wall, just on the other side.... No. He would not go there. Never there. And yet he couldn't return to the Valley either.

Suddenly, a bird dove into the lake and darted up with a big fish. The bird was big too, a kingfisher with blue and white feathers; Jonathon had never seen one quite like it. With the fish clamped in its beak, the bird flew over the water and into the brush sprouting from a small island.

The day faded fast. Jonathon paced the shore, fuming, brooding until cold and hunger drove him back up the steps in the bank. As he hurried across the clearing to the house, he half expected his grandfather to leap out from behind a tree and shoot him. He left his boots and socks on the porch. When he opened the door, the hinges squealed.

Inside, he curled his toes on the pine board floor, then stepped toward the fire snapping in the fireplace. A bouquet of yarrow stood in a blue jar on the mantle. A calico cat—sprawled over the seat of the chair nearest the fire—opened one eye. Jonathon stood on a woven rug beside the hearth, looking up at the strings of sausages and the braids of garlic and onions hanging from the rafters. An open chest overflowed with skeins of violet wool; knitting needles poked out like thorns. Jonathon found himself smiling and immediately stopped.

A strange noise, a soft thumping, came from the back of the house. He listened, turning before the fire until he saw his grandfather's bow—shed of its linen wrapping—leaning against the china cabinet.

Who had unwrapped it? His father and Uncle Wilford would never have touched it without asking. That meant—his grandmother. Jonathon walked toward the thumping sound, planning to tell her exactly what he thought of people who snooped. At the end of a long hall, three steps dropped down to a paneled door. He knocked. The thumping stopped.

"What!" his grandmother's voice demanded.

Jonathon stepped back.

"Well?" she called.

"It's me, Jonathon. Can I come in?"

Silence. Then, "Suit yourself."

When he opened the door, the thumps started again: his grandmother sat weaving at a loom, her feet working pedals, her hands sliding a shuttle back and forth. She leaned forward with her lips parted, concentrating. All around her, colors danced and shimmered and shouted. Huge tapestries covered two of the walls. Shelves along the third were stacked with skeins of wool and spools of thread. They gleamed every color and hue: indigo, yellow, crimson, peach, lime green, and a hundred others. Jonathon felt as though he had suddenly flown inside a rainbow.

"You would think," his grandmother declared to her loom, "they would give a person a little warning, instead of just popping in after all these years. They could have sent a message. Or something."

Jonathon nodded. "They never tell me anything either. They treat me like a little kid. I'll be fourteen in May."

His grandmother pointed the shuttle at him. "That's right. There's that to consider too." And she threw the shuttle across the loom.

Jonathon blinked, then remembered why he had come. "Did you unwrap my—"

She spun around on her stool. "Let's get something straight right now. Don't you realize that if I talk to you, you'll be real?"

"But I am real."

"No, you're not. If I let you be real, I'll feel all the pain of not knowing you for thirteen years. If you're not real, then I haven't missed anything, now have I?"

He looked at her. A web of fine wrinkles radiated out from

her eyes, which were the color of pine bark in the rain.

"So you'll understand if I don't talk to you?" she asked.

"Fine," Jonathon said, thinking again of all the trouble she had caused him by marrying a Dalriada. "If that's the way you want it, then I won't talk to you either."

"Good." Sephonie spun back and began to weave again.

As Jonathon walked toward the door, one of the tapestries on the wall caught his eye. A golden river wound like a snake through an orchard. The trees, stitched in fantastic shades of red violet, orange, and turquoise, bowed under their bounty of golden fruit.

"Did you make this?" he asked.

"No! The cat did." She sighed. "Yes. And I sell them, believe it or not. To the rich folk in Middlefield and Shilaree." Then she nodded down at the white damask forming on her loom. "But making cloth is my bread-and-butter work. I sent your ma a package every year."

Jonathon stood still. "You're the famous weaver? They never told me. Why didn't Pa want me to know about you?"

"I'll tell you why. Because I didn't approve of that so-called agreement he had with your ma—that business of not telling you about your Dalriada blood." Sephonie pulled back the comb on the loom. "So he refused to let me see you or even write to you. Afraid I'd spill the beans—I would have, too."

"Oh," Jonathon said, startled by her truthfulness and by the idea that a stranger knew all about him—knew more, in some ways, than he did.

"And Brian thought your ma might let something slip if she even mentioned me," Sephonie added.

Spill the beans, Jonathon thought, watching her hands work faster. Had he at last found someone who would answer his questions? Someone who would tell him the truth about everything he needed to know?

"What are those ruins up on the ridge?" he asked, testing her.

His grandmother looked straight into his eyes without

flinching, just as his mother used to do. "I thought we weren't going to talk to each other?"

Jonathon pulled up a stool, plopped down, and crossed his arms.

"Stubborn, I see," she said. "Wonder where you got that from?" Then, more softly, she added, "They haven't told you much, have they?"

"Hardly anything."

"I don't want to do this," she said. "I'm too old to relive it all again."

He looked at her.

"And I don't know that much," she warned.

He waited.

"I recognize that look," she said, sighing. "Let's start with the ruins. This place got its name from them—the high gate. Highgate. Once those ruins were the gate between the Valley and the Red Mountains. But that was way back in the Golden Age when the people were one."

"What people were one?"

"The Valley folk and the Dalriadas. Though no one in the Valley will admit it or even talk about it."

Jonathon's eyes widened. "What happened?"

"What always happens—war. It began when a trader from the Beyondlands brought the first horse to the Valley."

"Tell me more," he said.

She did.

chapter
twenty-one

Tatters of fog trailed over the lake through a sky inching toward morning. The log beneath Jonathon dipped as he cast his fishing line in a low roll; twenty feet out, his fly sank. During the past month, he had learned that the biggest fish fed in the gloom before dawn.

He twitched the line, hoping to lure one particular fish, a huge elger that frequented this shore. He had seen only traces of it: a ripple rolling like a dream, a shadow slipping beneath a bank. For days, all Jonathon had wanted to do was fish, fish and forget his troubles. At first, he had many questions for his grandmother—although some of them, like whether a Dalriada might be his father, he still had not found the courage to ask. Lately he had not visited her workshop at all. While not exactly happy, he felt content here—and safe.

He twitched the line again and glanced at the trees, wondering where the kingfisher was this morning. A week ago, Jonathon had thrown him a small elger; ever since, the bird hovered nearby whenever he was fishing.

As the fog dwindled, Jonathon looked up toward the pass

where the gray ruins loomed out of the mist. His grandmother had said the ancient war divided the people into Valley folk and Dalriadas. To protect themselves, the Valley folk built Highgate. Then, as the years passed, they moved south to safer and more fertile land even though the Dalriadas kept to the Red Mountains. Slowly, the wall had crumbled.

By the time war broke out again—the Encroachment War, then the Border Wars, and last, only four hundred years ago, the War of the Renegade King—the Dalriadas had found new ways into the Valley.

Jonathon cast the line again. The sun slivered over the eastern woods and lit the ruins; the stone turned rose, glittering with mica. What did the Red Mountains beyond them look like now in the sunrise? Dazzled, he lifted onto his toes when suddenly the kingfisher dove into the water next to him.

Jonathon teetered on the log; it rolled, and he fell chest deep into the icy lake. The kingfisher flew back into the air, his shadow brushing Jonathon's cheek as something big, something enormous, shot by his knee in the water. He peered down. If that had been the big elger, it was already gone.

* * *

"Good breakfast, Grandma," Jonathon said a few hours later as he searched through the cupboard for a dishtowel. She sat with his father and Uncle Wilford, drinking coffee at the table. The smell of ham and baking bread filled the kitchen. Blue curtains embroidered with daffodils hung at the window. The cat, speckled with flour, curled up on a mat beside the stove and licked his paw.

"Thank him." Sephonie pointed her teaspoon at Uncle Wilford. "He cooked most of it."

"I thought it tasted familiar," Jonathon's father said, laughing.

"He always cooked breakfast for Karena and me," Sephonie said. "One day he told me he preferred eating his breakfasts to mine, the corn muffins in particular, so he might as well cook for everybody."

Uncle Wilford smiled.

"Jonathon," she said, "the dishes will dry themselves before you find a towel in that cupboard. Look in the other one. Second shelf."

Jonathon opened the cupboard door. "I thought you had a good job with Grandma's folks," he said to Uncle Wilford. "Why did you quit and come up here with her and Ma?"

"Well, I thought a change of scene would be—"

"Nobody else would come," Sephonie interrupted. "I needed help, and my family disowned me. Tell the boy the truth for once."

Disowned for marrying a Dalriada, Jonathon thought, picking up a towel. In the back corner of the cupboard, he saw a clear crystal cup and lifted it out.

"Isn't this just like Uncle Wilford's special cup at home?" he asked.

No one spoke.

Jonathon turned the cup until the sunlight shining through the window sparkled on the glass. "Are there more?"

"Only two in the whole world," Uncle Wilford said, "brought from the Beyondlands." He looked at Sephonie; their eyes held for a moment, then she tapped her spoon against the table.

"Put it back, Jonathon," she said.

After he closed the cupboard door, he began wiping the blue and white china plates. "But Uncle Wilford," he said, "if Grandma needed help here, why did you move to Greengard with Ma?"

"Oh mind your own business, boy!" Sephonie exclaimed and pushed back her chair. She grabbed her teacup, walked over to the stove, and with her back hunched against them, poured more coffee. Surprised, Jonathon watched her, never before had she refused to answer a question.

"I hate to say this," his father said a moment later, "but we'd better be planning our trip home."

Jonathon dropped the plate; it clanged onto the floor, wobbled, and went still. A crack zigzagged through the middle. Home, he thought. The Valley. The pasture where his mother had died.

"I'm sorry," he said.

"Never mind." His grandmother picked up the plate.

"We'll leave day after tomorrow," his father said.

Jonathon looked up; three pairs of brown eyes were watching him.

"I'm not going back," he said.

His father frowned. "I know you've had fun here, but we have to go before the snow falls. And the Council's in session now. I have to get that waiver. And there's school, as well as work to be done at Greengard."

Jonathon stared at him. School? Greengard? His father spoke as though nothing had happened, not the blight, not the mob, not the murder of Old Man Craven.

"I can't go back," Jonathon said. "Can I stay here for a while, Grandma?"

"Fine by me."

"No," his father said.

"Just until spring, Pa."

"I said no."

"It's a good idea, Brian," Uncle Wilford urged. "Give Stonewater a chance to cool down some more."

"And it would give me a chance to visit with my grandson," Sephonie said. "After thirteen years."

Jonathon's father crushed his napkin in his hand. "The boy stays with me."

"But, Pa—" Jonathon began.

"I'll hear no more about it." His father pushed back his chair and left the table.

Jonathon spent the rest of the morning lying on his bed. He fiddled with his grandfather's bow while the knot in his stomach grew tighter and tighter. At last he opened a drawer and searched through his shirts until he found his pouch; his fingers gripped the leather, feeling the red rock inside. He stuffed the pouch into his pocket.

A few minutes later, he knocked on the door of his grandmother's workshop. Today, she sat sewing at her tapestry loom beside the window.

"I want to ask you something," he said.

She smiled. "Imagine that."

"Do you know who my real father is?"

Her needle stopped in midair. "What did you say?"

"There are some folks in the Valley who say, who said...."

"Well?"

"That Pa's not my father."

Her head tilted.

"Because of my blue eyes," he added. "And now the mark too."

"First I've heard of it," she said quietly. "Though come to think of it, it wouldn't be an entirely bad thing. It would certainly explain a lot."

"Then you think maybe Ma...."

She shot him a look.

"Well, Pa says she used to ride off alone into the Red Mountains even after they were married."

"So what?" his grandmother said. "Dalriada women go off alone all the time. And any woman married to Brian Brae would need to get away from him frequently. I never understood what Karena saw in him." She sighed. "But Karena did tell me she loved him. If he isn't your father, she never let on to me."

"But you think it's possible?"

"Could be. What does your pa think?"

"I think he wonders. How else could he have..." Jonathon had been about to say, how else could he have taken me up to the hills and left me to die? But he couldn't say it. "If I go back to the Valley," he said, "the men there will try to kill me again. I've got to stay here."

"Then you'd better work something out with your pa," she said. "That's your job."

"But he doesn't understand anything!"

"Not much," she agreed. "But I think he'll get an inkling, soon."

The day came to leave. Uncle Wilford walked out of the barn leading Minna and Steady; the pack horses waited at the hitching post. Jonathon stood in the cold wind beside his grandmother, who clutched a shawl around her head.

"Let's go, Jonathon," said his father, already mounted on Sammy.

Jonathon shook his head.

"No nonsense now," his father warned. "I've made my decision."

"I know," Jonathon said softly. "But I won't go back. I'm sorry, Pa."

"Get on Minna!"

"No."

His father dismounted and walked toward him. "Don't make me put you on that horse."

"Maybe you can," Jonathon said, backing away. "But you can't watch me every minute. I'll run off."

"Oh, leave the boy, Brian," Sephonie said. "He needs something you can't give him. You know that or you never would have brought him here."

Jonathon's father stopped, his feet planted, his face grim. The scar above his eye seemed to open like a raw hole of grief. With an effort, Jonathon looked away.

"I'm not leaving," he said.

"Yes you are, damn it." His father grabbed him and dragged him toward Minna.

"Let me go!" Jonathon yelled.

"Brian, you fool!" Sephonie cried. "Stop!"

"They'll kill me!" Jonathon said, struggling. "I don't belong in the Valley." The ache flared in his forehead. "You left me up in the hills once before, didn't you, Pa? Now's your chance to get rid of me. I'm staying here!"

Instantly, his father released him. "You don't know what you're saying." He shuddered at Jonathon's glowing forehead.

"All right. Stay if you want." Then his eyes filled with pain and love. "Jonathon?"

But Jonathon couldn't speak.

His father yanked up his collar. He strode toward Sammy, mounted, and rode away without looking back.

Wait, Pa, Jonathon wanted to call, the heat draining from his forehead. Wait. He took two steps after his father, then stopped.

"I can't let Brian go back alone," Uncle Wilford said. "He needs me."

"He needed Karena, too," Sephonie pulled her shawl tighter. "I'm tired of his needs. Does he think he's the only one who mourns? It's high time Brian Brae thought of someone else, his son, in particular."

"This isn't Brian's fault!" Uncle Wilford exclaimed. "Jonathon should have been my grandson, Sephonie. Then none of this would have happened. They both should have been mine—Jonathon and Karena. Should have been ours."

Sephonie stared at the lake.

Uncle Wilford sighed and turned toward Jonathon. "But then you wouldn't be who you are," he said, touching Jonathon's cheek. "And you're just fine, son. Remember that. Now don't stay too long. I don't want to have to come after you." He attempted a grin. "You're just like your ma, and I don't want to risk getting an arrow through another perfectly good hat."

Jonathon nodded.

"I'll be back, Sephonie," Uncle Wilford said. "I'm an old fool, I know. But I'll never give up hoping." A moment later, he rode away, leading the pack horses.

Sephonie put her hand on Jonathon's shoulder. "You were right, Jonathon," she said. "They don't understand much at all."

chapter
twenty-two

Out on the lake, Jonathon shivered above a hole he'd chopped in the ice. Winter had settled in swiftly during the six weeks since his father and Uncle Wilford had left. He dropped a fish into the bucket, then let his line sink back into the water, sink down where the big elger still swam in the darkness. Would the fish pull him in, if it ever bit, instead of him pulling it out? He warmed his fingertips against his throat; his woolen gloves stopped at the middle knuckle, leaving his fingers free to move. Every few minutes, he stirred the water with a stick to keep the hole from freezing over.

The kingfisher circled above, caught the fish Jonathon threw him, and flew away toward the rocky island. On the far shore, the pines looked gray, muted by the falling snow. Although he couldn't see the ruins, Jonathon sensed the Red Mountains waiting beyond them. Their call clamored inside him, swirling like the snow, harder, faster, pulling at his heart, until at last he wound up his line, took the bucket, and walked toward the house.

A half hour later, Jonathon knelt inside his grandmother's workshop warming his hands at the fire. After the gray outside, he felt as if he had stepped into a summer garden rioting with color.

"Have you been to the Red Mountains?" he asked her.

"I lived there one winter," she said from her tapestry loom. "After I was married."

Jonathon could not picture her living in a place of such unimaginable dangers.

"But it wasn't the life for me," she added. "I need a garden and a real roof. And I never learned much of the language." She poked the needle through and pulled the purple thread tight.

"I chose to live here between the Mountains and Valley so Karena could be near her father—he refused to live outside the Mountains. He visited though and taught her to ride and hunt. But when she turned twelve, he stopped coming."

"Why?" Jonathon asked.

"I don't know. Karena cried her heart out. She said the Red Mountains swallowed him up."

"How did Ma get his bow?"

"One spring when she was fourteen, she ran away. She came back months later with the bow. I knew when I saw it that he was dead. Karena would only say that she'd found it on Kalivi Mountain—that's the highest one."

Jonathon pictured the glittering peak he had seen from the sagebrush flat. "Kalivi Mountain," he tried saying the odd name and instantly felt its rightness—felt it resound in his mind as though he had always known it.

"Your mother brought a Dalriada horse, Windborn's sire, back with her too. Wilford and I had our hands full. I don't know what I'd have done without him."

Jonathon threw a log on the fire; sparks flew up. "Then why didn't you marry Uncle Wilford instead of a barbarian?"

"Your grandfather was not a barbarian," she snapped. "His name was Angarath."

Jonathon stared at her. "But that's my...." he stopped.

"Your ma was a Dalriada. Do you think she was a barbarian? And what about you, Jonathon A.—A for Angarath—Brae?" Sephonie leaned toward him. "If your grandfather was a barbarian and your mother was a barbarian, then just what does that makes you?"

"I've got wood to chop," Jonathon said. He went out and slammed the door.

The next afternoon, he was standing over the hole in the ice when suddenly the line jerked, yanking his arms down. Tension shot through the rod and into his hands as the fish tried to run with the hook in its mouth. Jonathon leaned back, fighting to dig his boots into the slippery ice. He knew it was the big elger he'd been trying to catch for the last two months.

The rod bent nearly double. When he tried to slow the line spinning out from the reel, it cut his fingers, and pain streaked through his arm. His shoulders, back, and even his thighs strained against the force, but still the rod tip inched closer to the hole until all the line was played out. He feared he might fall in—though part of him knew the hole was too small. His right foot slipped. He whipped out his knife and cut the line; the abrupt release of tension knocked him backwards onto the ice as the line snaked into the hole and vanished.

Somewhere in the deep, free and yet not free, the fish shook his head, trying to dislodge the hook embedded in its jaw. Jonathon sat on the ice, relieved, disgusted with himself, and, strangely enough, not disappointed at all.

* * *

For weeks, Jonathon avoided his grandmother's workshop, though they still spoke politely at meals. Then came a day he didn't want to spend alone: it was the day after Sunturn; it was the day his mother had died.

Jonathon picked up a skein of blue-black wool and turned it in his hands. Did his grandmother know what day this was? He walked over to the orchard tapestry, his lips dry.

"I made that when I heard you were born," his grandmother

said, winding a bobbin, "I would never sell it. I started this one," she nodded at her loom, "when I heard that Karena died."

A flame-colored border hung below the bottom of the tapestry. Jonathon lifted it and saw another tapestry fastened beneath. Yellow stars, green clouds, and purple moons—some full, some crescents—burst against a blue sky. A man, with red hair streaming out behind him, rode a white stallion across an orange mountain.

"A Dalriada," Jonathon whispered, remembering how they had pounded down the hill toward his mother. The red rock felt warm against his leg. He opened his hand, and the picture of the orchard dropped over the Dalriada.

"That one is for Angarath," his grandmother said.

"Why?!" Jonathon demanded.

"Why what?"

"Why him?" he cried. "Why did you have to marry a Dalriada?"

She looked at him. "You mean, why love? That is a question nobody ever knows the answer to."

"But they killed her! A year ago today they killed her!"

"I know," she said calmly.

"How can you love them when they killed her?"

"I don't love them, Jonathon. I loved one. Just as you loved one. A person, not a race."

He started toward the door.

"Jonathon," she called, her voice stern. He stopped but did not turn around. "I know about Rhohar," she said. "About how your ma died. And I'm telling you it wasn't your fault."

"What did you say?" he asked, spinning on his heel. Her eyes were as heavy and wet as two stones at the bottom of a river.

"It wasn't your fault," she said. "A Dalriada killed her. Not you."

"I'm a barbarian. Thanks to you."

Her chin rose. "You don't know what you are, boy. That's your trouble."

He ran outside.

Slowly, the winter passed. As the days lengthened, light seeped back across the stale snow. The call of the mountains persisted until by spring, Jonathon felt so restless that he could settle to nothing, not fishing, not chores, not his grandmother's stories. Highgate was safe, but he knew now that he couldn't stay here forever. Should he travel back to the Valley?

One night in April, Jonathon carried a lantern into his grandmother's workshop and set it on the window sill. He lifted the orchard tapestry enough to see the one of his grandfather beneath; the Dalriada seemed to leap off the wall in his power and glory while the silver threads on the horse's hooves and mane shimmered. If my father is a Dalriada, Jonathon wondered, will he look like that?

Two flames shone by the window; the lantern flame and its reflection in the dark glass. Outside, another golden light caught his eye—or was it some trick of the full moon? Up on the ridge, veins of light shimmered across the ruined wall, flickering like a beacon.

Come up, it said to him. Come now.

chapter
Twenty-three

Minna's hooves squelched through mud and snow as
Jonathon rode up toward the ruins the following
day, his grandfather's bow hanging over his shoulder.
Inside his saddlebags was a picnic lunch big enough to feed six
people as well as extra clothes, candles, a wax-treated canvas,
and even a bedroll—all packed by his grandmother.

"The sky may be clear now," she had said when he
protested against taking so much for only a day, "but around
here a storm can blow up before you can say boondoggle. Best
to be prepared."

Jonathon edged Minna around the fallen trees and moss-
licked boulders barring the way. No one had used this trail for
a long time. A few hundred feet above the lake, the snow
deepened, though signs of spring showed in the white satin
bells growing in drier spots. He heard the swoosh of wings and
saw the kingfisher land on a snag crowning a pine tree.

"What are you doing here?" Jonathon called. The bird
chattered, flapping one wing.

Jonathon rode on, crossing a stately stream that splashed down a stair of rock. The trail narrowed, veering around a cliff, and he saw the Highgate ruins rising like a song against the sky.

A stone wall soared seven times the height of a man; each end was anchored in the rock of the pass. Although the wall had crumbled in many places, the fallen stones piled high, too high to see the Red Mountains beyond. Disappointed, Jonathon slid off Minna and looped the reins over a bush. Had he ridden all this way for nothing?

He examined the gates in the wall—two double doors shut fast, perhaps twelve feet high—but saw no iron ring, no hinges, no way to open them. The only projection was a polished agate set in the stone above the doors. It was gold, the size of a platter and the shape of a teardrop. The ridge itself was too sheer to climb; the Valley folk had chosen their defensive position well. A stone house, an old guardhouse he guessed, leaned against the west side.

Jonathon walked along the base of the ruins, searching for a hole to look through or a place where he might scramble onto the rubble. High up on the wall, a walkway stretched below the top; high enough so that guards could see—and shoot—over the top, but low enough for the wall to protect them. Fragments of stairs led up to it, but none was solid enough to climb.

In several places, thick lines of dove-gray rock had been troweled and sculpted over the wall's surface. Jonathon backed up, trying to make out the design, but the holes where stones had fallen were like missing pieces in a puzzle. Finally, he shook his head, baffled. The pattern would not click in his mind.

A blast of wind blew off his hat, and he glanced up at a sky swollen with black clouds. He hurried back to Minna. By the time he reached her she was pawing at the ground while the trees lashed back and forth. The crack of thunder echoed off the ridge, and the horse reared.

"Easy girl," he said. "Easy." There was no chance of getting back to his grandmother's in this weather. He led Minna through the driving rain until they reached the guardhouse, where the kingfisher darted in ahead of them. Inside, part of the roof lay in a heap, but one corner was still intact. After he unsaddled Minna and calmed her down, Jonathon found a spot as far from the open roof as possible, scooted inside the bedroll, and ate a ham sandwich. Thank you, Grandma, he thought.

The wind howled; the rain hardened to sleet and then the ping! ping! of hail. As he listened to the storm, he thought of his father, Uncle Wilford, and Rosamund far away in the South Valley. A terrible sense of loneliness overcame him. Here he was, miles from anyone, from anywhere, in a place that was neither the Valley nor the Red Mountains, like him. He had nothing. No home. No people. He wasn't even certain who his father was. Jonathon huddled deeper into the bedroll, where he curled into a ball and fell asleep.

Plop.

Jonathon was staring down at a circle of stars, but they blurred, wavering, sending out crinkled rays of light that rippled into each other. Part of his mind protested, telling him he should be looking up at stars, not down. He saw his toes sinking into the edge of the circle. He wiggled them and again heard the plop and saw the rays ripple out. The circle was a puddle of water reflecting the stars above.

He stood beside the ruined wall, not far from the guardhouse, although he didn't remember coming outside. Had he been sleepwalking? When had the storm stopped? In the clear sky, the stars of the Cornucopia spilled from north to south. The constellation of the Horse had begun its ascent from the east. Jonathon walked back toward the guardhouse but stopped when he saw someone lurking by the door—the hooded man from his dreams.

"Go away," Jonathon said, reaching to his shoulder for his bow. It wasn't there. The man glided toward him; the red tassels on his belt swung as he walked.

"What do you want?" Jonathon asked, backing away.

The man held out his hand and pointed north toward the closed gate and the Red Mountains beyond. A light glowed from inside his hood, a golden light in the shape of antlers.

"You're a Dalriada!" Jonathon cried. "A barbarian!"

The man yanked down his hood, and Jonathon saw his own face, his own face twenty years older, looking back at him.

"No," Jonathon whispered.

Again, the man pointed north, then he vanished. Sobbing, Jonathon fell to his knees in the slush.

For what seemed like hours, his mind floundered, lost in the same blank place where he had existed after the mob had tried to kill him. Gradually, he became aware of a repeating sound: a boom...boom...boom...like the slow, steady heartbeat of the world. Jonathon began to anticipate it, to wait with longing for each one. All at once, he was holding the red rock, feeling a burst of warmth shoot out with each beat. The ground shook. All the power of the mountains seemed focused in the rock.

Jonathon heard an ancient, rasping voice calling him, calling him with words he heard with his soul, not his ears: Rise with the sun and go! Dalriada! The beauty of the Red Mountains is yours. Ride north, arise! My heart will guide your spirit through the wilderness; my blood give you sustenance. You shall not be lost, but found, if you come to me.

Jonathon felt a wild exaltation—until a pain stabbed his head. His eyelids opened, and he saw the guardhouse roof above him, visible now in the dawn. He was lying inside his bedroll.

"Ouch," he said, feeling the pain again; the kingfisher stood on Jonathon's shoulder tugging on his hair. Jonathon sat up. A few yards away, Minna stood with her head down and one hind leg slack. He blinked, confused. Hadn't he just been outside? Or had it all been a dream?

Jonathon looked down and saw he was still holding the rock. Another boom shook the ground—or was it only distant thunder? He listened but heard no howl of wind, saw no raindrops falling through the open roof. Again the boom sounded, shivering through his blood and his bones. The exaltation rose in him once more.

His body began to move of its own accord; his hands knew what to do before his mind told them. After he packed his gear, he saddled Minna and mounted. The rock pulled him— its call stronger each moment—pulled him out of the guardhouse toward the ruined wall. He stopped some thirty feet in front of the double doors and watched the kingfisher fly to the golden agate above them.

Chi-chi! Chit-a-chi! the bird cried, then flew away.

Jonathon stared at the agate, then took out the throbbing red rock and held it up. Everything else—Greengard, the Valley, his old life—was gone.

"I am a Dalriada," he said.

The rock grew hotter and hotter until the carved horse burned, and a beam of light shot through the air and struck the agate. It turned ruby red, glittering like a drop of blood. Curls of golden light whisked along the edges, then spilled out onto the dove-gray rock, surging along the pattern of curved lines, and leaping the gaps in the ruins. Shining across the wall, from cliff to cliff and top to bottom, was a great, golden tree laden with apples. Eddies of light spun off all the branches, dancing up and down, winking, then vanishing. Above the gates, the agate still glowed, a bright red spot in the heart of the wall, like a seed inside the tree's trunk.

Dazzled, Jonathon squinted; he was half-blinded, but unable to look away.

A rumbling shattered the dawn as stone grated on stone. The ground trembled and the doors swung open until they stood flat against the wall. After a final golden burst, the beam of light stopped. The rumbling faded, and the dawn was silent again.

Jonathon stared through the open gate: that was the way he had to go; that was where the answers to his questions lay. He could deny it no longer. He had to go while the call was still strong inside him, before his courage faded. His grandmother would understand. She already knows, he thought, remembering how she had avoided his eyes while packing his gear. She had known all along that he was leaving.

He squeezed his legs and Minna walked forward. The sun rose as they reached the threshold.

Ridge after ridge of crystal mountains rose up like a glorious tale, shining pink, orange, purple, and scarlet—shining every color of red in his grandmother's workshop and more. The land of the Dalriadas waited, as he had known all winter it would be waiting, only a few miles from his grandmother's house.

One peak, glittering like red glass, soared higher than all the others.

"Kalivi Mountain," he whispered and rose slightly in the stirrups.

Jonathon rode through the Highgate ruins toward the Red Mountains, with the kingfisher flying out before him.

part three

The Red mountains

chapter
twenty-four

Hooves rang on rock, bringing the day out of the night deep in the Red Mountains. Jonathon woke, curled on the cold ground, and saw a jagged cliff towering above him. The hooves beat louder.

"The Dalriadas!" he said, jumping up. "They're coming." It wasn't a dream this time. He grabbed his bow and ran, his boots sinking into the soft, spongy mud left by the melting snow. As hooves, too, clomped through the slush, Jonathon raced toward a huge boulder to his left, ran around the far side, and leaned against it.

I can't face them, he thought, panting; the mountain air was thin. But isn't this why I came? He bit down on the inside of his cheek and tasted blood. He remembered how his mother had stood alone in the pasture, facing the Dalriadas with her hand held out. Pride and anger surged in his heart.

"Enough," he said. "No more hiding." He scrambled onto the boulder, crusted with lime-colored lichen, and nocked an arrow—after three weeks in the Red Mountains, he had only one left. Trembling, he drew his grandfather's bow. He waited, though everything in him wanted to run.

Like a song of glory, the Dalriadas came. Nine horses—blacks, duns, red roans, and one golden bay—galloped across the slope. The Dalriadas leaned low over the horses' necks, their hair whipping back from their copper faces. Keen-eyed, long-limbed, they wore leather and carried gleaming bows.

Run, Jonathon told himself. No, hold. I can hold. His breath wavered in white clouds.

The Dalriadas saw him, shouted, and fanned out, raising their bows as they circled the boulder. The sun staggered up from behind a peak and poised on the edge; for a moment, the day seemed to hang in balance as though the sun might roll down the side of the peak instead of rising into the sky.

Jonathon's bow arm shook, but he held while faster and closer the Dalriadas circled around him. Turning and turning, he aimed at a roan's neck, at the ripple of dark and bright on the flank of the black, at a Dalriada in gold flowing up from the back of his golden bay. Their splendor seized him. Now he knew why his mother had not run.

High above, the cliff marched like an immense staircase. The voice of his grandfather's bow called him, its golden filigree shining. Everywhere there was light. Jonathon arched back, and his last arrow streaked like a shooting star straight up into the sky.

"Rhohar!" he cried, fearless, exulting. The Dalriadas might kill him, but he had faced them at last; he had held.

"Kenna Rhohar!" the Dalriadas cried. Slowly, the circle stopped. Sunlight sparked off a bronze belt—a row of owl faces linked together—as well as armbands, bridles, and nine drawn bows.

"Lata, Didorieth!" someone said.

Jonathon jumped off the boulder and turned defiantly toward the voice. The golden bay, magnificent and proud, wild to run, pawed at the ground; on it sat a man with fiery hair prowling around his face. Arrows sprouted from the quiver on his back. Jonathon stared up, not at the man's stormy blue eyes, but at the antler-mark sculpting his forehead.

"Ikennu, Didorieth—Rhohar?" the Dalriada demanded.

Jonathon shook his head. He felt ashamed of how he must look: ragged, thin, wanting to run—like a quivering rabbit. But I held, he thought, his chest lifting with pride.

"Ikennu, Didorieth, Rhohar?" the man repeated scornfully.

"Angarath?" Jonathon tried the only other words of their language that he knew. "Kalivi?"

"Angarath!" the man exclaimed, leaping off his horse. Tall and as powerfully built as his mount, he walked lightly, with such intensity it seemed as if he might spring without warning. He wore a gold deerskin tunic and leggings that were soft yet tight, molding every muscle beneath. His gaze, fastened on Jonathon, was arrogant and hypnotic, like a cat that has cornered a mouse.

Jonathon stepped back.

The man stopped, his lips curling in a contemptuous smile. On his shoulder was a silver brooch, a winged wildcat with the hind legs of a hare—a fantastic creature that reminded Jonathon of those in his visions.

The man took another step, when the air filled with a flurry of wings, and the kingfisher swooped down on him. The Dalriada flung up one arm to shield his face. Scolding, the bird circled his head and then landed on Jonathon's shoulder. All the Dalriadas laughed—except the man in gold, who jerked his sleeve straight, his eyes angry.

"How was breakfast?" Jonathon said softly to the bird.

The man thumped his chest. "Kiron," he said, then added, "Tiglat!" And held out his hand for Angarath's bow. When Jonathon hesitated, Kiron seized it, and for a moment they pulled in opposition until Jonathon let go. Kiron examined the pattern of horn, wood, and inlaid gold.

"Didorieth vertien Cahaud!" His eyebrows raised, and he gave the bow to the woman wearing the owl belt, who rode a black horse with a white blaze. Behind her stood a dapple gray with a deer carcass strapped on its back. Jonathon thought of roast venison, and his hunger howled inside him. He had last eaten two days ago, and that had been only a winter-starved red squirrel. All his provisions had disappeared when Minna had run away a week earlier. Since then, Jonathon had scrambled from ridge to ridge and from pass to pass, using Kalivi Mountain as a guide whenever he could.

The kingfisher tugged on his ear, then flew away.

Jonathon touched his throbbing arm, scraped raw by his bowstring in his desperate attempts to find food. Did he dare ask the Dalriadas for something to eat?

"I'm a Dalriada too," he blurted instead, but the words vanished in the high mountain air. He had no horse and was thin and draggled beside these glorious people whose words he didn't understand. As they stared at him, the moment of courage on the boulder left him. They're going to kill me, he thought, like Ma.

Kiron sprang forward. He grasped Jonathon's head and yanked his hair back, revealing his forehead.

"Bahn Deor!" he said, his fingers digging into Jonathon's scalp.

"Hey!" Jonathon yelped with pain. After a few more seconds, Kiron pushed him away.

"Didorieth," the others murmured, nodding. "Bahn Deor." The woman gave the bow back to Kiron, who walked over to the packhorse and shifted the deer carcass. He jabbed one finger at Jonathon, then jerked his head toward the horse.

So they aren't going to kill me, Jonathon thought, suddenly exhausted. Not yet, anyway.

"Give me my bow," he said, pointing.

"Na," said Kiron.

"That bow was my grandfather's." Jonathon shrugged off his quiver and showed them it was empty. "Now give it back!" Kiron only laughed.

As the drums began to beat in Jonathon's head, he strode up, grabbed the bow, and stared into Kiron's eyes—a hunted look lurked in their depths. Jonathon saw with shock and envy that Kiron was only a few years older, yet he was a man.

Jonathon pulled harder. He felt the ache, then the sudden heat, in his forehead as the mark glowed as hotly as a flame. Through the pounding in his ears, he heard Kiron's inrush of breath, saw him falter and look away.

"Megara! Megara!" the Dalriadas cried. Kiron released the bow, shrugged, and smiled the small, contemptuous smile again.

Jonathon blinked rapidly as the heat faded from his forehead. He slung the bow over his shoulder and tried to mount the packhorse, which stood at least fifteen hands. After his fifth attempt, Kiron picked him up, lifting him as though he weighed nothing, like air, like spirit, and plopped him onto the horse. Jonathon crossed his arms, his face rigid.

A rank, spicy smell came from the deer behind him. When the woman on the black horse offered him a thick strip of jerky, Jonathon seized it and tore salty strings with his teeth. Kiron sprang onto the back of his golden bay with one graceful leap.

"Steh ti," he called, and the Dalriadas started forward. The sun climbed higher as they rode north, deeper into the Red Mountains.

* * *

By mid-afternoon they had ridden over twelve miles. The timid grass of spring straggled up through mud and scabs of snow. The jerky had strengthened him, but Jonathon dug his nails into his palms, struggling to stay awake, to stay on the horse.

He smiled bitterly. Ever since he had first seen the Dalriada horses by the Mirandin, he had longed to ride one; now that he was, he could barely hold up his head. Kiron would probably need to tie him on, mere baggage like the dead deer behind him. By Valley standards, even this packhorse was magnificent. Kiron's horse was the finest Jonathon had ever seen except for Rhohar.

As the trail turned, mountains embattled with glaciers loomed up to the east, looking cold and remote, their beauty inhuman. Jonathon couldn't believe it was really May. In the Valley the days would be warm; the garden would be planted in orderly rows; and the trees would be blooming. His heart filled with homesickness.

It seemed longer than three weeks since he'd left his grandmother's house. The nights had been terrible, crawling with stars. No human voices or hands ever touched him, only the wind keening through the trees and ridges. Sometimes songs had risen up from the mountain where he lay, songs strangely dark. But I wasn't all alone, he thought now, watching the kingfisher fly ahead. The bird—Jonathon had named him Porter—had stayed with him for some reason and had even brought him fish a few times.

Jonathon had just edged the packhorse closer to the owl woman, working up his courage to ask for more jerky, when the Dalriadas formed a single line and rode onto a narrow ledge. On the right, a three-hundred-foot cliff plunged straight down. It shot up again on the left, where the layers in the rock—strata built over ages of time—wrinkled into lines. His gaze traveled up, then stopped, riveted on the perilous cornice of snow overhanging the top. If it broke, he would be buried in a roar of fear, falling, death. Jonathon focused on the plants clinging to the rock crevices and tried to look neither up nor down.

After a quarter of a mile the ledge widened. They rode onto a small saddle between two ridges, then dropped down, descending toward the sound of water. The Dalriadas stopped beneath a stand of fir trees, where the lowering sun shone through the branches and splintered the light into a dark, yellow haze.

Beyond the trees, etched against the sky, a young woman leaned forward on a mighty horse. Wind tangled her red hair, shining with stripes of gold.

"Athira!" the Dalriadas hailed her.

Jonathon started. He recognized her! She was the girl he had seen by the river on the day long ago in the Valley. Her horse tossed its head, flashing the stripe of gold in its mane.

"Rhohar!" said Jonathon.

chapter
Twenty-five

"Vayli!" Athira cried to the Dalriadas, raising her left hand. She sat straight, as slim as a willow wand.

"Rhoha Athira!" The Dalriadas pressed their palms to their hearts. "Halim Aer Deor."

She looked at Jonathon and frowned. "Didorieth?" As she had at the river, she wore the two-pointed hat, only now a blue sapphire flashed between the peaks. It looked like a third eye.

That flash pierced Jonathon's eyes and drove down and down until it lit the blackest place in his heart. He remembered the last time he had seen Rhohar, when his mother had faced the charging Dalriadas, the blue lining in her cloak flashing like a jewel. Red and white spots blurred his eyes.

"Barbarians!" he cried. "You killed her!" Squeezing his legs against the horse, he charged Athira. The Dalriadas shouted. Rhohar screamed, and Athira clung to his back as he reared into the air, higher and higher, in a stream of red hair and black mane, both swirling with gold. When Jonathon's horse shied, the deer carcass lurched against his back, and he fought to keep his seat.

Athira brought Rhohar down. Jonathon blinked, trying to clear the spots that still bubbled before his eyes. Up close, he saw that her horse was more chestnut than blood bay and that the white mark on the forehead was a blaze, not a star. It wasn't Rhohar; the golden stripes in the mane had confused him.

Kiron galloped up, yanked Jonathon off the packhorse, and threw him to the ground, knocking the wind out of him. The entire world was the pain of his bow digging into his back, the belly of the packhorse above—its hooves flashed dangerously close—and the reeling blue sky.

I've got to get up, Jonathon thought, but he couldn't find the strength and lay staring up until Kiron leaped off his horse and slid a knife out of a sheath on his boot. In an instant, Jonathon was on his feet. Kiron held up the knife; the blade curved, tapering like a silver tongue. It was dark on the flat side with light glittering on the edge. Jonathon froze, hearing in his mind the thud of his grandmother's loom, feeling the thread of his life knotting, ending.

The knife came closer and closer, broadside, until it stopped three inches from Jonathon's face. He saw his eye reflected in the metal; then his breath steamed over the blade, and his eye disappeared.

"Na," Athira called, but still Kiron stood, his knuckles white from gripping the knife's handle. A smear of dried blood was caught beneath the nail on his forefinger. Suddenly the knife seemed to be inside Kiron's eye, to be the pupil itself, the dark blade and glittering edge locked in battle.

"Na, Kiron! Naled!" Athira said, her voice commanding.

Kiron put one hand on Jonathon's chest and shoved hard. As he stumbled back, Jonathon felt his heart pounding again, felt the wind touching his skin, felt his hands and legs and arms moving—alive. Kiron held up the knife and showed it to the Dalriadas. No one spoke.

While Kiron remounted the golden bay, Athira walked her horse toward Jonathon; she stared at him, frowning, rumpling her antler-mark. She pressed both palms together and wiggled them like a fish swimming. Her mouth opened, then closed, as though she were searching for words.

"Mulgani," she said at last. "Mulgani! The River Boy has come!" Wheeling her horse, she rode down the slope, with the Dalriadas galloping behind her.

Jonathon watched them, amazed that Athira knew his language, but he was past wondering, drained almost past caring. Were they going to let him go? Should he try to escape? The wings on Kiron's wildcat brooch seemed to stretch over him, the claws on the hare feet extending. Jonathon suspected that Kiron or any other Dalriada could easily track him. And why run when he had come to find them? Besides, he was hungry, lonely, and had no arrows left.

Jonathon followed the Dalriadas.

* * *

A quarter mile down the hill, the trail opened onto a south-facing meadow dotted with tents, people, and horses grazing at the far end. Jonathon saw smoke coiling up from a handful of campfires. At the back of the meadow, a cliff sheltered the site from the fierce, alpine winds. I am part Dalriada, Jonathon thought, I have the right to be here. My real father might even be down there. Boldly, he walked into the camp.

Athira, Kiron, and those who had ridden with them dismounted near the largest tent. A blue banner with the image of a red, twelve-point buck fluttered above it. Dalriadas gathered around them, talking fast, pointing toward Jonathon, while others led the horses away. On either side of the doorway stood a female guard; each pressed a palm to her heart as Athira and Kiron stepped inside.

Jonathon walked on. Other tents, dyed red and yellow and green, sat beside boulders or beneath pine trees. Over each door hung garlands of dried lupine, herbs, and bits of antler and bone, rattling in the breeze. Color spiraled in pots and baskets, in woven mats of lavender, pink, and lime.

He passed an old woman stitching leather, two girls skinning rabbits, and a big man carving wood with delicate strokes of his hands. A group of children twirling sticks stopped their game and stared. Everyone wore layers of deerskin or coarse, bright cloth. Strange as these people are, Jonathon thought, at least they have blue eyes and the antler-mark—the adults anyway. In some ways their similarity to him seemed strangest of all.

His stomach rumbled at the smell of food, and he saw a boy about his own age stirring a pot suspended over a fire. The boy sat cross-legged, humming loudly, wearing a purple tunic crosshatched with red at the neck and sleeves. Jonathon walked up and looked down into the pot; a stew bubbled with slow pops, releasing fragrances of garlic, onion, and herbs he couldn't name. Swallowing hard, he looked at the boy, whose hair was carrot-colored and as tousled as a carrot top. The boy stared back, then his eyes shifted to Jonathon's bow, and his mouth fell open.

"Can I have some of that?" Jonathon asked, pointing at the stew. "Please. I'm awfully hungry." At that moment, Porter landed on his shoulder.

The boy grinned and dropped the wooden spoon into the pot, his brilliant turquoise eyes dancing with laughter. He reached toward Porter, then picked up Jonathon's wrist instead; the bones protruded, his blue veins showing through his white skin. The boy's grin faded.

"Tch!" he clicked his tongue. Then he saw the long infected scrape where the bowstring had cut Jonathon's forearm.

"Cleeto!" the boy exclaimed. He grabbed a cloth bundle and unrolled it on his lap, pulling a small leather bag from an inner pocket. Reverently, he poured a few herbs into his hand, crushed them, and dropped them into the pot. As he stirred the stew, he swayed a little with his eyes half closed. Then, scooping up a spoonful, he blew on it and tasted; his lips pursed. He frowned, added more of the herbs, stirred, and tasted again.

"Ah," he said, snapping his fingers. He ladled the stew into a wooden bowl, then rose, bowed, and offered it to Jonathon. When Jonathon took it, he felt the heat flow through the wood into his hands.

"Thank you," he said, bowing back.

The boy grinned again, speaking words Jonathon felt he almost understood. He carried the bowl over to a stump a short distance away, where he ate and ate, hardly pausing to breathe. The stew tasted tangy, wild, filled with chunks of venison; it gave him strength.

When Jonathon finished and looked up, he saw the boy beaming at him, so he patted his stomach and smiled. The boy laughed, then jogged away toward the center of camp. There, in front of the large tent, people were dragging logs into a shape like a wheel or a star lying on the ground. Others packed moss into gouges hewn in the wood. While they worked, the night poured up the sides of the mountains, chasing the light toward the peaks until it vanished, and the mountains turned completely dark.

As he watched the Dalriadas, Jonathon felt lonely again, not from his time in the mountains; the loneliness he felt was older and more familiar—the loneliness of being an outsider. What were they going to do with him? Kiron would have killed him if Athira had not stopped him.

More Dalriadas gathered around the logs, their voices rising, arguing. Someone broke away and walked toward Jonathon. Was it the cooking boy, Jonathon wondered, peering through the darkness? No, the person was too tall. Jonathon stood up, uneasy, as a man stopped in front of him.

Suddenly fire roared up from the log circle, shooting gold, red, and white flames into the sky, lighting the ruff of red hair that lashed around Kiron's face. Two diamonds of ice flashed in the blackness of his eyes. He seized Jonathon's arm and dragged him toward the fire.

chapter
Twenty-six

Kiron pulled Jonathon to the edge of the star-shaped fire, where the heat arched like a shimmering sentinel. "Let me go," Jonathon cried and wrenched away, but the Dalriadas closed behind him; he was trapped.

A bear reared up, swinging its head from side to side. Jonathon jumped back, then saw that the bear was only a head and pelt worn by a Dalriada. Three other Dalriadas, dressed as a wolf, eagle, and deer, danced beside the bear. Behind them, five women played drums, beating with hand and stick and bone, thumping, slapping, pounding the rhythm that Jonathon had often heard inside his head. A pipe wailed a high, thin melody like wind howling over a barren crag.

On the other side of the fire, the Dalriadas parted, and Athira walked forward between them. She now wore a hat with even taller points—still set with the sapphire—but woven in the same red and gold colors as her hair. Around her throat hung a necklace of burnished gold, a snake biting its own tail.

"Rhoha Athira!" the Dalriadas called.

An old man in a white robe threw a handful of dried flowers into the fire; sparks exploded, hissing, and a sharp, sweet smell drifted on the smoke. When Jonathon breathed in, he suddenly felt dizzy.

The old man's antler-mark branched into six points on each side, with spurs that curled and twisted as though the roots of a tree had grappled into his skull. He lifted his hands in a gesture of invocation and spoke. "Warion Aer Deor. May the path through the night, netan et doria, lead us to the stars."

His mind whirling, Jonathon coughed, still breathing the smoke. He had understood some of the words! Was the old man mixing the languages of the Valley folk and the Dalriadas?

"Equos. The Horse rises as the Tree sets." The old man pointed to each constellation. "The Finding Star holds at the center of the Cornucopia."

As Jonathon understood more and more, he realized that the words were not Valley. He was hearing a language he had always known somewhere in his mind, somewhere deep down. His body seemed to sway, and he recalled arms around him, rocking him, a voice teaching him—his mother's voice, saying remember, Jonathon, remember. She must have taught him Dalriada when he was very young. Had the smoke from the flowers somehow awakened his memory?

Athira held up one hand, and with a final burst, the drumming, piping, and dancing ceased. Her white deerskin dress glimmered, waving in the heat.

"We ignite the star-fire to discuss the tidings of the Mountains," she said. "And the coming of the Didorieth."

Didorieth? Jonathon struggled to find the word's meaning; then it came to him.

"Dirtdweller?" he said aloud, startled. "Is that how you think of us?"

The Dalriadas murmured.

Kiron turned to him. "Why did you pretend ignorance of our language?"

"I…didn't know I knew it," Jonathon said, stumbling over the strange words. "Until the smoke."

The old man nodded and whispered to Athira.

"Then stand forward, dirtdweller," she said.

Jonathon ran his fingertips along the bow, which still hung over his shoulder; even without arrows he drew strength from it. Was his grandfather still alive? Was one of the men standing here his father? But what if, Jonathon thought, he doesn't want me anymore than…than Pa did?

The Dalriadas waited, flames flickering like daggers across their faces. The antler-marks on their foreheads varied; some had more curves; some more branches; some were pale, almost gold; while others were brown or a freckle-colored red.

These people looked so beautiful and strange, so noble and yet terrifying, that Jonathon felt giddy. He could not believe he was with them at last. He had come far to find them, had come freely into the Red Mountains—not knowing what he hoped for, but only that he had hope. Jonathon threw back his shoulders and stepped forward.

"Why do you come among us carrying Angarath's mighty bow?" Athira asked, her voice distorted by the fire between them. "The bow out of song, Cahaud, the ancient one? How do you, a dirtdweller, come to carry one of the treasures of my people?"

"My mother gave it to me," Jonathon said. Again, he had spoken in their language; the sweet-smelling smoke still danced through his brain though the dizziness had passed. "Angarath was my grandfather."

"The resemblance is striking," said the old man.

"The boy is Megara," said the owl woman who had ridden the black horse. "He has the gift of fire in his forehead, as his grandfather did."

"I am Owalen, a seer." The old man pressed his hands together. "You are the grandson of the Weaving Woman who lives at Highgate?"

"Yes," Jonathon answered, surprised. "Is…my grandfather here?"

"Angarath rides now with the Eldest Deer," Owalen said. "He is one of the Watchers, buried in the Great Snake Glacier high on Kalivi Mountain. He was a noble, worthy man—and my friend."

Jonathon felt a weight in the pit of his stomach, but how could he grieve for someone he had never known?

"Grandson of Angarath," said Athira. "Why have you come to the Red Mountains? Mulgani, my mother, who was a Seer, said that you would. The day I saw you across the river she told me: 'He is one of us but does not know it. Someday he will come. Remember. The people will need him.' So I ask you now, why have you come?"

"There are lots of reasons," Jonathon said. "First, because I'm trying to find out if my father's a Dalriada."

Athira glanced at Owalen, who shook his head.

"I don't know who your father is," he said.

Jonathon's hands fell to his sides. He stood, disappointed and relieved—confused at feeling both. His father might still be a Dalriada even though these people didn't know who he was. But did he want his father to be one or not?

"What are the other reasons?" Athira asked.

"Well, I want to be a Dalriada now, and..." Jonathon hesitated, unwilling to tell strangers of the longing he had felt or the call he had heard. "And I wanted to know what was here," he finished.

"There is trouble here," she said. "How can you help us?"

"Help you?"

"Why else would the Eldest Deer have sent you?"

"No one sent me," Jonathon said. "What kind of trouble?"

"It all began when the Farlith was lost," said Owalen. "And it grows worse with each new moon." He turned. "Kiron?"

Kiron stepped forward; the topaz eyes on the silver brooch scintillated in the firelight. "Queen Athira," he said, bowing.

Queen? thought Jonathon. Athira was the Dalriadas' queen? She didn't look more than his own age.

"My people," Athira said, "although the snow still lies

deep, Kiron and his riders have spoken with many in the other brisols. Tell us now what you have learned."

"The tidings are bad," Kiron said. "I speak for the Hunters. Bird and bear have grown sparse, the deer thin. For a year and a half, the white hare has hidden. Soon we will grow hungry."

"I speak for the Singers," said the owl woman. "The song in the world wanes. Southwind blows from the land of the dirtdwellers—blows and blows. Where is clean northwind?"

"The mountains lose their voice," warned another woman. "The marmot's whistle fades."

"I speak for the Artisans," called a man dressed in green. "The ways through the mountains, the roots of Making, and the places of vision are all vanishing."

"Yes," said Owalen. "The paths on Kalivi grow faint. If this continues, we shall perish."

"But what of the Promise of the Farlith?" cried a man.

"The Farlith is still lost." Owalen bowed his head, and the pipe wailed again.

"What is this Far-lith?" Jonathon asked; there were still words he didn't understand.

Owalen stepped nearer the fire. "Back in the Golden Age, when we were one people with the dirtdwellers, our ancestors were the Makers. They explored the spirit, bringing back songs and shapes from the whirlwind. They ate of the First Fruit from the First Tree—the Tree that Grows No More. But ever their spirits sought deeper. Their hearts cried to go to the Red Mountains, but they could not for fear they would be lost.

"One day the Farlith came down the River. The Farlith is a drop of blood sprung from the Red Hart, the Eldest Deer who runs on Kalivi Mountain. It took the shape of a stone, which spoke, saying: My blood will sustain you if you come to me. Take this as sign and symbol that your spirits will not perish in the Red Mountains. So the Great Promise was made.

"The Makers kept the Farlith secret. They still did not go to the Red Mountains because they could not follow the deer fast enough. Then the first horse came from the Beyondlands.

Patiently, with secret purpose, we learned their ways. Ever we lifted our eyes to the Red Mountains rising on the edge of the northern sky until our eyes turned blue with our desire. Then those with blue eyes and the horse wisdom were named Sky Riders—Dalriadas.

"As our powers increased, the others, who kept their eyes only on the brown earth, began to fear us. The dirtdwellers fought us, tried to keep us from our freedom. They feared and still fear, visions, passion, and the powers of Making. They do not believe that the fruit of the spirit is given to us.

"So we separated into two peoples, and the First Tree withered and died. One night when the moon shone full, the Dalriadas rode away. So fast and strong were we that the dirtdwellers could not stop us. We thrived in the Red Mountains because we had the Farlith; the horses gave us speed, and the deer gave us life.

"In all the ages since, the Farlith has been held for the Dalriadas by the queen or king." Owalen fell silent as the fire roared like a beast.

Athira spoke. "A year and a half ago, in the land of the dirtdwellers, I lost the Farlith. That is when the trouble began. Soon after, Rhohar was stolen from us."

"Stolen by dirtdwellers." Kiron scowled at Jonathon.

"Without the Farlith," Athira added, "each day grows darker. We are fading. And now come among us is a dirtdweller with blue eyes, such as we once were—and not just any dirtdweller, but the River Boy, the Boy Who Catches Fish with Singing Thread, as Mulgani foresaw." Athira's eyes, bright and dangerous, turned on Jonathon.

"Why did you attack me?" she asked. "Have you come not to help but to destroy? Is it to be again as it was in the past between our peoples? Murder and war?"

Jonathon looked at the curve of her throat encircled by the snake, then at her curling strands of hair—like flames themselves—falling past her waist. Power radiated from her. Now there was fire between them instead of a river. He felt something inside him reaching out to match her. He wished he were cleaner, older, and stronger, wished his clothes were not rags.

Kiron drew his knife.

"Answer," Athira commanded. "Kiron holds your life breath on his blade. Why did you attack me?"

"I thought your horse was Rhohar," Jonathon said. "I was angry because you, one of you killed my mother."

"You lie," Athira said.

"My father stole Rhohar. My mother was about to take him back. She was half Dalriada, Angarath's daughter...." Jonathon was shouting now "...and you killed her!"

"That Valley woman was Akarena?" Owalen cried.

"Her name was Karena!"

The Dalriadas pressed their palms over their hearts and their voices rose in a keening chant. Moving stiffly as though he'd suddenly grown old, Kiron slipped his knife back into its sheath.

"Misfortune hounds us ever since the Farlith was lost." Athira took a vial from her golden belt and unstopped it. "Behold. Melted ice from the Great Snake, the sacred glacier on Kalivi Mountain." She threw the water onto the fire.

"The Dalriadas call to the Red Mountains!" she cried, lifting her bare copper arms. "We seek your voices. Bear and Wolf speak to us now. Great Fish whisper of the deep places. Wing of the Hawk call to us. Our ears grow deaf, your voices faint. Guide us now! Why have you sent the River Boy?"

Owalen unwrapped a bundle by his feet, held up the head of the doe that had been strapped onto the packhorse, and threw it into the fire.

"We call upon the Red Hart, the Eldest Deer on Kalivi Mountain!" the Dalriadas cried. "Speak to your people!"

As the head crackled in the fire, smoked billowed high, writhing, blackening, rolling into the shape of a deer's skull. The heat redoubled, and the fire leapt, bounding into a single blue flame; in its heart was the face of a woman.

"Ma!" Jonathon called, stretching out his arms.

Dangers, she seemed to say, dangers you can't even...then a log broke, and the face vanished in a burst of sparks. The Dalriadas chanted on. The drums beat; a strange music rushed, and Jonathon sensed what was coming and knew he could not stop it. The smoke swirled into the shape of a human skull that arched out of the fire toward him.

Jonathon cowered. He had lost everything. There was nothing left except this; nowhere else to go, only here....

He felt a warmth in his pocket and pulled the rock from the pouch. The carved horse pulsed, glowing red. An apple shone in the teeth of the skull in the fire, an apple flickering with golden highlights.

Jonathon lifted the rock; he knew what he held.

From across the star-fire, he heard Athira cry...

"The Farlith!"

chapter
twenty-seven

You must eat!" exclaimed the boy with the carrot-colored hair the next morning. "Eat and eat! You are thin as a minnow!" The boy, whose name was Barli, handed Jonathon a piece of flat bread.

"Thanks," Jonathon said, relieved that he still remembered the language awakened by the flowers in the smoke. He knelt on a woven mat, took a bite of the bread, and huddled closer to the fire—the sun had not yet climbed above the eastern ridge.

When the star-fire had burned low last night, and all the Dalriadas had returned to their tents, it was Barli who had led him back to the cooking fire, Barli who had given him a sleeping skin. Jonathon had curled up with one hand on his bow and the other clutching the Farlith; he had refused to relinquish it. Athira had threatened to take it by force, but Owalen had intervened.

Now, as Jonathon chewed slowly, he felt the familiar weight of the rock inside his pocket. Although he had always known that it held power, he had not known how much until last night. He felt awed that he had carried such a thing, unknowing, for so long.

With a soft whoosh of his wings, Porter landed on Jonathon's shoulder and eyed the bread.

"Here you go." Jonathon broke off a few crumbs, and the bird pecked them from his hand.

"Ah," said Barli, bowing. "I can see that this is indeed a wise bird, a bird of discerning taste. My bread is very good, is it not?" Then he glanced up at the sound of hooves; a man rode into camp on a horse whose coat was the dappled gray of light bouncing on water. He dismounted and entered the queen's tent.

Jonathon took another bite of the sour, chewy bread. His mouth watered at the thought of corn muffins, ham, sausage, and eggs scrambled with onions—one of Uncle Wilford's enormous breakfasts. He felt an ache of homesickness. Did his father, if Brian Brae were his father, miss him even a little? But this is my home now, Jonathon reminded himself, if the Dalriadas will have me. He wasn't at all certain they would.

"And here comes someone else with discerning taste," Barli said, watching the man leave the queen's tent. As he crossed the camp, the sun slid over the ridge, and his pale gray tunic shone like the silvering on a tree. He stopped in front of Jonathon.

Chewing fast, Jonathon rose to his feet. Something about the man seemed not to demand respect, as Kiron did, but to evoke it. With the bread still in his hand, Jonathon swallowed and looked warily up at the man's face.

"So you are Angarath's hungry grandson," said the man, laughter sparkling in his blue-gray eyes. On his left shoulder hung a silver brooch fashioned like an arching wave, finely worked in filigree. He was short and stocky with a wide, deep chest.

"Yes, sir," said Jonathon.

"I am Tlell. Your grandfather was my friend. I also had the honor of meeting your mother once. Are you…" then he saw

Jonathon's bow leaning against Barli's tent. "Cahaud!" he exclaimed. "So it is true." He reached for the bow, then checked himself, asking, "May I?"

Instantly, Jonathon gave it to him.

"Old friend," Tlell murmured. "The last time I saw you, I had lowered you into the crevasse beside…" he looked keenly at Jonathon. "Where did you find this?"

"My mother brought it back from Kalivi Mountain. She gave it to me the night before she was—killed."

Tlell's eyebrows rose. "I regret that I met her only once. She was obviously a person of great courage." He ran one hand down the bow's limbs and strung it as effortlessly as a boat glides over a pond.

"This bow," Tlell said, "was made from the wood of the First Tree. It has the perfect combination of heartwood, which is flexible and drives the arrow far, and sapwood, which is strong enough to keep the heartwood from breaking. It knows the secret of perfect balance." He looked into Jonathon's eyes and plucked the bowstring; as it vibrated, Jonathon felt something flow from the man, felt something measure and hold him.

"What's your name?" Tlell asked, unstringing the bow and handing it back. "It seems no one has had the courtesy to ask."

"Jonathon Angarath Brae."

"Hmm," said Tlell. "Jho-nan-thon. That is difficult for my tongue. Take good care of Cahaud, Jhonan—. Yes. If you are agreeable, I think we will call you Jhonan."

As Jonathon reached for his bow, Tlell saw the infected scrape on his forearm.

"Why hasn't that been tended?" Tlell asked.

"I told them about it last night," Barli said, shrugging. "They didn't seem to care about the pains of a dirtdweller. Or perhaps my message has flown away from their heads."

Tlell frowned. "Then I shall bring it back again." And he walked away. Jonathon knelt on the mat, surprised to find the chunk of bread still in his hand.

"How come he knows so much about my bow?" he asked, his eyes following the man.

"Because he is Tlell," said Barli simply. "The Master Bowman."

* * *

For three days and nights, Jonathon ate from Barli's pot and slept beside his fire. The hard, hungry weeks alone in the Red Mountains had caught up with him; he could barely keep his eyes open long enough to eat before he was dozing off again. A healer came daily and changed the dressing on his arm. By the fourth morning, Jonathon felt wide awake, tired of his strange dreams, and ravenous.

"So, Jhonan," Barli said, handing him a bowl full of a steaming, grain porridge. "You are wide awake at last. But you are still too thin. Eat!"

"Why doesn't your mother cook for you?" Jonathon asked after swallowing a mouthful.

"Because I like to cook, and she does not. She's a leatherworker. You should just see the saddles she makes. She's the plump woman with the necklace of white stones who eats here at night."

Jonathon blinked. "You cook for your mother?"

"Here we do the kind of Making we like," Barli explained. "Which is usually what we do best. I am no good at leatherworking or horse training or hunting, no good at all. But cooking!" He snapped his fingers. "Yes! That is my gift. I also know much about plants and herbs—as a cook must.

"Once I wanted to be a healer," Barli added, "because they know the secrets of the plants, many mysteries, many songs. But no, I decided, if you are a healer, everyone you see is sad. I like to make people happy, see them rub their bellies with contentment." He laughed. Jonathon smiled, thinking that Barli seemed nothing like a barbarian.

"But if you don't hunt," Jonathon asked, "where do you get your meat?"

"The others bring gifts in exchange for my cooking. You

have seen Maland, that man with the crooked nose and long chin who eats here? His gift is hunting. But cooking—ha! He would burn his long chin in a pot, I am sure."

Barli sliced a potato into a simmering stew. "Kiron is the best hunter in our brisol—though he has only sixteen summers. He already wears the pin of mastery in case his boasts are not loud enough. But he eats at the Lady's fire."

"The Lady?"

"Queen Athira." Barli pressed one hand, even though it held half the potato, to his heart. Jonathon remembered the flames flickering up her bare arms, then pictured the terrible skull of smoke, and a shiver ran up his back.

"And have you noticed that girl with the face as sweet as honey?" Barli asked. "Gatea? You have seen her eating here?"

"I noticed her," Jonathon admitted. He had also noticed a tall girl with big hands, who watched him gravely.

"Gatea sings for me in exchange for eating at my fire." Barli dropped in the last chunk of potato, his smile fading. "But not often enough."

"I see; you trade for everything. I'm afraid I don't have anything to give for all the food you've cooked me."

"It will be gift enough to see you with meat on your bones. Besides, you have brought the Farlith back. Anyone would be honored to serve you." Barli fed another stick into the fire. "But what was your gift of Making? In the land of the dirtdwellers?"

Surprised by the question, Jonathon put the bowl down. He thought about home, the Valley, the fledgling orchard of Ruby Spice seedlings, and the porridge formed a lump in his stomach.

"I suppose," he said slowly, "my gift was making things grow."

"Making things grow? The trees, the grass—" Barli waved one hand at them. "They grow without any help."

"We grow fruit, grain, and vegetables," Jonathon explained. "Then we preserve them to eat through the winter."

"Yes, we preserve food too. We gather all we can find; there are brisols who do only that. But we don't have to make things grow. How do you make something grow? Bah!" Barli shook his head. "What a strange land you come from, Jhonan. I am afraid your gift will not make a good trade here."

Jonathon thought for a moment. "I'm pretty good at fishing."

"Ah!" Barli flourished his spoon. "Now that is what we will do. You will catch me fine fish, fat fish, beautiful fish! That is what we will do. I will cook them with zannia or perhaps wrapped in tolof leaves...." His eyes grew dreamy. "You will grow fat, and we will both be very happy."

"All right," Jonathon said, laughing. He was wondering whether the noble Dalriada horses would mind having their tails plucked for fishing line, when Kiron walked up.

"Come with me, dirtdweller," he said. "Now that you have finally crawled out of the sleeping skin."

Jonathon glanced at Barli, but he only shrugged and rolled his eyes.

"And bring Cahaud," Kiron ordered.

Jonathon followed him up a trail to a meadow above the camp where daisies and lupine winked in the tall grass, bending as though blown by a great breath. The flowers reminded him of his mother's garden. So many things in the Red Mountains reminded him of her, but he pushed the memories away.

A waterfall curved down a swag of rock, pooled, and dropped into a creek that snaked across the meadow. Suddenly, the waterfall moved toward him. Jonathon blinked. Then he saw Tlell, who in his gray tunic had looked like part of the falls.

"Thank you, Kiron," Tlell said when they reached him, "for bringing Jhonan."

"My honor," Kiron said with a mocking bow. He folded his arms across his chest and waited, a small smile curling his lips.

"I will not keep you longer," Tlell said. "I know you have important matters to attend to."

Kiron jerked his arms open, his hands falling to his sides. Tlell raised one eyebrow. In the silence, the waterfall rippled like a harp. Then, with a curt nod, Kiron stalked away.

Tlell turned to Jonathon and held out a leather arm guard. "This is old and worn, but it will protect your sore arm from the bowstring."

"Thanks."

"When you have learned to shoot properly, you won't need it. Now please put it on. I wish to see what you know of this bow you have inherited. Will you shoot for me?"

Jonathon felt his face grow hot. He opened his mouth, but no words came out. How could he fumble with his grandfather's bow before the eyes of the Master Bowman?

Tlell studied him, then sat down on a log. "Please join me."

Jonathon sat beside him, feeling the bark from the log press through one of the holes in his pants. His face grew hotter. Porter flew up, circled, and skittered low over the creek, landing on a branch where he could eye the water.

"Your grandfather," Tlell said, watching Porter, "did not inherit this bow until he had twenty summers. Angarath was a big man, but in spite of his strength, it took him three years to learn to shoot this bow."

"Why so long?"

"Because the bow is ancient and has a spirit of its own. Cahaud was made in the Golden Age by a Master Bowman named Calderstune. To shoot it accurately, you need excellent technique, but you must also be able to join its voice with your own. That's difficult. If you have tried to shoot it, you must have felt its spirit calling to yours."

"Yes," Jonathon said slowly, "I've felt something like that."

"What have you felt?"

"What have I felt?" Jonathon repeated, startled; the question seemed enormous. It echoed through his mind as though hurtling through a long passage to a place he didn't want to go. What could he say? That there was a red rock and a colt of fabulous beauty? That his mother had died because of him? That he had grown up in fear of madness? Or that the

Valley folk had wanted to kill him? Or that his own father had left him to die? Tears hammered against his eyes, but he forced them back.

"I see that much has happened," Tlell said. "Much that you have not allowed yourself to feel." He looked back at the creek, at the water wearing its way over the rocks, at the motionless, patient bird.

"So, Jhonan," he said, "will you shoot for me?"

chapter
twenty-eight

Tlell said what?" Kiron exclaimed later that day when Jonathon came down from the high meadow.

"Tlell said," Jonathon repeated, alarmed by the dismay in Kiron's eyes, "that he asks you to be my Atenar and to take me to…Elanae." Jonathon's tongue twisted over the words; some still puzzled him. "But he didn't explain why."

"My old teacher asks much!" Kiron said, his hands curling and uncurling. He pivoted on one foot and glowered up toward the meadow. On the back of his leather shirt was a shiny streak where his quiver had rubbed it raw.

Jonathon slid one heel back, then looked up at the fir trees bordering the meadow; one of them forked into two dead snags. Jonathon had shot beneath it three times. Though one arrow had landed in the stream, and two in the brush, Tlell had only nodded, unconcerned, and asked for the honor of teaching Jhonan. The honor, Jonathon thought now and slid his heel forward.

Kiron turned. "When the sun is a hand's breadth from

Dunadun," he said, pointing to a claw-toothed peak on the western ridge, "I will take you to Elanae. As for being your Atenar..." he seemed to choke on the word and strode off.

Jonathon felt his heart racing, as it always seemed to do around Kiron, and began breathing in the new way that Tlell had taught him. First, he inhaled deeply from the bottom of his stomach, then expanded the breath up into his ribs, and last, filled his chest with air. To exhale, he pushed his stomach up slowly without collapsing his chest, spinning out the breath for as long as he could. This was the foundation for the Dalriadas' archery techniques.

"I am afraid Kiron despises dirtdwellers," said a voice behind him.

Tired of being insulted, Jonathon spun around, but checked his anger when he saw Athira. She wore a blue cloth tunic edged with gold, with the sides slit over deerskin leggings. The heavy snake still hung around her throat, but she wore no hat, only her braided hair circling her head like a crown.

"Where I come from," Jonathon snapped, "we call Dalriadas barbarians."

"You dare insult me?"

"Well, 'dirtdweller' insults me."

She put her hands on her hips and seemed about to blurt something out, then let them fall back to her sides. "Yes, you are right. Although we have little respect for dirtdwellers, you bear the Farlith and Cahaud and have been chosen by a bird-spirit. You are Megara. And you are Angarath's grandson." She inclined her head. "All reasons why you are of high rank."

Jonathon said nothing.

"Forgive my ignorance," she added, "by teaching me how to refer to your people with respect."

"They aren't my people anymore," he said, surprised and a little distrustful. "But they're called Valley folk."

"Then, River Boy, Boy Who Catches Fish with Singing Thread, Kiron dislikes the Valley folk. He also does not wish to face his responsibility for..." she stopped.

Jonathon tensed again, resentful of being called boy by someone who—according to Barli—was only a year older. He could see the iron in her, the determination in her wide mouth, the quick intelligence in her eyes.

"I wish to speak to you about the Farlith," Athira said. "Isn't it time for you to return it?" Her eyebrows raised, rumpling the antler-mark, which emphasized her question. On her, like the others, the mark shifted with each mood, as though it were another way to express thought and emotion.

"Well?" she asked.

Jonathon hesitated. The Farlith was his link to something, his only link, though he wasn't sure to what. He couldn't part with it yet.

"It does not belong to you," she said.

"Tlell says the Farlith has a mind of its own. He says that it found me for some purpose."

"Yes, of course." Athira waved her hand impatiently. "So you could bring it back to us. It belongs to the Dalriadas. You know how desperately we need it. Without the Farlith, we will die."

"I'm a Dalriada," Jonathon said. "Besides, the Farlith is back in the Red Mountains now. That's what's important, isn't it?"

"But I am the queen," she insisted. "It is my place to hold the Farlith for my people, not yours, River Boy."

Boy again. "Then you shouldn't have lost it," Jonathon said.

Athira's face turned as red as her hair.

*　*　*

Later that day, when the sun stood a hand's breadth from Dunadun and the shadows cast by the mountains made pools of night, Kiron walked through the camp in his golden leather shirt. Women stopped what they were doing to watch him pass.

"Come then," he said when he reached Barli's fire. Somehow the morning's rage had left him, though he didn't look happy. "I have chosen to take you to Elanae, but you will wear these." He tossed Jonathon a bundle of clothes. "I won't take you to my sister looking like something a coyote has chewed up and spit out. You would frighten her." Kiron walked a short distance away and waited with his arms crossed.

"Elanae is his sister?" Jonathon asked Barli.

Barli nodded. "Their mother died birthing her. Then the Mountains swallowed up their father when he fell from Portal Peak. Elanae is Unta—you will see." Barli reached out and touched the clothes. "I wonder how many deer Kiron traded for these. Only people of the highest rank or skill can afford such quality."

"Well, I won't wear them," Jonathon said. "I don't want anything from him."

"If you don't put on these clothes, Jhonan, all the cooking I have done for you will be wasted! Thrown away, pffft!" Barli snapped his fingers.

"Why?"

"Because for such an insult, Kiron could have you exiled."

For the second time that day, Jonathon followed Kiron through the camp, feeling like a stray dog. The clothes felt odd but comfortable, like a new skin that fit exactly right. Worked to a fine softness, the white leather tunic brushed the hair sprouting on his chest; it fell almost to his knees over a pair of brown leggings. His leather shoes were neither boots nor shoes but something in between, something softer, lighter.

The sun sank, spangling the mountains red, purple, and pink; cloud ribbons in the same colors chased each other across the sky. Kiron stopped at the far edge of camp where a curve in the cliff made a hollow protected from the wind; it was narrow at the opening like a womb.

"Walk softly," he warned. "Elanae is shy as a leaf blown from a tree. If you frighten her, dirtdweller, you will pay dearly for it no matter what Tlell says."

Inside the hollow, a girl crouched over a fire burning beside a purple tent. Her hair, the same cinnamon color as Kiron's, hung down like a veil. She began to smile, but when

Jonathon came up she cowered back, swung her hair over her face, and hid behind her hands.

Kiron pointed to a mat beside the tiny fire. "Sit there," he told Jonathon. "And don't move."

Jonathon knelt.

"Little sister," said Kiron softly.

Jonathon was amazed at the gentleness in Kiron's voice.

"This is Jhonan," Kiron said. "Though he is part dirt-dweller, he has brought the Farlith back. Tlell asked me to bring him to you."

The girl moved her hand and peered at Jonathon with one frightened eye that was as blue-black as midnight.

"Tlell would not ask lightly, Elanae," Kiron said. "You will see why. Give her the bow, dirtdweller."

Jonathon held it out. Her hand, spindly and slight, with long sensitive fingers, took the bow. The sheet of hair swung back, and her eyes shone like obsidian.

"Yes," Kiron said. "It is Cahaud. And Tlell has asked me to be Jhonan's Atenar. So, in a way he is also yours."

"What does Atenar mean?" Jonathon asked.

Kiron glared at him. "It means Hart brother. Now be silent."

Hart brother? Jonathon thought, horrified. Kiron was the last person he would want for a brother. What was Tlell thinking? Elanae caressed the bow as if it were a kitten. She stared at Jonathon, dipping her head from side to side as though in rhythm to a song that only she heard.

She looks very young, Jonathon thought. Perhaps eleven. What was it Tlell wanted her to do?

Wings swept down from the sky, and Porter landed on Jonathon's shoulder. He cocked his head, looking at Elanae, who laid Cahaud across her knees and smiled. Jonathon felt his soul crack as her smile reached inside him. When she held out her hand, the bird flew to it. Never before had Jonathon seen him go to another person.

"His name is Porter," he said softly.

Elanae stroked his feathers, then gently plucked a few from his wings while he chattered. She gazed at Jonathon again and tilted her head, her smile gone. Although it hurt him to look into her eyes, he found he couldn't look away.

All at once he saw a tree, a shining tree that rose from a dark place to greet the stars, a tree more glorious than any he had ever imagined. Its mighty limbs grew, spreading and branching, putting forth leaves that glittered like green glass. Just as he felt the tree would burst out of his head, Elanae looked down, and the image faded. Porter flew off. She turned away with the bow in one hand and the feathers in the other.

"Thank you, little sister," said Kiron. He stood, nodding to Jonathon to follow.

"But my bow," Jonathon protested.

"Come you!" Kiron grabbed his arm.

When they emerged from the hollow, Jonathon shook off Kiron's hand. "What about my bow?"

"Do you understand nothing? She must have the bow to make the arrows. Already she has measured you with her eyes and heart."

"What arrows?" Jonathon asked.

"Surely Tlell told you that Elanae is a Master Fletcher. Though she is only fourteen, her arrows are the best and the truest. She makes very few, usually only for the Lady, Tlell, and me—the Making saps her strength. You could see that she isn't strong."

"Yes," said Jonathon. "But why didn't she talk to me? Or to you?"

"Because she cannot speak, except through her arrows." Kiron turned his face away, and his voice filled with grief. "Elanae has never spoken."

chapter
twenty-nine

Brilliant and swift, the arrow sliced through the air like a shooting star. Jonathon held the position of release and watched it fly. When the arrow missed the target by an arm's length, his shoulders sagged.

"I'm trying," he said to Tlell, who had just demonstrated again all the proper forms for standing, nocking, drawing, holding, and releasing. "I'm trying hard."

Tlell nodded. "You're trying too hard, Jhonan. Relax. Shoot as a river flows, as a bird flies. Focus on your breathing. With practice, you won't need to think of so many things at once; they'll become part of you. Try again."

Jonathon sighed. Two weeks had passed since Kiron had taken him to see Elanae. This morning, Tlell had at last brought the eight new arrows. Jonathon pulled one from his quiver. Wind seemed to be caught in it, wind and stars and a dazzle of light. The shaft was straight and true, painted with gold cresting that echoed the design on Cahaud's handgrip. The vanes were fashioned of golden grouse feathers speckled with brown. The blue cock feather was from Porter's wing.

"I'd hoped," he said, "that with such fine arrows, I'd shoot better."

"You are," Tlell said, "but the arrows, like the bow, must be matched by the archer. You must learn to aim from a place inside your heart. Elanae crafted the fletching to reflect your spirit, which, in turn, will help you to find it. That is her gift. Each Dalriada has a unique pattern of fletching, different from anyone else's."

"I will catch Elanae lots of fish," Jonathon said. "Fine, fat, beautiful fish, as Barli would say."

Tlell laughed and twirled his bow. "I see Barli has explained how we trade, but did he also tell you that children receive freely from everyone until after the Ridgewalk?"

"The what?"

"The Ridgewalk—a test of the body and spirit. Late in August, when the highest snows have melted, each child with fourteen summers must take the Ridgewalk to Kalivi Mountain—Mountain of Vision. If you wish to stay with us, you must take it too. If you return from Kalivi—Sol Faringen we call it—you are then considered an adult."

If you return? Jonathon brushed away a bee buzzing near his face. He thought of his mother's shooting test, of her refusal to let him go to the Red Mountains until he turned fourteen.

"After you cross the summit," Tlell added, "and come down onto Kalivi Plain, a horse will choose you."

"Me? A Dalriada horse?"

Tlell smiled. "That's the only kind we have here. Barli takes the Ridgewalk this summer. The risk is great—some die."

"Die?" A spasm skipped over Jonathon's back. He turned and looked behind him, but no one was there. He stared at the target near the edge of the meadow; behind it, a grove of white pines grew close together, their trunks dark on the north side. He had left the Valley to avoid dying, now he could not stay in the Red Mountains without facing it again.

"I wish I'd known that before I..." he said slowly. "But I do want to stay. I can't go back to the Valley."

"Why is that?"

Jonathon shifted his feet. Although he wanted to trust Tlell, he felt wary; he had trusted men before—like Mr. Landers—and been betrayed. The sun flashed off the wave-shaped pin on Tlell's shoulder, and Jonathon felt words surging up inside him. He told Tlell a few facts about his life: facts only and not all of them, his voice sounding as distant as though he were talking about someone else—until he came to his doubts about his father.

"...and because of what Ma did, and the antler-mark, my blue eyes, and hearing the Red Mountains' call so strong—all of it points to my blood father being a Dalriada. But I'm not really sure if I want that or..." Jonathon skipped on to tell about meeting his grandmother. He didn't mention the hooded man or his father leaving him to die.

Tlell listened. In the intensity of his attention, Jonathon could feel the sedges listening, the stones in the river listening, even the mountains seemed to be listening. When Jonathon finished, Tlell stood silently.

"The Ridgewalk will hold great peril for you," he said at last.

"Why?"

"You wouldn't understand, even if I could explain. But if you learn to shoot Cahaud, to hear the bow's voice, it will help you to survive and to understand all that has happened in your life. After you master the techniques, you will learn to find a way through your feelings and thoughts and finally reach your own heart and spirit." Tlell paused. "Will you take the Ridgewalk, Jhonan?"

"I..." Jonathon rolled Elanae's arrow in his fingers and looked up at the mountains. Back home on the sagebrush flat, they had looked beautiful and perilous; that was even truer now. But in spite of the danger, he could not ignore the voice that had called him to the mountains—that still called him now. Was it Kalivi? Urging him to come, come and understand?

"I'll go," Jonathon said.

"Good. Then we have much to do in three months. Shoot again, please."

Jonathon did.

As the days lengthened, he practiced shooting, made a fishing line and hooks, and enviously watched those a year older learn to shoot on horseback. Three weeks later, the queen's brisol packed up and rode to Low Summer Camp, following the deer; the animals moved higher as the snow melted.

"Why do you always choose a practice site near water?" Jonathon asked Tlell one day while they set up a target in a new meadow with a waterfall at one end.

"Because I wish to shoot like water flows," Tlell said. "And live the same. Water yields to everything, flows around the boulder that splits its path. Yet, in the end, the water wears down the boulder."

*　*　*

The next afternoon, Jonathon cast his new fishing line into a crescent-shaped pool in the stream; at last he could begin repaying his debts. He could wait until after the Ridgewalk, but what if he didn't survive? That was a definite possibility since he had so little time to prepare. The other fourteen-year-olds had been preparing all their lives.

The current dragged the line downstream too quickly. Jonathon fumbled with the pole, feeling the wood of the poplar switch dig into his hand. He had fashioned crude wooden guides and wrapped them on with waxed string. The reel wasn't a reel at all, but merely a hunk of wood to wrap the line around. Any moment now, the entire contraption might fall apart. He recast and the worm plopped on the water. As soon as he found the right materials, he would tie a few flies.

Meanwhile, he needed fish for Barli, Elanae, Tlell, and Kiron, too, in exchange for the clothing. Although Jonathon knew Kiron had given the clothes grudgingly, he didn't want to owe him for anything. Jonathon avoided his "Hart brother" as much as possible, which was easy because Kiron spent most of his time out hunting—or with Athira.

Jonathon whisked the line through the air and glanced up at the sky, arching as if it were a radiant blue bowl flipped over the mountains. The sun burned on his hair, bleached almost white from living outside.

"Hello, River Boy," Athira said, walking up with a bow over her shoulder and a brace of rabbits dangling from a thong in her hand. "Have you caught anything yet?"

"Just started," he said, glancing at her curved shape in the soft leather tunic. She laid the bow and rabbits in the grass.

"The Dalriadas don't fish in this manner," she said, watching him cast. "The day I saw you by the River, I was entranced by your Singing Thread—this line that flies through the air as you seek fish. If we could see thoughts, they would be like that, flying out from us like a thread on the wind."

"Why were the Dalriadas in the Valley that day?"

"Because I was born with the golden thread in my hair and so would become queen."

"I've been wondering—why does that make you queen?"

"Those with the golden thread led us in our quest to the Red Mountains. So now it's the sign of highest royalty from those ancient times. But it isn't passed in a straight line," she added, fingering the snake necklace. "The last in my family to bear the golden thread was my four times great grandfather."

Feeling a sudden tug, Jonathon jerked up the line; a fish had nibbled the bait, then run.

"I still don't understand why you were in the Valley," he said.

"Because a queen must know her people's enemies—their land and language. Once, hundreds of years ago, we tried to make peace with your people. A king's envoy journeyed to your great gathering place, a place of Dark Stone Rising."

Jonathon thought of Middlefield, of the old council building that sat so heavily on the land. "What happened?"

"The storytellers says that the envoy fell in love with a woman, a noble brown and gold Valley woman. They conceived a child and the dirtdwel…the Valley folk killed the envoy. No one remembers what became of the woman or their child."

A gust of wind pressed her tunic against her body. As Jonathon's eyes skimmed over her, he mistimed his cast, and the hook snagged a huckleberry bush. Athira brought it back.

"Thanks," he said, but when he held out his hand, she closed her fist over the hook, worm and all, and stared straight into his eyes.

"Lady!" a voice said.

Jonathon turned. Kiron stood behind them, frowning, bare-chested in the heat.

"You're needed in camp," Kiron said. His muscles bunched beneath his skin, which stretched taut as a drum. Over his heart was a red scar—an upside down V with a swirl beneath.

"What's that scar?" Jonathon asked. He had seen it on others too.

"The O-Bredann, the mark of adulthood," Kiron said, his eyes still on Athira. "Given by Owalen to those who Sol Faringen—return from the Ridgewalk."

Athira traced the scar with her finger. "This represents the peak of Kalivi Mountain, and this curve below is the Great Snake Glacier, where the Watchers—noble Dalriadas like Angarath—are buried in crevasses."

As Kiron stared down at her finger, a muscle twitched in his jaw.

"So, who needs me?" Athira asked, stepping away from him. She smiled at Jonathon and gave him the hook.

"Have you nothing better to do than play with a little dirtdweller boy?" Kiron asked.

"Jhonan is the grandson of Angarath," she said, her cheeks reddening. "His Megara is stronger than yours. He carries a mightier bow than yours, and the Farlith too."

"He's only a boy—until the Ridgewalk, which I doubt he will survive. And he cannot shoot Cahaud. I've watched him flailing around in the meadow. I don't know why Tlell bothers with him."

Furious, Jonathon jammed the end of the poplar rod against his waist.

"But—" she began.

"You are the queen," Kiron interrupted. "By associating with him, you dishonor us all."

Athira's eyes flashed. "I do not need you to tell me what I am. Only to remember it yourself."

"In the Valley, Kiron," Jonathon said, "we say that Dalriadas bring blight and barrenness to the land. But now I know that what you bring is much smaller."

"You are insolent, Atenar. Shall I teach you manners?"

Jonathon was about to throw down the rod and clench his fists, when he heard the waterfall splashing down the rock stair steps. He took a deep breath.

"Have you nothing better to do than fight with a little boy?" he asked, raising his eyebrows with an expression of mock innocence.

"I will not waste words with you." Kiron turned back to Athira. "Owalen is asking for you, Lady."

She picked up her bow and the rabbits, still arguing with Kiron. When they were halfway across the meadow, he grabbed her arm and kissed her, but she shoved him away and whacked him with the rabbits, leaving a streak of blood on his skin. They walked off in opposite directions.

Jonathon felt a burst of jealousy as he untangled the line and recast it. Why could Kiron be gentle with Elanae but with no one else? Perhaps because she was his sister, and no one could take her affection away from him.

An idea shot through Jonathon's mind. Kiron was jealous of him! Afraid that Athira cared for him more. But why would she? Kiron had everything: strength, intelligence, a magnificent horse, the O-Bredann, even a pin of mastery for hunting. What did Jonathon have that could possibly compare with that?

The hook, drifting unattended, caught on a branch where the stream curved. Jonathon tugged, imagining how he would kiss Athira. First, he would reach out gently to touch her cheek; if she turned away, he would wait for another time, as patiently as Porter waited for fish. If she didn't pull away, he would lean closer and—suddenly her face changed. Instead, Rosamund's face flashed before him as the hook came free.

Rosamund with the garland of sunflowers on her head;

with her skirt covered in dirt from planting the tree; and with the two white socks hanging from her pockets. He smiled. What was happening at home? It was July, almost time for early harvest.

Jonathon shut his eyes. No. That life was over. He wanted to stay in the Red Mountains, to belong here, to be a Dalriada. First though, he had to survive the Ridgewalk. He put the fishing rod away and strung Cahaud; perhaps the debts could wait after all.

Although he shot arrow after arrow until darkness fell, not one hit the target.

chapter thirty

Jonathon ran, gasping for air as the trail climbed inexorably up. His knees burned, and pain sliced his lungs, but today he was determined to run all the way to the lake. Ahead of him ran the girl with the big hands, behind him, a boy named Siear. The trail dipped, and for a moment Jonathon seemed to fly. Then the path shot up again, up to the final switchback. Breathe, he told himself, breathe.

The girl, named Halla, pulled farther ahead. Siear drew closer; Jonathon heard the brush slap against his leggings. The trail crested the slope, and at last he saw the grove of mountain hemlock that bordered the lake. After another thirty yards, he swept beneath the branches where Halla was walking now, back and forth in the shade. Jonathon forced himself to walk beside her even though he wanted to collapse. The trail from camp climbed nearly two miles to Lake Trayna, gaining two thousand feet in elevation.

"You ran well, Jhonan!" said Halla, barely out of breath.

Siear raced up, panting, and pounded Jonathon's back.

"You did it!" he yelled, scrunching his thin, pointed face and his thin, pointed nose.

Too breathless to speak, Jonathon grinned at his new friends. For a month now he had been running with Halla, Siear, and Barli. Now it was his turn to carry the rucksack. They were all fourteen.

"We won't walk the Ridgewalk," said Halla. "We'll run to Kalivi!"

"In six weeks we will run," cried Barli.

"Run to the horses," said Siear.

They stopped walking and looked at each other with shining eyes.

"Imagine hunting on our own mounts," Halla said, "instead of some old packhorse who only wants his supper." Tall and rangy, she was the best runner among the fourteen-year-olds in their brisol and hoped to be a Master Hunter someday. Siear didn't know what he wanted to be yet, some days one thing, some days another, as fickle as a mountain wind. All of them had met around Barli's cooking fire.

"Straggler," Barli called as Porter flew to a branch over their heads.

Jonathon wiped the sweat between the ridges on his forehead and looked up at Mount Trayna; the white snout of its dome gleamed in the afternoon sun. One of the mountain's shoulders sloped down and cupped the sparkling lake, like a mother holding a child on her lap.

"To Old Man's Chin!" Jonathon yelled. Whooping, they sped off again, running toward the western shore where a chin of rock jutted over the water. They shrugged off their bows and quivers, then pulled off their clothes. Jonathon kept his eyes down, even though the others thought nothing of being naked.

Halla walked out onto Old Man's Chin and peered down at the lake thirty feet below, checking for logs.

"Clear," she called.

Jonathon tried to keep his gaze on her head, but it kept

sliding down her long, red braid; sliding down her back, with its mole like a brown spot on a golden pancake; sliding down her round hip…he looked away. He thought about the Joining Night, the seventh night after the Ridgewalk, when all those who had Sol Faringen could seek mates if they wished.

Halla bent her knees and sprang, her long arms sweeping over her head as she arched through the air. When she sliced the water, only a single white-edged wave scattered through the ripples.

"You next, Jhonan," said Barli. "You were second to reach the grove."

Jonathon walked to the edge, feeling the warm stone against his feet. He looked down at the water below; it sparkled, as brilliant as the sapphire in Athira's hat. Every time he had tried this before, he had stood staring down, his hands shaking, then backed away. No one had ridiculed him. Today, though, he had run all the way to the lake; maybe today he could dive.

He waited, breathing as Tlell had taught him, until a song seemed to come over him, a song of the lake, of blue water and sky. He rose on the balls of his feet. Without making a conscious decision, he let go, was flying and the lake seemed to rise up to meet him….

The cold shocked every inch of his mind awake. He shot down deeper and deeper, feeling a moment of panic at the bottom. He opened his eyes, somersaulted, and kicked up, and his lungs demanded air, and the water turned lighter and bluer, and his head emerged in a great splutter, and he breathed.

Feet first, Halla paddled toward him on her back. "Your reward for bravery, Jhonan!" she called and kicked her legs, splashing him with cascades of water. Siear and Barli dove in to help. When they had finished swimming, they climbed back to Old Man's Chin, dressed, and lay on the rock. Jonathon watched Porter fly toward the far shore where Mount Trayna towered up.

"How many don't come back from Kalivi?" he asked. There

was a silence. He felt guilty, as though he'd suddenly tossed a skunk cabbage into their midst, but they were all haunted by Kalivi; it stood between them and the rest of their lives.

"The number varies," Halla said. "Never in memory have all Sol Faringen."

"What will happen?" Jonathon asked.

"Who knows?" Barli flopped onto his stomach. "No one will talk about it. Their mouths are shut tight."

"And even if they did, it wouldn't help," Siear added. "The way is different for each."

"You mean, there's more than one trail?" asked Jonathon.

"The paths on Kalivi shift," Barli explained, "they are never the same. The Seers say we each take our own path with us to the Mountain. I say it is time to eat." He unpacked lunch, laying out venison jerky, bread, wild greens, and purple-black crowberries.

"I want a black horse," Halla said, her pale eyes dreamy.

Jonathon chewed a hunk of flat, chewy bread and thought of Rhohar running free somewhere, but Rhohar was the horse for a king.

"He'll be black as candle-soot," Halla added. "And as noble and swift as Kiron's Wistar."

"Then you could learn to hunt as well as he does," Siear said.

"Perhaps." She sighed. "Teaching is one of the duties of mastery, but Kiron always hunts alone."

"Bah!" Barli waved one hand. "Kiron cannot be bothered with anything that doesn't puff up his pride."

"He's going to teach me to hunt," Jonathon said quietly. The others stopped eating.

"He is?" Halla asked. "I will push you off the rock out of envy. How did you manage it?"

"I asked him. He's my Atenar, after all. He had to agree."

Halla looked at Barli, who looked at Siear, who sat with his jaw hanging open, staring at Jonathon.

"But, Jhonan," Barli protested. "You will be alone with him in the forest and far from help."

"So?" Jonathon softened a piece of jerky with his fingers.

"So anything could happen out there," Halla said, "and be called an accident."

"I'll be all right," Jonathon said, trying not to think of the faint smile on Kiron's lips when he had agreed. "What kind of horse do you want, Barli?"

Barli pointed at him. "You are trying to change the subject. But, let me think." His eyes closed. "I want...yes! I see it! Such beauty awaits me on Kalivi Plain. An orange steed, with weeds for a mane, and a purple tail—so fleet and fast the field mice scatter before it."

They laughed.

"Though I want to survive for other reasons too," Barli added.

"Gatea?" Jonathon suggested. "Doesn't she seem to be eating at Dorand's fire a lot lately?"

Barli frowned. "If your eyes are so big, Jhonan, why can't your arrows hit the target?"

Jonathon ripped a shred from the jerky. Everyone knew that even after two months of rigorous practice, his shooting showed little progress. He shoved the jerky into his mouth and remembered his lesson with Tlell early that morning; not a single shot had hit the target. Jonathon had thrown down the bow. He had stomped over to the creek, picked up a heavy stone, and hurled it into the water, where it sloshed, clanking against the other rocks.

Tlell had walked up behind him. "You have improved tremendously in two months, Jhonan, believe me."

Jonathon shook his head and blinked hard at the clusters of wild lilies growing along the bank. True, he had learned a few things. He understood now that he didn't draw the bow, but the bow drew him. His arms and shoulders no longer trembled; soon his muscles would rival Kiron's. Yet, what good was any of this when he couldn't hit the target?

"You must be patient," Tlell said. "As patient as Porter waiting for fish. I have watched him perch on a branch, motionless, for hours. Mastery is long patience."

"But I don't have time to be patient!" Jonathon exclaimed.

"The Ridgewalk is only a few weeks away." He wished he had never seen Cahaud or Elanae's beautiful arrows. He was tired of trying and trying without ever succeeding. "I just can't seem to make it work."

"Making is not forcing. Making is the opposite of forcing." Tlell took a drink from his water-skin.

"I don't understand."

"You told me once that your gift of Making in the Valley was helping fruit trees to grow."

"Yes, but—"

"You tend the tree and provide the soil with water. You plant the tree where it can greet the sun. You keep weeds and insects away. All these things you do so the tree may grow, but you don't make the tree grow. It grows of itself from the song that is in the world." Tlell paused and put the stopper back in the water-skin.

"When you shoot," he continued, "you practice, you provide the bow, the arrow, the technique. But you don't make the shot, the song that is in the world makes the shot. Your task is to learn to enter into the song, your song, through your own heart. You must let go of yourself and aim from your heart for your heart. That is the true target."

Now, as Jonathon sat on Old Man's Chin above the lake, he looked down at the jerky which he had shredded to bits. I have to let go of myself, he thought; it's just like diving.

"I am sorry, Jhonan," Barli broke the silence. "I grow sad, and my meanness streaks out because Gatea looks at Dorand instead of me."

"I've seen her looking at you," Halla said.

"Yes," said Barli, "when she craves an extra helping from my cooking pot—her favorite is pheasant stewed with huckleberries and a touch of mint."

They laughed gently.

"Does Gatea look at me like the Lady looks at Jhonan?" asked Barli, his eyes sly.

"She looks at Kiron," Jonathon said, startled.

"She used to," Siear said.

"But she's the queen," Jonathon said. "I have the Farlith, and she wants it. That's all."

"Perhaps." Halla squeezed water from her braid. "But I think it's more than that."

Jonathon tried to keep his expression blank. Was it true? Did Athira care for him—as a mate? Then why did she always call him boy? Now that he thought about it, she hadn't lately. In a few more weeks, after the Ridgewalk, he would be considered a man by all the Dalriadas. Then….

"But Kiron won't give her up without a fight," Siear warned. "She chose no mate after her Ridgewalk last year."

"The queen had enough worries," Halla added, "with all the trouble in the land. She didn't need to add Kiron to them."

"But why would she want me?" Jonathon asked. "There's a good chance I'm not even half Dalriada."

"Jhonan!" said Barli, exasperated. "Where are your eyes?"

"You bear the Farlith," said Halla.

"And Cahaud," Siear added. "Elanae made your arrows."

"Angarath was your grandfather," said Barli. "And only the highborn are Megara."

"You have honor enough and more to be consort to the queen," Halla said. "Kiron knows that."

So, Jonathon thought. There must be a chance, a real chance.

"Kiron is troubled, maybe dangerous," said Barli softly. He shook his head. "Please, Jhonan, do not go hunting with him."

chapter
Thirty-one

Jonathon's foot snapped a twig.

"Step softly," Kiron whispered over his shoulder. "The deer."

Jonathon gritted his teeth and followed him on through the dusk. But we're hunting bear, he thought, not deer. Pine needles poked his face. He ducked beneath a branch, then banged his knee; the trunk of a fallen spruce barred his way. Even on its side, it stood higher than his chin. Kiron simply flowed over it. Jonathon rubbed his knee, searched for a handhold in the wood, and hauled himself up.

They were six miles from the Dalriadas' new camp near the Brosinga Ramparts and on their fourth hunt in three weeks. So far Kiron had taught him nothing. Every step that Jonathon took was simply a struggle to keep up, to keep quiet. Was Kiron trying to wear him down?

You will be alone with him, Jhonan, far from help.

Jonathon dropped with a thud on the other side of the spruce and scrambled after Kiron. They crept up a narrow draw where shadows hovered behind trees, drooped under hanging moss, and lurked between rocks. Near the top of the draw, the woods thinned. A wolf howled. Jonathon froze, and Kiron stopped to listen as the cry lengthened, crescendoed, and was answered by a second wolf.

Jonathon's blood banged in his ears. The first star glittered between two owls, black silhouettes on the branch of a pine tree. Kiron glanced at Jonathon as the wolves howled again.

Anything could happen out there and be called an accident.

Moving fast, crouching low, Kiron turned north. His body blended into the woods, into branch and leaf and shadow, almost became the woods. He seemed to be only eyes, gleaming, pure, without body, without thought of himself. Jonathon followed, panting through his mouth to keep quiet.

Kiron squatted by a thicket. His nostrils flared, and he opened his mouth, tasting the air. Jonathon did the same, but smelled only the sharp scent of juniper. Quick as a cat, Kiron slipped into the thicket, leaving Jonathon to struggle through the whorling branches. One branch slapped his forehead, and he thrust it away. Why could he never do things with ease, the way the Dalriadas did?

Kiron was kneeling in the heart of the thicket when Jonathon caught up. Bear droppings piled on the ground—fresh, pungent, and smelling of elderberries.

"Not far," Kiron mouthed. They followed the path the bear had taken in and out of the thicket, a path as clear as though axes had blazed the way. The ground sloped up to a pass, where groups of dark firs rose like arrowheads. Kiron stopped behind a tree with a twisted crown.

"We wait," he whispered. Jonathon nodded. Wind hit his face, pouring over the pass in a cold, steady stream.

Kiron pointed across the gap. Towering in the twilight, Kalivi Mountain reared up not twenty miles away. Faintly, as lighter shades of black, Jonathon saw the ramparts and spires on its crusted flanks. Never before had he been this close. Although its call had been constant since he had come to the

Red Mountains, it remained in the background, unnoticed, in the same way that his lungs breathed and his heart beat. Now, it welled up again; he felt dread and longing. In eight days, he would be walking—or dying—somewhere on those sacred slopes. An acid taste lined his mouth, and he scraped his tongue against his teeth.

Kiron, too, seemed transfixed by the dark mountain. They stood with their arrows nocked but not drawn. The nighthawk swooped, crying, oo-rue! oo-rue! Jonathon felt something rising out of himself, felt something coming forward to meet him. He held Cahaud tighter.

"Elanae is fourteen," Kiron whispered. "She goes on the Ridgewalk this year."

"What?" Jonathon asked, startled. "Elanae? But how can she?"

"It is the law."

"But she's...that's like...trying to force a star to walk on the world!"

Kiron looked at him, his face softening. "Yes."

"Don't they make any exceptions?"

"For the sick, for those with broken bones or the long fever. And even then it's only delayed. I have tried and failed to get an exception for her. She must go. The law claims to treat all equally, but to treat people the same who are not the same—that is not justice." Kiron shook his head, whipping his ruff of hair.

"Elanae is Unta," he went on, "a spirit who has come as a gift to us all, a spirit so bright she needs but a frail body. Yet the test we give her depends on the body's strength. I say it is wrong!"

While Kiron glared at the mountain, the moon, three quarters full, rose over the western ridge. Jonathon thought suddenly of another law, a Valley law.

"Elanae must go," Kiron said, tears falling down his high cheekbones. "And my heart warns me that she will not Sol Faringen."

Shocked, Jonathon stared; he had never seen a man cry

before. Kiron was strong and courageous, admired by everyone, a mighty hunter high in the queen's favor. Yet he didn't seem ashamed or try to stop his tears.

"Kiron," Jonathon whispered, "I—" He stopped. Not thirty yards away, a shadow separated from the bulk of the night and moved fearlessly across the pass. The bear.

They froze, their bows still undrawn. The bear sniffed, its head swinging from side to side, and they saw the rampant gleam of an eye. Then it was gone. As the moon soared, Kalivi Mountain threw off its dark cloak. The glaciers blossomed, white, dazzling with light, spilling like frozen rivers over the red flanks.

"Kiron," Jonathon struggled to speak. "In the Valley we also have a law." Pain shot into his heart, but for the first time, he did not try to escape it. "A law that says blue-eyed babies must be taken into the hills and left to die."

Stunned, Kiron's eyes widened.

"My father obeyed this law," Jonathon said fiercely.

Their eyes locked. The Megara sparked in Jonathon's forehead, then in Kiron's, and the light glowed between them.

When the bear growled in the distance, Jonathon shook Cahaud. Kiron nodded and raised his own bow. Their lips smiled, hard and grim, as a song seized their hearts. They turned away and together began to hunt.

chapter
Thirty-two

T here!" Barli exclaimed, reining in his horse. "The Kaliod Pinnacles—the Ridgewalk!" Jonathon looked up from the packhorse he rode and saw a chain of five peaks rising like stair steps against the sky.

"They're too steep!" he said.

"We climb around some of the steepest parts," Halla said, bringing her horse closer. "Along the connecting ridge."

Siear pointed. "The ridge leads like an arm up to Kalivi. It's hiding behind those clouds."

Jonathon stared at the clouds, trying to see the mountain beyond. I'm almost there, he thought.

They had left the Brosinga Ramparts a week ago. As the eagle flew, Kalivi wasn't far, but mountain travel took time, and the Dalriadas savored the journey. Scattered in small groups, they rode through the glory of high summer in the high country: along red, rocky slopes; beside alpine firs; over meadows rollicking with lupine, daisies, purple windflowers, and the occasional late-blooming hyacinth. The vastness of the mountains staggered Jonathon's mind. Yet, he never forgot that he was riding toward Kalivi and the end or the beginning of his life.

"I just want to get it over with," Siear said now.

"Me too," Barli agreed, his usually happy face glum.

As they rode forward again, bear teeth clacked on a thong around Jonathon's neck. Kiron had claimed the pelt because his arrow had killed the animal. Panicked, Jonathon had shot first, hitting the bear's right shoulder, which had only enraged both the bear and Kiron. Never would he forget the sight of the bear rising up and up, forever up—its back to a tree, its coat silvery gray in the moonlight. It charged him as he had reached for a second arrow. At last Kiron had shot; though for a moment, a long, horrible moment, Jonathon had not believed he would.

Once the bear lay dead, Kiron had smeared its blood between the ridges on Jonathon's forehead. Together they had shouted their triumph. The next day, however, Kiron had been his old surly self, ignoring Jonathon as though none of it had ever happened.

Now, looking up at the pinnacles, Jonathon wondered if he had only imagined Kiron's slight hesitation. He knew that Kiron could have let the bear kill him—an unfortunate accident. He could have given the Farlith to Athira and been assured of her affection. What had stopped him?

Jonathon pressed his thumb against one of the bear teeth, still amazed by all he had gained from trading his half of the bear. Not only had his debts vanished, but he also owned a sleeping skin, a bowl, and another set of clothing. Best of all, Gatea had sung two beautiful songs for him.

"Jhonan!" Barli exclaimed.

"What?" said Jonathon, startled.

"I have spoken to you three times! What are your ears dreaming of?"

"Hunting."

"Ah," Barli said, grinning. "Yes, that was fine eating we had. But it was nothing, I tell you, nothing compared to the feast we will have after the Ridgewalk."

"That good?"

"Better than you can imagine." Barli smacked his brown lips. "It's all to make strength for the Joining later. We will be men then and need all our strength to make the women happy!"

His ears hot, Jonathon looked at Halla, but she only flipped her braid over her shoulder and glanced at him from the corners of her eyes. Ever since the bear kill, other girls—and even some of the young women who were fifteen or sixteen—looked at him in a way he was beginning to understand; it was a slow, sideways look beneath the eyelashes. He liked it. A moment later, he spotted Athira standing beside a shallow tarn while Rhoha drank. She was the one he wanted, but would she choose him?

After five more miles, they rode into the camp of the Tendars, the brisol that trained the horses. Dalriadas from all over the Red Mountains—the families and friends of the fourteen-year-olds and anyone else who could make the long journey—had already arrived. They surged forward to greet the queen.

"Hail Athira! Hail Rhoha!" The Dalriadas fluttered strips of red cloth or waved their bows in salute.

"Greetings!" she called, raising one hand. "Greetings to the people of the Red Hart Who Runs on Kalivi Mountain!"

A small man came forward and pressed his palm to his chest. "I, Keelas, leader of the Tendars, welcome the Queen." As thin and wiry as the horses they trained, the Tendars lived here from the time the snow melted in July until it fell again in October. Then they rode south to Hidden Sun Hold, a place where many brisols gathered for winter, where Making and storytelling filled the days. Jonathon planned to make more fishing lines and better rods that winter—if he survived Kalivi. His shooting had not improved.

"And welcome to you, Ridgewalkers," Keelas called. "Please leave your mounts and follow me. The next horse you ride will be your own."

"Hail and Sol Faringen!" the Dalriadas shouted.

Jonathon took his gear and, with the other fourteen-year-olds from his brisol, followed Keelas to a meadow reserved for the Ridgewalkers. One hundred and thirty-nine would go this year, Keelas told them, a small group.

Many Dalriadas watched Jonathon pass. News of him, the Farlith, and the bow he carried had spread through the land during the summer. His blonde hair shone like a beacon among the variously shaded redheads. Porter perched on his shoulder. Whispers erupted in their wake, and Jonathon felt the bitterness of being an outsider again, a feeling he had almost forgotten.

*　*　*

"I can smell the horses," Jonathon said later, a light in his eyes as he unloaded an armful of firewood.

Barli snorted. "That, my friend, is only because you smell like one yourself."

"We could all use a swim in Lake Trayna," Halla said, unrolling her sleeping skin. Porter came winging over, flapping and chattering.

"You want some bread?" Jonathon asked him, but Porter flew off, flew back, circled, and darted away again. He repeated this aerial dance until Jonathon understood and followed him. About a hundred yards away, the bird landed on the branch of a noble fir.

Below it, Elanae curled in a bowl-shaped hollow in the ground. Small white flowers speckled the grass. Each blossom had five petals, and six blossoms grew on each delicate stem, drooping under the weight. They smelled sweet and sharp like the dried flowers from the bonfire, the ones that had awakened the Dalriadas' language in his mind. Elanae had woven them into her long tangled hair where they glimmered like stars. With her knees pulled up to her chin, she stared out at the clouds wreathing the pinnacles and pulled a strand of hair against her cheek.

"Hello, Elanae," he said gently. "It's me, Jhonan."

He sat with her for a while and later left her some stew.

When he came back again, the bowl was empty, except for a single white flower in the center. He tucked it in his breast pocket, then draped a sleeping skin around her.

When at last he slept that night, he dreamed of the dark skull looming out of the bonfire while he screamed and screamed. The Farlith burned in his hand, guiding him through a forest of bones, the bones of deer, bears, birds—and humans.

*   *   *

At dawn, Jonathon washed in the icy stream until he was wide awake, his skin tingling. He would go to Kalivi clean. Was he really going there at last? Today? He looked to the northeast, but the clouds still drifted low. He pictured the mountain as he had seen it from the sagebrush flat above Greengard: beckoning, ominous, glorious.

When he was dry, he pulled on his best tunic, the white one that Kiron had given him. He rubbed the leather pouch that contained the Farlith, comforted by the solid feeling of the rock inside, then stuffed it in his pocket.

Others were donning luck charms too, a copper bracelet, a beaded belt; one girl slipped on a sash made of raven feathers. The Ridgewalkers were not allowed to eat or speak— both difficult for Barli, who patted his stomach sadly.

When Owalen came for them, Jonathon picked up his bow, quiver, and knife—all that they were allowed to take— and followed him to the main camp. Hundreds of people stood on stumps and rocks or sat on horses and each other's shoulders to see the children for perhaps the last time. Some even perched in the trees; it looked as though a flock of large, colorful birds had suddenly landed.

Athira stepped forward in the white gown that reached to her ankles. Her hair blew loose, red gold in the early morning sun, curling against the golden snake that glittered around her neck. Owalen, Tlell, Kiron, and a few other Masters and Seers, gathered behind her.

"Our spirits go with you on the Ridgewalk, the way to

Kalivi Mountain," Athira said. "May the Watchers and the Great Snake help you. May the Red Hart guide your footsteps. We await for you to Sol Faringen, to return to us as women and men."

The Dalriadas cheered.

She held up one hand. "This year, the Ridgewalk is a time for special celebration because Jhonan has brought the Farlith back to the Red Mountains."

"Hail the Farlith!" the Dalriadas shouted. Tlell and Owalen glanced at her. She's up to something, Jonathon thought, his hand tightening over the rock.

"It seems a suitable moment for us to honor Jhonan," Athira said, "and for him to return the Farlith to its original owner." Her eyes triumphant, she held out her hand. The crowd hushed.

Sensing trouble, the other fourteen-year-olds, including Siear, edged away from Jonathon. Barli and Halla stood fast beside him. Jonathon looked into the expectant faces of hundreds of Dalriadas; when he made no move to give Athira the Farlith, many of the faces turned angry. People began muttering.

Like the night in the smoke-filled Valley, again he faced an angry mob. They're not demanding my life this time, Jonathon thought, but they may as well be, since they're demanding the very thing I need to survive. Without the Farlith, he would not Sol Faringen—he believed that with every bit of blood and bone in his body. He felt the rock grow warm, felt its pull, as though the Farlith itself were urging him to keep it.

Athira's hand did not waver.

"The Lady awaits your answer," Kiron said.

"You may break your silence," Owalen told Jonathon.

"I thank the Lady for the honor she would do me," Jonathon said; the words seemed to come through him from somewhere else. "But the original owner of the Farlith is the Red Hart. How can I offer the Farlith to The Eldest Deer Who Runs on Kalivi Mountain until I'm there?"

Athira's eyes flashed. One corner of Tlell's mouth twitched. Owalen murmured something to Athira and then stepped forward.

"There is wisdom in the boy's answer," Owalen said. When the other Seers nodded in agreement, the crowd fell silent. "Now let us give the Ridgewalkers our final blessing." Owalen's hands raised, his long white sleeves fluttering. "We rejoice in your journey and your returning."

As cheers rang out once more, the hammering in Jonathon's chest eased, but he still clenched the rock. Owalen led the fourteen-year-olds across the camp to a path that sloped between the buttresses of a cliff. After they had climbed half a mile, they reached a glimmering cirque.

"You will wait here beside Durulin until you are called," Owalen said. "Keep the silence." He walked toward an enormous rock severed in some age long past. Two slabs leaned against each other, leaving an archway between—the beginning of the Ridgewalk. Owalen passed through it and disappeared.

Porter skimmed over the water, while Jonathon paced along the shore. White flowers, like the one Elanae had given him last night, clustered in the grass. Barli had told him that the flower was called a pinnea, and that it grew only around the Kaliod Pinnacles.

Every few minutes, Owalen returned and called a name; Halla's was one of the first. Ignoring Siear, she smiled at Jonathon and Barli, raised her bow over her head, and ran up the path.

As name after name was called, the waiting grew unbearable. Each time Owalen stepped through the arch, all eyes fixed on him. Jonathon wondered if the names came to him spontaneously or if he had a list in his mind. When Siear's turn came, he walked with his toes turned in, something desperate in his pinched face.

"Barli Tatovian Ina," Owalen called fifteen minutes later. Barli sighed and stood, brushing pine needles from his seat. He twirled his bow, grinned a lopsided grin, and was gone. At that moment, Jonathon realized he might never see Barli again. That fear ignited another, older pain, and he sat down and bowed his head.

An hour later, Owalen walked over to Elanae, who sat huddled away from the others. "Elanae," he said, stretching out his spotted, old hands. "It is time. The Mountain and the Eldest call you now, my child."

She took his hands and stood up: thin, frail, her eyes bright. Jonathon wondered what visions she saw. Inside the archway, she stopped and looked back at him. She stretched out her arms, placing one on each slab of rock. Their eyes held, and the image of the tree with green glass leaves towered up in his mind. Then she turned, her hair floating out, and disappeared up the trail.

Still waiting at midday, Jonathon slumped against a log. He twirled Elanae's pinnea in his fingers, counting the spins, trying to contain his fear. When Owalen appeared again, Jonathon didn't even bother to look up.

"Jhonan Angarath Brae," said Owalen. "Kalivi Mountain awaits you."

chapter
Thirty-three

With every sense on guard, Jonathon walked up a hill screened by cliffs from the cirque. He half expected some creature to attack him, but saw only the red trail winding away like a thread between the trees. The noble firs soared, banded with shafts of sunlight. Porter skimmed in and out of the blue-green branches. As the trail ascended, the nobles dwindled, giving way to meadows and the smaller alpine firs with their spire-like crowns. Wild lilies still bloomed here where the summer came late. When Jonathon reached the timberline, the humped back of the first pinnacle sloped ahead.

His fingertips tensed on his bowstring. There was only one way to Kalivi Mountain, where the horses waited, where the rest of his life waited, and that was across the Kaliod Pinnacles. Torn and ragged, a wound against the sky, the pinnacles swept up toward the cloud-wrapped mountain and vanished into the fog.

Jonathon began to climb. Three horses could have ridden

abreast across the first bit of the ridge, although he did have to scramble around a sheer outcropping near the top. High on the second pinnacle, the wind gusted. On the third, the ridge narrowed to a spine. He held on to the stunted, wind-sculpted trees, whose roots grappled into cracks in the rock. By the fourth pinnacle, Jonathon was straddling the ridge, scooting forward inch by inch, groping for holds. He stopped, suddenly afraid he might fall off the face of the world, and looked out.

The clouds had begun to clear. To his right, the slope pitched to the root of the vale that curved toward the camp. To his left, lower ridges swelled with miles of forest. He saw no sign of his friends or anyone else. Kalivi was still hidden by clouds, though its surrounding white peaks thrust up like vassals. Jonathon scooted forward again, but now a vibration buzzed through the ridge, buzzed into his hands and thighs as he dragged them over the rock. Although he couldn't see the mountain, its voice was filling him, and he began to move with quick, unthinking grace.

Walking upright, almost oblivious to the danger, he crested the fifth and final pinnacle as the clouds blew away. Then the ridge dipped, curved, and he stood face to face with Kalivi Mountain.

The mountain exulted, sparkling like a diamond. Filigrees of ice spiraled in fantastic shapes, unnamable shapes, shapes found only in his dreams. Towering spires cast blue shadows bigger than lakes. Walls of red rock burned like fire through rents in the snow and ice.

"Kalivi," he whispered with a fierce joy. He leaned forward, about to run the last distance, when the sky thundered. He shrank back. For the first time since he'd rounded the bend, he looked down. Eight feet ahead, the ridge ended, plunging into a crater of ice. The sky thundered again. A colossal shard of ice cracked away from the crater's side; it toppled, trailing long white teeth, and crashed into the cauldron of ice and rock and water. Mist shot up. It arched higher and higher, until drops sprayed his face. The crater was half frozen even at the height of summer.

The roar faded, but Jonathon's ears still rang. On the other side of a forty-foot gap, the ridge started again. It merged briefly here with the perimeter of the crater, like a strip of bacon nestled against a fried egg. Bridging the gap was a fallen tree.

He climbed over to it and saw that several feet of the trunk extended onto a ledge, the roots jamming into the rock. When the tree was a seedling, it had split into two trunks which had grown around each other in a long, tight spiral. The tree was only a foot wide, sagging in the middle from its own weight.

His hands grew cold, and the taste of metal coated his mouth. He could see no other way across the abyss. Had any of the others crossed here—Barli, Halla, or Siear? If they had fallen onto a floating chunk of ice, wouldn't he be able to see? He kept his eyes away from the bottom.

Porter flew across the gap while Jonathon backed away from the brink until his shoulders pressed against the rock. How long did he have until someone came and witnessed his cowardice? Then again, perhaps no one would come. Hadn't Barli said that the mountain created a different path for each person? If that's true, Jonathon wondered, why didn't I see any forks in the trail?

He stared at Kalivi Mountain. He had traveled so far to answer its call, traveled all the way from Greengard. Now, when he was nearly there, a crater of ice stopped him. He kicked the log. Although it didn't budge, he was still afraid to step on it; slicks from the spray shone on the wood.

"I have to go back," he said, though he knew that Dalriadas either completed the Ridgewalk or died trying. Nobody returned through the archway to Durulin. If he did, he wouldn't get one of the magnificent horses; Owalen wouldn't cut the O-Bredann into his chest; and Athira would never choose a coward. The thought of Kiron's laughter made Jonathon wince. Cross the log and risk dying or leave the Dalriadas—that was his choice. After all, he had known all along that he might die on the Ridgewalk. Hadn't he?

He hadn't really believed it—until now.

Blood pounded in his face. He was furious at being put

into an impossible situation. "Be angry," Tlell had said once when Jonathon had stood in the meadow holding his bow at full draw. Cahaud had pulled him down where his anger churned, rabid and deadly. Startled, Jonathon had eased the tension on the bowstring, but Tlell had said, "Hold. Be angry. Stand with it and feel it deep—when you are alone—so its weight will be gone."

Now, Jonathon closed his eyes and imagined himself ripping apart the log, tossing hunks of ice into the crater, smashing, rending, punching, until his anger eased. He breathed deeply until he felt as if he were breath itself. An eagle called…what is fear? And the scent of the pinnea drifted on the wind, creating a quiet space inside him.

He was alone; no one would come to help. His actions and decisions, his very life, depended on him alone. His eyes opened on the radiance of the mountain, on the red rock marbled with white snow. Jonathon stepped onto the log, walked steadily, and did not look down. When he was almost across, the sky cracked again; another shard of ice howled down into the crater.

The shock jerked the log, and his back foot slipped. As he fought for balance, his head snapped down, and he saw a body on the ice below. Both legs twisted in impossible positions; a brown boot gleamed on one of them. Jonathon's head snapped up. He flung out both arms, found his balance, and took five quick steps to the other side.

Porter flew around his head, scolding. Jonathon burst into a run and ran until the gap was far behind. When night fell an hour later, he found a small dead pine—few grew this high up—and kindled a fire. He lay back and looked at the stars clotting the sky. The wind blew, muttering of ice.

I am on Kalivi Mountain, he thought, astonished. If he climbed high enough and looked far enough, he would see the sagebrush flat above Greengard. Somewhere above him were the Watchers, buried in the Great Snake Glacier; Jonathon hoped to avoid it. And somewhere behind him, a body bent backwards on the ice. Were any of his friends' boots that shiny? He pictured their boots tossed in a heap on Old Man's Chin, then they blurred and became his father's boots and....

Jonathon blinked across the embers at yet another boot, this one with a buckle on the ankle. Embers? What had happened to the fire? He must have fallen asleep. The boot moved, stirring the hem of a robe.

"Barli?" Jonathon asked, yawning, and looked up. He saw the tasseled end of a gold belt, then a brown cloak, then—Jonathon grabbed Cahaud and sprang up. It was the hooded man.

"Get away from me," Jonathon said.

The hooded man held out his hand, imploring, and pointed up the mountain. The full moon sailed like a white ship behind his hood. Jonathon shuddered, wondering if the man's face were still an older version of his own.

"Are you one of the Watchers?" he asked.

The man pressed his hands together, raised them above his chin, and opened them in a wide circle over his head. He pointed up the mountain again, his body flickering, then he faded and finally vanished.

Jonathon closed his eyes, willing himself to wake. He knew this dream, knew he could wake up and be home in bed under his quilt. But when he opened his eyes, he saw every detail of the slope before him—the angled rocks, the path, the overhanging ice—revealed by the moonlight shining on the snow. There was now enough light for him to go on as the man had urged.

"Porter!" he called, "Porter!" A moment later, the bird came flying toward him. Jonathon broke camp and climbed on up the mountain, which seemed wakeful and aware, an imminent presence. Water trickled, melting off snowbanks and ice fields. Cold crawled beneath his tunic, and he sighed for the campfire he had left. After nearly two miles, the trail began to fade in and out, then forked for the first time.

"Which way?" Jonathon asked Porter, who perched on his shoulder. The bird only pulled on his earlobe.

Both trails led up. One crossed a bank covered with slush;

it smelled dank, like stale, standing water. The other plowed through a tumble of scree and rounded a cliff where a whitebark pine stood etched against the sky. The steepness of the cliff and the sharply curving trail made it look as though he would step off into space, into the vastness of the stars. The sheer, stark beauty terrified him.

Hold. Stand with it.

He climbed the trail of scree, his breath short in the high, thin air. Now the path was clear, except for an occasional streamer of fog. A mile farther, he skirted a ridge and stopped.

Starlight slid down a glacier twisting between fangs of rock. Waves of ice lapped one over the other, surmounting up and over the summit. Beautiful and perilous, the Great Snake Glacier ate its way down Kalivi Mountain. Although Jonathon had been told it slithered only a hand's breadth in a year, it looked as though it might come crashing down at any moment. Awe seized him: a joy and terror of the rock and ice that crowned the top of the world.

He then realized he had reached the place he'd hoped to avoid. Deep in one of those crevasses was Angarath's grave, where his mother had found Cahaud. How had she retrieved it? A picture of her crumpled body in the pasture flashed before his eyes, but he pushed the memory away.

He saw, still far up, the pass on the mountain's neck. Over that pass were the horses; over that pass his life waited; over that pass he had to go. But the trail ended here. Even in daylight he could not cross, not without axes and ropes, perhaps not even then.

Porter flew off his shoulder and Jonathon turned, watching him land on a lip of stone on a cliff ten feet away. Below him, in the solid rock of the mountain, was a wooden door. It looked ancient, carved with flowers, stars, and a deer whose antlers twisted into a tree. Was there a way through the mountain? A way beneath the ice? But wasn't that where the Watchers were? Jonathon looked back at the glacier; he could not cross.

He touched the door with one finger. Fear howled through the wood, and he jumped back, twisting to the left and landing in a half-crouch where he faced—a boy.

The boy huddled on the left side of the door, his knees drawn up and his head buried in his arms. He sat so still that Jonathon had mistaken him for a rock.

"Siear?" Jonathon asked, touching his shoulder. "Barli?" But the boy, immobile, as cold as ice, no longer saw or heard. Jonathon backed away. Whoever he was, he must have been paralyzed by fear, unable to go on. He was dead. Dead.

Jonathon's heart pounded, rushing, throbbing, screaming words to his brain: Be afraid! Be afraid! He reached forward and with all his strength, yanked open the door in the mountain.

chapter
Thirty-four

The door opened on utter blackness. Jonathon grabbed an arrow and drew Cahaud, aiming into the shadows. A ribbon of fog skimmed out of the doorway, wrapped once around his knees, and vanished. For a moment, he saw his grandmother's hands flying across her loom.

"If my grandpa's in there," Jonathon said, "he wouldn't want to hurt me."

Suddenly, Porter unfurled his wings and darted up from the stone over the door. Jonathon watched him fly toward the pass on the mountain's neck, growing smaller and smaller until he disappeared.

"See you on the other side," Jonathon said, his throat tight. He felt abandoned, but knew he had to go alone.

With Cahaud fully drawn, Jonathon stepped over the threshold into the blackness. It swallowed him, crawling on his skin like some living horror he could neither see nor brush away. He took three steps, then another and another. He glanced back at the doorway—a rectangle of grayer darkness sprinkled with stars—and saw the silhouette of the dead boy's elbow. After three more steps, his foot hit something. He cried out as claws scrabbled on his face, but when he reached up to fling them off, there was nothing there.

Breathe, he told himself. He reached out with his foot and slid his toe up the surface he had struck. Rock? A wall? After eight inches, it leveled out. He inched his foot forward; again, his toe hit rock, and again it leveled out—a staircase.

Jonathon began to climb: one step, then another, up and up. The stench of rotting meat fouled the air. All the bulk of the mountain seemed to crush him, suffocate him. His muscles burned from holding Cahaud at full draw and he eased the tension. Then a crosscurrent of air touched his left cheek. He stopped, his hand groping forward in the dark, and discovered a second staircase angling off from the first. Now which way? He listened, but only a faint humming rang in his ears.

"If only I had some light," he said. All at once, he felt the Farlith growing warm. Would it shine? Jonathon slung Cahaud over his shoulder and reached for the pouch, but when he held the Farlith near his eyes, he couldn't even see it in the blackness. Nothing happened.

He sighed and was about to put it back, when the carved mane began to glow. Blinking, Jonathon turned the rock. The horse's body sparked, then the legs. The hooves and tail burned, brighter, hotter, until his hand was suffused with a red gold light. A huge reflection of the horse sprang onto the wall where it flickered like fire. Although warm, the Farlith no longer glowed; all its force lived in the horse of light.

Jonathon squinted and watched the horse run—still flat on the wall—into the branching passage. He hurried after it, climbing more stairs into the mountain's throat. His knees began to ache from bending and straightening. The horse of light plunged into one new passage after another. All of them led up. Only one thought burned in Jonathon's mind: keep following the horse. Up and up it galloped, sometimes close and sometimes so far ahead that Jonathon saw only the tail whipping out of sight.

When the tunnel split again, a blast of foul air from the right nearly knocked him down.

"You're not my son," a voice called from the same direction, shattering the silence. Jonathon froze; he knew that voice.

"Pa?" he called, but how could his father be here in the mountain? Jonathon peered into the passage. The fiery horse ran that way, and Jonathon followed.

"You shamed me!" his father's voice shouted, all around him now, ringing off the stone walls. "You ruined my life."

Jonathon cringed.

"I left you to die," the voice accused. "Why didn't you die instead of your mother?"

Jonathon stumbled on, away, as the voice echoed behind him. The tunnel branched again, and another crosscurrent of putrid air carried another voice.

"You're not of the Valley," Mr. Landers' voice said, and Jonathon followed the horse toward it. "Not of the Valley, not of the Valley...."

"Barbarian!" Mr. Dakken yelled. "Loony-blue!"

The voices beat against Jonathon, faster and harder, blasting the air, echoing through the passages until they filled all his soul.

"Dirtdweller!"

"Not of the Dalriadas...not of the Valley...."

"Kill him!"

"Life breath on my blade...."

"You're not my son, my son...."

Jonathon staggered, bent double against the wind sweeping through the tunnel, but still he followed the horse. A chasm loomed to the left. Above it, gigantic bones streaked with flesh hung from the ceiling; the smell made him reel. To cross the chasm, he would have to touch them, swing himself hand over hand to the other side. He shuddered and turned away. Then a high voice, throbbing with pain, pierced above all the others.

"Jonathon, help me!" his mother's voice cried from the chasm. The horse of light galloped straight toward it.

"No!" he cried. "No!" He fell forward, and the edge of a stair cut his elbow. He lay; his heart dimmed in agony. Only when the horse had jumped the chasm, leaving him surrounded by darkness again, did Jonathon finally crawl forward. He put the Farlith in his pocket, grasped the bones, and swung out over the chasm.

"Don't leave me," he called. "Not in the dark."

"Save me from the Dalriadas, Jonathon!" Her voice swirled around him.

"Ma!" he sobbed.

"You loved Rhohar more. You were angry with me. Why did you kill me?"

"I didn't." He grabbed one bone, then another. "I never did."

"You killed me, you killed me, you killed me...."

"No!" Jonathon shouted, dropping down on the other side of the chasm: "I loved you. I love you, Ma!" His shout reverberated through every chamber of the mountain.

He saw the horse of light race up a spiral staircase like a fiery whirlwind. After clutching Cahaud in one hand and the Farlith in the other, Jonathon followed.

Fresh air blew in his face as he entered a vaulted cavern near the top of the mountain, faintly lit by the horse pulsing on the far wall. Jonathon wiped the back of his hand against his eyes and looked up at the ceiling. Stars shone through two round windows, through a rectangle, and lower, through a jagged opening like a mouth with teeth.

Jonathon screamed. The windows were eye sockets. He stood inside a vast skull, looking out from death. Words burst out from deep in his belly: "I don't want to die!" But the skin seemed to slide off his face until he was stripped to the bone before the stars emblazoned above death. High, high up flew the shadow of a bird. With all his strength, Jonathon threw the Farlith up through the eye of the skull.

Hooves thundered through the mountain, and the Red Hart came leaping into the cavern. His antlers branched into hundreds of points, each striped with gold.

Jonathon drew his bow. His head began to ache as light

B London

burned from his forehead. Cahaud sang him down and down—come deeper, come deep—until Jonathon was aiming for, aiming from the very chambers of his heart. Elanae's arrow glittered beside his cheek. The Eldest Deer kept coming; his eyes, which were human and deeper than human, fixed on Jonathon.

Jonathon's arrow flew and pierced the Red Hart's chest. He stumbled, his legs collapsing beneath him, his beauty, power, and splendor bleeding away. Although his eyes filled with pain, they still looked at Jonathon with something…was it love? Then they closed; his head bowed; and he died. Glorious music resounded off the cavern walls.

Weeping, Jonathon flung himself down beside the Red Hart and into the blood flowing over the floor. One drop sprang into his hand, sparkled, coalesced, and became the Farlith. He laid it between the Red Hart's antlers, and they began to grow. They thickened, branching and spreading into a tree, which rose higher and higher until it soared through one eye of the skull. Jonathon grasped the antler-branches and climbed. All around him, leaves opened, buds bloomed, and the fragrance of apple blossoms sweetened the air. Instantly, the apples ripened. He picked one, tucking it inside his shirt to eat later. He climbed up and out of the skull, then swung onto the snow beneath the stars.

Shining in the moonlight, a horse galloped up, and Jonathon sprang upon its back. They raced down Kalivi Mountain to the sound of drums beating; drums dancing like feet on a wooden floor; drums pinging like raindrops on a tin roof; drums creaking like cradles before a hearth. His skin throbbed, became a drum skin playing all the rhythms of the seasons and tides, of life and death. Jonathon turned his head and saw the Red Hart leaping beside him. He was alive! Astride, her frail hands clinging to the antlers, was a girl whose cinnamon hair streaked out behind her, trailing stars.

"Elanae!" cried Jonathon.

"The Promise," sang Elanae. She swung one arm and threw the Farlith toward Jonathon. It flew up; he caught it, and she was gone.

chapter
Thirty-five

Jonathon crouched low on the horse, galloping onto Kalivi Plain as the dawn challenged the night. When the sun skipped over the eastern peaks and speckled the grassy plain with light, the horse slowed. Jonathon sat up. Only then did he see the color of the mane flowing over his hands; it was black with golden stripes.

"Rhohar!" he cried, elated. Rhohar flicked back his ears, whinnied, and stopped. Jonathon threw his arms around the horse's neck, then slid down his side, wondering if his feet would ever touch the ground. Once they did, Rhohar turned and thrust his muzzle into Jonathon's hair.

"You grew up," he said, remembering the long-legged colt. "And you've chosen me after all," he added, amazed. "Me!" What was the word his mother had used? Consent. Rhohar had consented. "I wish she could see us now," he said, stroking the horse's cheek.

Instead, he saw her in his memory as she stood chopping carrots at the kitchen table. It brimmed with herbs, bowls of cream, honey, and frothy eggs as well as pans of bread just out of the oven. She laughed, her eyes sparkling, and suddenly whirled him around the table.

Jonathon leaned his forehead against Rhohar and smiled, relishing his first joyful memory of her since she had died.

He opened his hand. The Farlith looked the same as before—still a red rock carved with a horse—unchanged by its journey through the mountain. Up on Kalivi, amber clouds dabbed the summit like beads tossed by the sunrise. The mountain lived inside him now, its root in the dark places of the earth, its peak touching the sky.

He put the Farlith in his pocket, wishing he had some of his mother's bread. How long since he had last eaten? Two days? He remembered the apple from the tree in the cavern. Jonathon took it out of his shirt and was so startled he almost dropped it. Stripes of gold glittered across the red apple, stripes of gold like those in Athira's hair, Rhohar's mane, and the Red Hart's antlers. Words from the *Ballad of the Firegold* flashed in his mind:

> Oh, apples sweet and red as wine
> And gold as a leaping flame.

This apple had to be a Firegold. Here in his hand was the treasure sought by generations of his family. No wonder they had never found it. They would never have dreamed of looking in the Red Mountains or, stranger yet, inside a mountain. Was the apple even real? It smelled sweet, felt heavy and solid in his hand. But what should he do with it?

Chi-chi! Chit-a-chi! a bird called, dipping and darting around him.

"Porter!" he shouted as the bird landed on Rhohar's head. The horse snorted.

"Well," said Jonathon, laughing. "If you two are ready, let's go find the others. And maybe some breakfast. I'm hungry, but I don't want to eat this apple." Considering its origin, the apple had to be magic, and the thought of eating it made him shiver. Besides, there was nothing else to show that Kalivi had ever happened: no blood on his shirt, no dirt on his hands, only the Firegold.

He climbed onto one of the flat boulders that littered the plain—the weather-sheared roots of an even older mountain than Kalivi—and threw his leg over Rhohar's back. The horse bolted down the plain. "I'm alive!" Jonathon sang as the sun wheeled higher. "Alive! Alive!" He had Sol Faringen.

Most of what had happened on the mountain he didn't understand, but, as Tlell would say, it was not the mind that understood such matters. Jonathon couldn't wait to see him. And what would Athira say when she saw him on Rhohar? She could no longer call him River Boy; he was a man now.

A half hour later, he rode toward the temporary shelter the Tendars ran for the returning Ridgewalkers. It was a place to rest and eat before riding southeast to join the main host of the Dalriadas waiting at High Summer Camp. Jonathon dismounted and found the shelter deserted. He knew the Tendars left on the fifth day of the Ridgewalk, but he had only been gone for a day. They must have left early. He decided to sleep before he tried to find the camp.

When he woke in the afternoon, he followed a trail scarred with the recent tracks of horses. He rode across the lumbering flanks of Kalivi, across water running from snowbanks, where buttercups flourished in the damp soil. The trees began to grow taller and closer together. As the day waned, he entered a canyon thick with aspens; the black ovals leered like eyes on the white bark. Rhohar slowed, his nostrils flaring. Jonathon smelled smoke. He rode forward until he saw two orange flames rising from a campfire; even as he looked, one flickered out. A man knelt beside the fire; he turned toward Jonathon and stood up.

"Rhohar?" Kiron asked, one hand pressing his heart. There was no small, contemptuous smile on his face now, only fear. "Is that you, Jhonan?"

"I'm back," Jonathon said, high on Rhohar. He felt triumphant.

"I was uncertain," Kiron said. "You ride like something out of a dream. I saw a shimmer of light that became a man and horse stepping out of the twilight. I thought it was some vision..." he stopped. "Joy that you have Sol Faringen, Atenar," he added, taking refuge in the ritual greeting, but he did not look joyful. "Rhohar chose...?"

"Me," Jonathon said.

Kiron's jaw tensed, and yet wonder filled his eyes. He seemed torn, at a loss. Something about him had changed; the bluster was gone, replaced by a heaviness in his face, a sag in his shoulders. His shaggy hair sleeked back from his temples, revealing his finely shaped head. He turned away, picked up a stick, and prodded the coals where he had something buried, roasting. The worn spot on the back of his tunic looked bigger.

Jonathon wondered whether he should ride on, but Rhohar dropped his head, looking for grass. Porter flew away through the aspens.

"I would be honored, Jhonan," Kiron said, "if you would share my meal."

Surprised, Jonathon dismounted and walked over to the fire, where Kiron offered him a bowl of roasted grouse.

"Thanks." Jonathon took it, then sat down. "Why was nobody at the Tendars' shelter?"

"They all left. You have been gone for six days."

"Six days!" Jonathon exclaimed.

"Yes. We counted you among the lost. No one in memory has Sol Faringen after so many days on the Mountain. I rode from High Summer Camp to the shelter hoping to find Elanae. I lingered there until dawn, then at last gave up all hope."

"I'm sorry," Jonathon said. "Elanae's arrows," he paused, remembering the one that had pierced the Red Hart. "Her arrows were true."

As they ate, they kept glancing at each other, aware of all that had shifted between them, but uncertain of what new tone to take.

"How many didn't Sol Faringen?" Jonathon asked.

"Fifteen—no, fourteen now—of the one hundred and thirty-nine. The Mountain was hungry this year."

"Barli? Halla—"

"I don't know. I saw only my grief."

There was a silence. Then Kiron added, "The Seers say that the greater the horse, the greater the challenges faced on the mountain."

Their eyes held until Jonathon looked away, scuffling one foot on the ground. When they finished eating, Kiron unrolled a grass mat, laid out his arrows precisely—the shafts parallel, the points lined up—and examined them for damage. Again Jonathon thought of Elanae; the pinnea she had given him still lay inside his breast pocket.

"You took one of the paths through," Kiron asked, "not over."

"There's a way over?"

"Several. Safer, if one wishes to avoid one's spirit rather than face it and learn." Kiron tested an arrow head.

Jonathon remembered the fork in the trail, the dank path he had bypassed. "But for Tlell and Elanae and...you—"

Kiron cocked an eyebrow with some of his old arrogance.

"—I wouldn't have made it," Jonathon finished in a rush.

"I'm not so certain," Kiron answered. "You might not have gone through, but you would have gone over. And a nag would have chosen you instead of Rhohar." Jonathon looked through the aspens, stark as ribs in the moonlight, but Rhohar and Wistar had run off somewhere. Kiron put one arrow down, picked up another, and ran the heel of his hand along the shaft.

"You're a man now, Jhonan," he said. Their eyes met again. For a moment, Jonathon saw red hair shimmer and dance between them. Tomorrow night was the Joining Night. Tomorrow night, Athira would choose one of them, only one of them.

Jonathon tilted his head back and looked at the familiar stars, glad he was no longer seeing them through the eye of the skull on Kalivi.

"I saw Elanae on the Mountain," he said softly.

Kiron's hand snapped shut over the arrow. "Tell me!"

"She was...riding the Red Hart."

Kiron pressed his hand to his breast. "You saw the Eldest?"

"Yes. And I heard Elanae sing."

"She spoke! She sang?" Joy replaced the grief in his eyes. "Then my little sister is well, though she will make me no more of these." He opened his hand and looked down at the arrow.

Then Jonathon too was staring at the arrow, at its unique pattern of fletching. Every detail—the vanes of speckled grouse, the cock feather of white swan, the red cresting on the shaft—pierced into his mind. The arrow blurred before his eyes; then he saw it again, embedded in a brown cloak on the snow.

"It was you!" Jonathon cried. "You killed my mother!"

chapter thirty-six

Jonathon snatched the arrow from Kiron's hand and sprang to his feet. "An arrow like this killed her!" he cried. "Only your arrows have this fletching."

"I—" Kiron stood up. "You speak the truth."

All thought seemed to stop in Jonathon's mind; his entire being focused in the sudden, raging pain in his forehead. He threw down the arrow and pulled his knife from its sheath.

"What I did was without honor," Kiron said. "I was just back from Kalivi, newly a man, full of myself and my strength. And full of rage that the dirtdwellers had stolen Rhohar." His eyes flicked to the knife.

When Jonathon tried to speak, something clawed in his throat.

"I was a fool who thought he was being a man," Kiron said, squinting at Jonathon's glowing antler-mark. "I regretted it long before you told us who she was. There was something about her courage, the way she stood alone, unarmed, facing us all...." he shook his head. "The Seers censured me for it. I should have told you myself, as Tlell urged."

"Tlell knew about this?" Jonathon exclaimed. "You're lying."

"I do not lie." Kiron yanked down his sleeve. "Everyone knew. Why do you think Tlell made me your Atenar? To take responsibility for what I had done to her, and to you."

Jonathon scraped his thumbnail back and forth along the knife's hilt, faster and faster, as though trying to dig a hole in the wood. He saw the stain spreading over his mother's cloak—the arrow above it twisting, blurring—then felt the hot pain in her heart, in his own heart.

"I know," Kiron said, "that I can never make amends for such a grievous loss. But I am sorry, and now I know how it must feel because—"

"Here's how it feels!" Jonathon shouted and charged forward, swinging his knife. Surprised, Kiron ducked. Jonathon spun around, then attacked again.

"Jhonan, wait!" Kiron jumped to the left; from his relaxed stance, he appeared to believe Jonathon posed no threat. Jonathon lunged. His knife slashed Kiron's golden tunic.

"Stop this!" Kiron said.

Jonathon switched his knife to his left hand and sliced Kiron's forearm from wrist to elbow. Blood ran down. Kiron yelled, at last reaching for his own knife, but Jonathon kicked his arm. A mistake, because Kiron grabbed his leg and wrenched it. Pulled off balance, Jonathon threw all his weight forward and, in a tangle of arms and legs, knocked Kiron over.

They rolled on the ground. A root jammed into Jonathon's ribs as Kiron pinned him, digging his fingers under the base of his skull. Pain shot through his head, but all the old lessons under the oak tree at Greengard came back to him. Jonathon shoved sideways with his shoulder and butted with his knee, twisting until he was on top. His knife arm was free. He shoved Kiron's jaw up, exposing his throat.

Now, Jonathon thought. Kill him.

A roaring filled his ears, and he seemed to be back inside the skull cavern on Kalivi. A thread pulled through his grandmother's loom, making the picture of this moment.

When the stitch tightened, this moment would become a part of forever that would not change. As Jonathon's knife poised, the pinnea fluttered from his pocket and landed on Kiron's throat. There it lay, white, fragile, its fragrance still fresh.

Elanae.

Jonathon jumped up and saw Rhohar beside the fire, his ears flattened. With a shout, Jonathon grabbed Cahaud and his quiver, then leaped onto the horse, who galloped away into the night. Jonathon's stomach churned, heaving with Kiron's grouse until he leaned over Rhohar's side and threw up. He took the Firegold out of his tunic—the white one Kiron had given him—then tore off the tunic and flung it away. The wind blasted against him. Although the cold air chilled his skin, it couldn't stop the burning inside him.

Horror rode with him, horror that he had wanted to be like Kiron, that he had admired the man who killed his mother. How could Tlell have kept the truth from him? Everyone knew. Halla. Siear. Athira....

"Barli," Jonathon cried. Even his best friend had said nothing. He thought of Mr. Landers, who also had seemed to be a friend but wasn't. Was the world full of people who deceived and betrayed? His mind turned black, and he seemed to be riding though a dark forest hung with webs, sticky webs of lies waiting to snag him. In the middle of the forest, his father held up the largest one of all. Jonathon blinked, shaking the vision from his head.

Rhohar ran where he willed; his speed never slackened. Above, the stars of the Cornucopia spilled like white stones across the sky. Even if I had known earlier, Jonathon thought, I wasn't strong enough then to challenge Kiron—like I am now.

You've got to be able to defend yourself, or someone else, he remembered Uncle Wilford saying. For a moment, Jonathon wondered if he had failed his mother by sparing Kiron's life. I was just back from Kalivi, newly a man, full of myself and my strength. And full of rage...Jonathon frowned. Those words applied to him, too.

There was a difference between killing for defense and killing for revenge—one was murder. In his fury, only Elanae had stopped him from that, only one white flower on a slender stem.

Jonathon began to sweat.

* * *

After midnight, he brought Rhohar to a halt beside a grove of yellow cedar. They watched the half-moon set behind a crag—an odd experience when only last night, or so it seemed to him, the moon had been full. For the first time, he really believed he had been on Kalivi for six days.

Jonathon found a sheltered spot inside the grove, broke off some branches, and made a bed for protection from the freezing air. He woke at dawn, still clasping the Firegold; by some miracle it hadn't been bruised during the fight. A stream bubbled nearby. When he knelt to drink, he saw dried blood on his hands and arms—Kiron's blood. He stared at the red-brown smears, then plunged his arms into the water and scrubbed them until his skin was raw.

Porter flew up.

"Sorry I ran off without you last night," Jonathon called, but Porter only scolded, darting off downstream to a salmonberry thicket.

"Breakfast." Jonathon's eyes lit up. After gorging on the berries, he tore a strip from his leggings and made a sling around his waist for the Firegold. Then he rode on. Last night, when he had let Rhohar run free, the horse had taken them farther east, closer to High Summer Camp.

At midmorning, Jonathon finally saw the tents sprawling over a chain of meadows. A glacier that he guessed was the lower tip of the Great Snake veered southward. His fingers tightened in Rhohar's mane, and he looked down at the golden stripes; for an instant, he saw red hair instead of black. He smiled, imagining Athira's joy and admiration when she saw him on Rhohar.

As they rode into the camp, he heard the music of pipes, harps, and drums. A group of Dalriadas held hands, singing and dancing in a long, snaking line that imitated the glacier. One little girl sat on her mother's shoulders holding up a red streamer that billowed out behind her.

"Rhohar! Rhohar!" People cheered when they saw the horse. They rushed forward, but as soon as they recognized Jonathon, they fell silent, their faces filling with astonishment, then disbelief. Jonathon sat straighter.

"Rhohar has chosen," a tall, bearded man cried, pressing his palm to his heart.

"Rhohar has consented," said another. Others took up the cry, passing it through the camp as if tossing a ball from hand to hand. "Rhohar has chosen. Joy that Jhonan has Sol Faringen!"

Someone elbowed through the crowd, and a familiar tousled head popped up by Jonathon's knee.

"Jhonan!" shouted Barli, brandishing a wooden spoon still dripping with gravy.

"Barli—you made it!" Jonathon slid off Rhohar and grasped Barli's shoulders. He glanced at Barli's soft boots, brown but not shiny. A moment later, Halla came running over and hugged him.

"Oh, oh," she said again and again, tugging on her braid with one hand while stroking Rhohar's nose with the other. Siear walked up. Neither he nor Barli wore a tunic. Instead, both proudly displayed the O-Bredann freshly cut over their hearts. Halla's was cut higher, above a wide band of leather laced around her breasts. Jonathon's own bare chest felt naked in comparison.

"We should have known our Jhonan would come home with the king of horses," Barli said.

"Think of the hunting you'll do with him," Halla said. "Even Kiron will not be able to match you."

"Your feet did not hurry, did they, Jhonan?" Barli waggled the spoon. "We thought the Mountain had gobbled you up in its belly. Just when I'd gotten you fattened up too. But I should have known you'd pop up in time for the feasting—

and the rest." He danced a few steps and grinned. "Gatea returned too. Her eyes have been sticking to me like sap."

Halla smiled. "Come and see our horses, Jhonan."

"You there, Dareth!" Barli handed his spoon to a small boy. "Watch the stew," he said, and then led the way to the horses. They were all conscious of the envious eyes of those a year younger. In a sprawling meadow east of the camp, the horses grazed freely, watched over by the Tendars.

"Her name is Bronwing." Barli pointed to a splendid white horse, perfectly proportioned, with powerful hindquarters, a flowing blonde mane and tail, and a mischievous glint in her eye. Jonathon looked at his friend with even-greater respect.

A dapple gray trotted up behind Bronwing. "That's Ikino," Siear said. Though a good horse by Valley standards, Ikino's ewe neck made him mediocre here.

Halla whistled a high, trilling note, and a jet-black horse with elegant lines trotted up, stepping high. Halla's wish had come true.

"Jhonan, meet Tralath," she said.

Even as he admired the horses, Jonathon eyed his friends, still baffled by their silence about his mother and Kiron. He would have to find the right time to ask them, but this wasn't it.

"Where is the Lady?" he asked instead.

"Off mourning somewhere," Barli answered.

Jonathon's hope surged. "Why?"

"She grieves for Elanae," Halla said. "And for the others who didn't Sol Faringen. As we all do."

"Oh," Jonathon said. "Right."

"The camp held the mourning ceremony last night," Siear added.

"But now there is one less to grieve for." Halla glanced sideways at Jonathon. "And tonight we celebrate life."

"Our tents are in the south meadow, along the copse," said Barli. "I have your saddlebags and gear. But now I must return to my fire. I'm sure that scalawag boy has burnt my stew. Boys!" He sniffed.

"Boy yourself until four days ago!" Halla teased.

"You cruel woman." Barli groaned. "Don't remind me. I—"

"Who is this fine young man?" a voice interrupted. Jonathon turned and saw Tlell, who looked at him with mock sternness, then grinned and embraced him.

"So," Tlell said to Rhohar. "You knew it too." He paused. "Your grandfather would have been proud of you, Jhonan. You learned much on the Mountain."

"Yes," Jonathon said. "But I learned one of the most important things after I came out." A question formed in Tlell's eyes. Jonathon looked at his teacher, and suddenly his doubts vanished. Whatever Tlell's reason for concealing what Kiron had done, it was a good reason, for Jonathon's good. As with his friends, they would talk later. Now, he wanted to find Athira.

With Porter following, Jonathon rode up a wooded rise and searched through the meadows until he spotted her in a field rippling with silver, green, and pale yellow grass. Athira stood with her back toward him. She nocked an arrow, drew, then held the bow at full draw, each movement flowing gracefully into the next. Jonathon had never seen her shoot before. When she released the arrow, it whoomped into the center of the target. He dismounted.

She heard him and glanced over her shoulder.

"River Boy," she said. Then the joy in her face changed to shock as she saw Rhohar standing beside him.

chapter
Thirty-seven

Athira ran up and touched Rhohar—his nose, his withers, his flank—then combed his mane with her fingers, examining the golden stripe.

"It is Rhohar," she said. "It really is."

"Hello." Jonathon pressed his hand to his heart. "I'm back."

She turned toward him. "How dare you ride Rhohar," she asked, her antler-mark throbbing. "You, a dirtdweller? He can't have chosen you. He can't!" All her dignity lost, she shook her bow in his face.

Jonathon stared at her, his stomach sinking. He turned away.

"Wait!" she called, but he walked the forty yards to the target and yanked out her arrow. Elanae had made it fitting for a queen; the vanes were goose feathers dyed gold, the cresting pure gold leaf.

Across the field, Athira slung her bow over her shoulder. She seemed miles away. She doesn't love me, Jonathon thought, rubbing the side of his head. How could she have said those things if she did? Nothing had changed—no matter what he achieved, he would always be a dirtdweller to her. As he walked back, he felt that even when he reached her, he would not meet her. He felt that the field could never be crossed, that the tall grass would swish forever against his leggings.

He gave her the arrow. "I'm a Dalriada now," he said. "I completed the Ridgewalk, and Rhohar did choose me."

"My words were unkind." Calm again, Athira smoothed a strand of hair behind her ear. "Forgive me. I was...startled. This is a grave matter that I don't think you understand." She paused. "Royal horses choose only those with royal blood."

Jonathon laughed. "Not this time."

She didn't laugh. "You are Megara. You have the Farlith and now you have Rhohar, too. All that you lack is the stripe of gold in your hair. And since your hair is all gold, who is to say?"

"What do you mean?"

"I mean," Athira said, "that amazing as it seems, perhaps you, Jhonan of the Valley, are meant to be king of the Dalriadas."

"Me?" Jonathon stared, laughing again, but the laugh emerged as a cross between a squeak and a cough. "I'm no king. Rhohar just remembers me from before. Besides, the Dalriadas already have a queen. You."

"Both can lead. If they are...." Her voice faded, and she tugged on her gold snake necklace as though it were choking her.

"What's wrong?" he asked.

Instead of answering, Athira looked out at the snow-creased ramparts to the north, then at Kalivi to the west. Sadness pulled down her face, but, as she kept looking at the mountain, her hand fell to her side. Her back straightened, and her face took on the strength of rock and ice and fire. She seemed like a bird who had instantly matured from fledgling to adult. For the first time, Jonathon knew how it felt to look at a queen.

Now resolute, her eyes appraised him as if she were seeing him in a new way too. Over the summer his body had hardened; his muscles had developed, and his voice had deepened.

"I see that my River Boy is a boy no longer," she said, twirling the arrow.

Their eyes held. She did love him! Heat zinged through Jonathon's body, making his skin tingle. The wind carried the music up from the camp, and the notes seemed to spin around them. When he reached for her, she gave a tiny smile and drew back.

"Find Owalen," she said. "He will give you the O-Bredann, the mark of a man. Then…." With two cold fingers she touched the bare skin over his heart. He tensed, staring at the curve of her chin, at the full red brows that arched above her eyes.

"I'll find Owalen right now," he said.

* * *

Jonathon was naked, standing before Owalen in the icy headwaters of the Mirandin River, where the Great Snake Glacier transformed to water. As he curled his toes over the wet stones, he wondered how long the water would take to flow down to Greengard, down to the place where the boulder split the river. He remembered his mother's words: *You're not a man yet, though I believe you're becoming a fine one.* Jonathon threw his shoulders back, determined not to flinch when the knife cut him; at the same moment, he thought of the bloody slash he'd made on Kiron's forearm.

Owalen chanted on and on, holding the knife high above his head. He wore a long blue tunic streaked with water around the hem. Beneath it, his bare calves were as thick as the ropes that climbers carried. Two pouches hung from a leather belt around his waist: one contained a mint salve that he had smeared over Jonathon's heart, the other a powder that would stain the scar red.

As a current of cold air swept off the glacier, Owalen stopped chanting and lowered the knife without touching Jonathon.

"I cannot give you the O-Bredann," he said.

"What? But why not?"

"I do not know. This has never happened before."

"But I completed the Ridgewalk," Jonathon protested. "The Red Hart came to me, and Rhohar chose me."

"The Red Hart?" Owalen raised his eyebrows, compressing the massive antler-mark on his forehead. "Usually the Eldest appears only to those destined to be Seers. There is no question that you have earned and are worthy of great honor." Gently, he placed his spotted hand on Jonathon's chest and listened. Around them, the new river skittered over the stones, surprised by its birth and its sudden escape from the ice. A chain of stepping stones didn't quite reach the far side.

Owalen shook his head, then sheathed his knife. "Your heart is not whole."

"I don't understand!" Jonathon exclaimed.

"It is not given to us to understand all things. I am sorry, but I cannot give the O-Bredann to one whose heart isn't whole. The reason may be that you are half Valley." Owalen paused, then added, "though your mother was given the mark."

"But this is my home now. I'm Dalriada, not Valley. No one in the Valley wants me."

"What about your father? Surely you are dear to him."

"My father," Jonathon's voice rose, "left me to die in the hills because my eyes were blue. The Valley has nothing to do with the Red Mountains. I have earned my place here."

"Yes, but a man is not half. I cannot give you the mark of a man."

Jonathon shivered. "Then you're telling me I must leave."

"No, Jhonan." Owalen gazed at him a moment, his pale cerulean eyes troubled. "I am saying that you must become whole. It is up to you to find the way." With that, he turned away and waded up toward the glacier.

Jonathon stood staring after him. Come back! he wanted to shout. Wait! A spasm of cold shook him; goose bumps reared on his skin. He turned, sloshing over the stones to the bank, where he grabbed his leggings and pulled them on.

Cast out.

He was cast out again, just when he thought he had found his place in the world. Exiled from the Valley, now he would be exiled from the Red Mountains too. He looked out at the white peaks with their forests like ruffled, green collars, then looked up at the sky. At this altitude, it was as blue and brilliant as a cornflower. He loved the Red Mountains, loved his life here. Why was everything he loved always taken away?

He reached for the Firegold's sling, then stopped with his hand in mid air. "Athira," he said, almost choking. Without the O-Bredann, there could be nothing between them. Jonathon picked up the Firegold and smelled it. He closed his eyes, took five deep breaths, and tried to call on the new strength he had found on Kalivi.

"I won't lose this place," he said. "If Owalen wants wholeness, whatever that means, I'll just have to get it somehow. Then I'll come back." But that plan seemed hopeless since he didn't know how or where he would find it, or even what *it* was.

In the south meadow by the copse, he found Barli's camping spot, recognizing the tent with its purple and orange flap and the dented copper pot simmering with stew over the fire. No one was there. Just as well, Jonathon thought, although he had wanted to say good-bye. Barli would have tried to persuade him to stay, but he had to go now, before the Joining Night began.

He stirred the stew once with the familiar wooden spoon. "Good-bye, Barli," he said.

Next to his gear lay a light saddle worked with twining leaves and flowers, and inlaid with gold along the edge. It had a high horn on the pommel which held the reins while a rider shot his bow. A saddle this magnificent could only be a gift for Rhohar, probably from Keelas or Tlell.

Hoofbeats sounded nearby, and Jonathon looked up. His jaw tightened when he saw Kiron riding along the other side of the meadow. Jonathon hurried now, taking a few loaves of bread—he didn't think Barli would mind—and repacking his saddlebags. He strapped on his quiver. Although his chest felt naked, he didn't pull on a tunic. "Let everyone see that Owalen wouldn't give me the mark," he muttered. "I don't care." He slung Cahaud over his shoulder, picked up the saddle and saddlebags, and went up to the horse meadow to get Rhohar.

Athira stood watching Rhoha and Rhohar chase each other through the grass, the chaser and the chased constantly switching in an elaborate dance.

"Lady," he said.

She turned, beginning to smile. "Oh, it's you," she said, her smile fading. Dressed for the feast, she wore the white deerskin dress and the two-pointed hat woven of red and gold. Her eyes dropped to his bare, unmarked chest.

"Why haven't you gone to Owalen?" she asked.

"I did."

"Then why hasn't he given you the O-Bredann yet?"

Because he is a fool! Jonathon wanted to shout, but he didn't. "Owalen says I'm not a man," he said, as steadily as he could.

"But you have Sol Faringen, you have Rhohar—"

"Owalen doesn't think all that's enough," Jonathon interrupted. He looked at her, imagining the night that would have been, certain she would have chosen him. But not now. He whistled, and Rhohar came trotting over. "I'm leaving," he added, saddling the horse.

Athira held her hands behind her back. "You can't—"

"Do you think I could stay here after this? Without the O-Bredann? Still considered a boy when I've done all and more than the others have?" Jonathon tightened the cinch. "And I'm won't stay here tonight and see you with Kiron."

"But—"

"No. I'm leaving. It seems I can't stay anywhere ever. Maybe I'll go to the Beyondlands."

She stood silently, as though weighing something in her mind. The sun sparkled on the snake necklace and flashed on the sapphire on her hat, making her regal with gold and blue light.

"I didn't say you can't leave," she said at last. "I meant that you can't take the Farlith or Rhohar away from the Red Mountains. I will not allow it."

Jonathon stared at her, appalled. She had been thinking about that when he had thought, had hoped, that she loved him?

"I see," he said. "But since I'm not considered worthy to be a Dalriada, I don't think you have any authority over me."

She shut her eyes, then opened them again. "Try to understand. I must do what is best for my people."

"But you don't really think of me as one of your people, do you? Even though an hour ago you were afraid I might be king."

Athira sighed.

"Look," Jonathon said. "Rhohar won't come with me if he doesn't want to. That's his choice, not yours."

"That is true," she said. As their eyes held, he remembered that hers were the first blue eyes, other than his own, that he had ever seen. That day when they had been children by the river in the Valley seemed like a long time ago, years and years ago.

He took the leather pouch from his pocket, held it in his hands a moment, then pulled out the Farlith.

"Here," he said, holding it out. "You're right about this. It belongs in the Red Mountains—Tlell says they're growing strong again. The Farlith stays. I want to know that it's here. That all this is here," he nodded at the surrounding peaks and swallowed hard. "And that it's well."

Reverently, Athira cupped the Farlith and pressed it against her antler-mark, standing with her head bowed. When she straightened, the little crinkles of tension around her mouth and eyes had disappeared.

"I honor you," she said. "We will be here and well, thanks to you. Return when you can, Jhonan," she added, still looking down at the Farlith. "You will always be welcome."

Jonathon threw his arms around her, his body pulsing with a wild, burning ache, but she didn't return his embrace. He vaulted onto Rhohar. As he rode away, he looked back over his shoulder and saw Kiron walking toward her. Jubilant, dancing, Athira ran to him with her hands cupped in prayer, holding the Farlith up to the sky.

chapter
Thirty-eight

His mind in turmoil, Jonathon rode toward the Beyondlands because he didn't know where else to go. He could live alone in the Red Mountains. He knew enough now to survive although he had doubts about the winter. No more people, no more people, Rhohar's hooves seemed to drum over and over. No more attempts to make himself into something other people wanted, only to be tossed away. If he lived alone, being a half-blood wouldn't matter, but to be always alone was more than he thought he could bear.

"She thinks I'm a king, just like you are," Jonathon said to his horse. If that were true, he was a king without a country, without a people, without even a home. Nothing had changed since he had left his grandmother at Highgate. Where is my life? Jonathon wondered, his shoulders sagging, but the only answer was the cry of the wind in the fir trees.

After five hours of hard riding, they stopped briefly while Jonathon pulled on more clothes. The sun had slid behind a summit to the west, leaving the air cold. He left his outer tunic unlaced so that Porter could curl up inside it. Then Jonathon mounted again. Something inside him was driving him forward, propelling him as if he were an arrow shot wildly in pain and anger, but toward what end? As the sky reddened, they galloped onto a pass with a sweeping, northern view, where the wind redoubled, becoming a roar. Rhohar halted and Jonathon looked out.

Below, beneath the uncertain slip of a waning moon, the Red Mountains melted into foothills. These rolled for many miles, then flattened, merging into the distant, misty line of the Beyondlands. They looked bleak.

"Is that where we're going?" he asked. Rhohar only flicked back an ear, and Porter, tucked inside Jonathon's tunic, didn't stir. Without thinking, Jonathon reached for the Farlith, then felt a sudden ache when he remembered it was gone. It couldn't guide him now. Instead, he took out the Firegold and pressed his thumb against its skin; still firm, still fragrant, the apple hadn't changed since he had picked it on Kalivi.

He knew how much it would mean to his father to see the Firegold, to see his dream and the dream of his ancestors come true. But was Brian Brae really his father? Did it matter? That thought startled him so much he dug one knee into Rhohar's side, and the horse looked round at him. Surely you are dear to him, Owalen had said. Jonathon fidgeted with the knot on the sling. Yes, his father had left him to die in the hills, but he had also raised him, protected him, and been willing to die for him—like the Red Hart. Jonathon felt that a piece of the puzzle was missing, as he had at Highgate when he'd tried to find the pattern on the ruined wall.

His hand tightened on the Firegold, and the golden stripes began to glow. He smelled earth, Valley earth, rich river-bottom loam. He saw rows of trees hung with fruit that gleamed like gems in the sunlight.

"Home," he said.

Suddenly Jonathon laughed at himself. In his despair at being denied the O-Bredann, he had forgotten what he had learned on Kalivi: the arrow must aim toward the heart's truth.

Here, over a hundred and fifty miles from Greengard, in sight of the Beyondlands, his heart urged him to take the Firegold home to his father—even if Brian Brae wasn't his father—to ask hard questions, and to run toward something instead of away.

You must become whole. It is up to you to find the way.

Still, Jonathon hesitated a moment longer. What if the farmers tried to kill him again? Then he smiled.

"I was wrong," he said. Something had changed since he had left his grandmother's. He had changed, even if the world had not. "Rhohar to Greengard!" he shouted. Wheeling sharply, Rhohar turned south.

*   *   *

At dawn, he stopped on a meadow overlooking a three-horned summit to the southwest and Kalivi to the east; it still dominated the skyline. While Rhohar grazed, Porter perched on a bush beside him, eyeing a stream that looped across the grass. Jonathon tried to sleep but kept wondering whether his father would welcome him or not. Surely you are dear to him...am I dear to him...played over in his head until he finally fell asleep.

Three hours later, he woke and ate some bread, but his jaw felt stiff, as heavy as a bucket full of lead. If everything had not gone wrong, he would have spent this morning with Athira. The thought he had refused to face last night tumbled out in the morning light: she had never loved him. She had wanted him only because he might be a king, and their union would strengthen the Dalriadas. Even while he glowered, part of him grudgingly admired her. She had been willing to sacrifice her love for Kiron to help her people.

With an effort, Jonathon dragged his attention back to the southwestern range. He feared that any route he chose to the Valley might end in impassable cliffs, resulting in endless backtracking. He was tempted to return through Highgate and see his grandmother again, but afterward he would have to travel down the Mirandin through a gauntlet of Valley folk. With Rhohar and Cahaud, not to mention his strange clothes, blue eyes, and antler-mark, he would be certain to draw unwanted notice. The best course was to swing southwest, around Sleeping Fire Mountain, through the Hills of Enchantment, and then down the Ptarmigan Ridge. But he didn't know the way, and that brought him right back to his original problem—those impassable cliffs. He sighed.

Porter squawked and flew into the air as hooves thumped across the north side of the meadow. For one ecstatic moment, Jonathon thought that Athira had come after him, but it was only Kiron riding Wistar.

"Atenar," Kiron called.

Wary, Jonathon stood.

"I have caught up with you at last," Kiron said. "Swift as Wistar is, he cannot match Rhohar's speed. I feared we would never catch you." Shadows smudged his eyes, but he didn't look angry or act as though Jonathon had tried to kill him two days ago. The only sign of their struggle was a bandage on his forearm.

"What do you want?" Jonathon asked.

"It's three weeks hard riding to your part of the Valley—"

"How did you know I'm going there?"

"You started north for the Beyondlands, then turned. Riding south southwest where else would you be going? But you don't know the country. I do. There are rough places. So I'm coming with you for part of the way."

"But—"

"Nothing you say will change my mind."

"What about," Jonathon said, "what about Athira?"

Kiron dismounted. "I have been waiting for Athira since I was five. I can wait a little longer." He loosened the cinch on the saddle. "Tlell caught Barli and Halla about to ride after you. He persuaded them to let me come instead."

"So Tlell sent you."

"No. I came of my own choosing."

Jonathon rolled his foot back and forth in the grass.

Although he no longer wanted revenge, he neither trusted Kiron nor wanted anything to do with him. The impassable cliffs rose before his eyes again; with guidance, the journey would go faster. Jonathon didn't know how long the Firegold would last.

"Listen," Kiron said. "I don't know what happened between you and Owalen, but I consider you a man, O-Bredann or no. Rhohar is proof enough of that."

Surprised, Jonathon patted Wistar's nose.

"Besides," Kiron said, grinning, "I would lose every shred of honor if I let my Atenar go back to the Valley looking like a starved rabbit."

Jonathon remembered the cold spring day when they had first met. "All right," he said, though he remained wary.

While Kiron ate, they discussed possible routes. They had just decided upon one, when they heard a splash and saw Porter fly up from the stream with a fish in his mouth.

"Kiron," Jonathon began, but stopped, and tore off a strip of jerky.

"What?"

"The queen thinks I may be…a king."

"So does Rhohar," Kiron said dryly. "So, actually, do many of us."

Jonathon blinked. "You?"

"Yes."

"But would you accept a…dirtdweller for your king?"

"I no longer think of you as a dirtdweller. I underestimated you, Atenar, in many ways. I will not make that mistake again."

Jonathon raised his eyebrows. Kiron was full of surprises today.

"Then I shouldn't leave," Jonathon said. "But I can't stay either, not now, not until…." He shut his eyes. He was tired of being half Valley and half Dalriada, tired of not being whole.

"If you are a king, you are—leaving won't change that. And you've already done your people a great service by returning the Farlith."

My people? Jonathon dropped the jerky.

"So seek what you must," Kiron added. "Someday you'll return, and I for one will be glad of that day."

"Now that you're sure of Athira," Jonathon said.

Kiron looked at him, his storm-blue eyes honest. "Yes," he agreed. Then he yawned. "I must sleep a while." With one hand on his bow, he stretched out on the grass and closed his eyes. Jonathon was amazed that Kiron trusted him that much.

Not feeling that trusting himself, Jonathon climbed up a crag behind the meadow and looked out at the mountains he had grown to love. "I'll be back," he said. Everything I love is always taken away, he had thought when Owalen had denied him the O-Bredann. Now, Jonathon realized the truth: the Red Mountains were a song inside him, and no one, no mark or ritual withheld, could ever take them away.

Two hours later, they were ready to ride.

"Jhonan," Kiron said.

Jonathon turned and saw Kiron standing five feet away, his knife in his hand. Part of Jonathon wanted to laugh. His ordeal on the mountain had taught him to face whatever threats he had to face. Didn't Kiron understand that yet?

Kiron turned the knife, extending it hilt first. "Take it," he said.

"What for?"

"My knife has held your life breath since the day we first met," Kiron said. "Take it now and wash it in the stream. Then you'll be free of its power."

Jonathon eyed him coldly. "Wash your own knife."

"It will have no meaning unless you do it."

Jonathon opened his mouth to refuse, when the sun flashed on the blade. He blinked. As though in a dream, he took the knife, walked toward the stream, and knelt, plunging the blade into the icy water. The cold stung his hand. Twigs, leaves, and a few mayflies floated past on the current. He remembered how his breath had fogged the blade and felt a sudden relief as the water poured over the metal. His reflection in the stream seemed to sharpen. He rose and gave the knife, still dripping, back to Kiron. Their eyes locked.

"All is now well between us, Jhonan," Kiron said quietly. "As well as it can ever be, I think."

Jonathon shook the water from his hand. "Agreed," he said, and the two men mounted their horses and rode toward the South Valley.

chapter
Thirty-nine

Jonathon stopped Rhohar on the edge of the sagebrush flat and looked down on Greengard. The cultivated patchwork of green—jade, olive, moss—startled his eyes, accustomed as they were to the wilder land of the Red Mountains. At least one thing was familiar—the blue Mirandin winding through the Valley. He could hear the river's steady din.

"Are we home?" he asked. Rhohar pawed the ground, making eddies of dust that smelled of sagebrush and cattle, while Porter squawked and flew off his perch on the saddle horn. Kiron had left them a week ago. To the north, many miles away, the tip of Kalivi Mountain shimmered on the horizon, but Jonathon saw only Greengard.

Even though he was looking down at his home, it still seemed far away. The house looked as small as the birdhouse he had built for his mother, and the round window in the attic twinkled like a distant star. Directly below him was the pasture where he had planted the Ruby Spice trees; from up here on the flat, their leaves had the same nubbly texture as one of his grandmother's tapestries. The sweet, heavy scent of ripe fruit came lilting on the air.

Jonathon noticed a band of brown beyond the cornfield and stood up in his stirrups to get a better look. The Greentales, the most productive crop on the orchard, leaned against each other, hacked, pulled down, their leaves brown and dying. Farther south, some of the Penna Pears had been ravaged too—their roots pointed toward the sky. Over half the orchard had been laid waste. What had happened?

He squeezed his legs around Rhohar, who started down the hill. Heat writhed up from the dust, and the Ruby Spice trees wavered, then disappeared. Instead, Jonathon saw a woman shove a boy between bales of straw; saw a colt with a golden striped mane run across a pasture; then saw the woman hurry forward with her palm held up, her cloak awhirl. Jonathon and Rhohar plunged down the hill toward them. Down and down they rode, skirting boulders and brush, until with a great leap Rhohar sailed over the deer fence. When Jonathon was in midair, the vision faded, and the Ruby Spice trees stretched before him again.

He slowed Rhohar to a walk, noticing the lushness of the leaves, the redness of the fruit. They turned the corner by the old barn, and Rhohar whinnied. Out of the trees stepped a statuesque young woman with a braid the color of corn crowning her head. She didn't run when she saw him but stood with her face uplifted, her feet firmly planted.

"Jonathon!" she cried. "You've come home!"

"Rosamund?" he asked, blinking. She wasn't a little girl any longer. He slid off Rhohar, and they smiled at each other.

"Just look at you," she said. "You look like something out of a song. What a beautiful horse!"

"Thanks." He paused while she stroked Rhohar's muzzle. "Rosamund, what's happened here? I was up on the hill just now and saw the Greentales. Was it the blight?"

"No," she said. "It was those horrible men. After you and your father left, they came over and tore up the orchard."

"It made me so mad!" she added, bunching her skirt in her hands. "All that about you bringing the blight. I knew you'd never hurt anyone. So I..." her voice drifted off.

"What?"

"I came out and made them stop."

"You?"

Rosamund nodded. "I told them the land would be worth more intact, and they should try to get it for themselves—I thought it would buy time until your pa got back. I knew their greed was the only way to make them stop.

Jonathon stared at her. He wasn't the only one who had faced danger.

"Then your pa came home with the waiver," she said. "They couldn't do anything then."

"What are you doing here now?"

"Well, I...." Rosamund swung her toe, tracing circles in the dirt. "I live here now."

Again, Jonathon stared.

"I left my father's house," she explained. "I refused to live with someone who would do such things. When your pa came home, he told me I could live here as long as I wanted. That was nice, because he's poor now you know, and not well. I—I hope you don't mind." She glanced at him shyly.

"I don't mind," Jonathon said, his heart in his throat, barely able to speak.

She looked away. "I walk out here by the Ruby Spice trees sometimes because this was where..." she paused. "You probably don't remember that day we planted the tree."

"I remember. Look what I brought home." Jonathon reached into the sling around his waist and handed her the Firegold.

"How wonderful!" she said. "The gold is almost like lace over the red. What kind of apple is it?"

"It's a...Firegold."

Her eyes shone. "Like the ones in the old stories, the magic apples?"

He nodded, and she raised it slowly to her lips as though

in a trance. Surprised, fearing what the magic might do, Jonathon reached out to stop her when a blow on his side knocked him to the ground. A boot swung toward his chest. He flung up his arms, deflecting part of the kick, but it still left him gasping. Rhohar reared, his hooves flailing. Then a young man with curly black hair grabbed Rosamund. It was Timothy Dakken.

"That apple's poison," Timothy shouted. "Don't eat it, Rosamund!" They fought for the apple, while Jonathon staggered to his feet with one hand clutching his ribs; it hurt to breathe.

"Jonathon!" called Rosamund, raising her arm. "Catch!" Her forearm swung back; her lace sleeve slipped down, and she threw the apple. When Jonathon caught it, the golden stripes began to glow.

"It isn't poison," he said and bit into the apple. Sweet, tangy, almost sparkling juice ran over his tongue. The apple tasted as fresh as spring, with hints of nectar and cinnamon. His eyes blurred. He saw the peaks, glaciers, and flowering meadows of the Red Mountains. He saw the orchards, vineyards, and fields of the Valley. He felt the water flow from Kalivi and journey down into the Valley soil, where the two joined with a powerful magic to bring life to the land.

Again, he bit the apple. With its roots in the earth and its branches in the sky, the Firegold Tree formed a bridge between the two. Jonathon felt something snap together inside him.

Lines from the *Firegold* ballad flashed in his mind:

> The world was whole, a garden green;
> The Tillers and Makers were one.
>
> Eat of the Firegold from the Tree!
> The earth rejoins the sky.
>
> The Song in the World shall soar!
> The Firegolds bloom forever more.

The Dalriadas called themselves the people of the sky.

Now Jonathon understood! He was whole, both Valley and Dalriada, as all the people had been in the Golden Age before the great rift. He had always been whole, but since he'd denied first his Dalriada half and then his Valley half, he had never realized it before. Why should he have to choose one or the other? He could be both—he was both. They could live together inside him.

Juice from the apple dripped onto Cahaud. Spellbound, Rosamund and Timothy watched as the golden inlay grew brighter and brighter, glowing with a fierce light. Tlell had said that Cahaud was made from the First Tree, the Tree that Grows No More. That tree, Jonathon guessed now, was a Firegold. He took bite after bite until only the core remained. His ribs no longer hurt, and though the heat burned in his forehead, it didn't ache.

"Let me go!" Rosamund said, elbowing Timothy.

"You're coming with me," Timothy said. His lower lip twisted in a permanent scowl—a result of his father's beatings.

"Leave her alone," Jonathon said.

"Go back where you came from, barbarian."

"I have. Now leave her alone."

"She's mine," Timothy said. "Like I told you a long time ago."

"I don't belong to anybody, Timothy Dakken." Rosamund slipped from his grasp and ducked into the orchard. When Timothy tried to follow her, Jonathon blocked his way.

"Don't," Jonathon said.

Timothy stared at Jonathon's bow, knife, and necklace of bear teeth. Then he glanced at Rhohar, who still showed the whites of his eyes. With his fists bunched, Timothy sidled away and ran toward Ironhill.

Jonathon took two steps after Rosamund before he realized he was still holding the apple core.

"What did I do?" he said. How could he have eaten the Firegold before his father saw it? And after bringing it all this way to show him? Jonathon sighed, dug each golden seed from the apple's core, and dropped them in his pouch. He aimed toward the place where he thought his mother had died and tossed the core into the Ruby Spice trees. At that moment, he heard the supper bell ring in its old, gay rhythm—only his mother rang the bell that way.

"Ma?" Jonathon said, then sprang onto Rhohar. As they rode off, Porter came flying up and clutched Jonathon's shoulder.

* * *

A few minutes later, Jonathon dismounted and stared at the rusty, iron bell on the porch; it hung heavily, motionless. No one was around. Light flashed off the round attic window, and he saw something move behind the glass. His father? Why would he be in the attic? Rosamund had said he wasn't well.

Inside the house, Jonathon ran upstairs as the grandfather clock chimed the quarter hour. The severe eyes of the Brae ancestors looked out at him from their gilt-encrusted frames. He hurried down the hall, passed his old room, and started up the attic stairs with Porter flying behind him. Dust coated the steps. The same faint fragrance, sharp yet sweet, still lingered in the air; only now it seemed familiar. When he reached the landing, Jonathon glanced at the portrait hanging in the shadows. The man's flat, brown eyes stared blankly back.

Jonathon touched the frame, tracing the intricate carving. On the top, a snake writhed through stars and moons; on the bottom, a deer's antlers swept up and curved into a tree—a tree laden with apples. Jonathon shut his eyes, breathing fast. He saw, quite clearly, the carved door on Kalivi Mountain; the carving was the same. He opened his eyes, lifted the portrait off the wall, and carried it the last few steps up to the attic.

Light streamed through the round window. Hot, stale air hovered over him as he looked around for a place to put the picture. Stacked along the walls beneath the sloping roof, were crates, trunks with battered brass corners, baskets, a dressmaker's dummy, and a rusted bed frame. Mice had nested in the cushions of a once-grand, rose brocade sofa. Beside it, a three-legged chair leaned against the wall.

Porter perched on top of an old, paint-spattered easel.

Jonathon walked over, put the painting face down on the ledge, and pried open the backing wood with his knife. After it popped off, he slid out the painting, which had ornate writing scrawled in the lower left corner:

> Raymont Brae of Greengarden. Self-Portrait.
> Bastard son of Amberly Brae.
> The Year of the Ninety-Eighth Council.

"Greengarden?" Jonathon said. "The ninety-eighth Council?" That was nearly four hundred years ago. He flipped the painting over and stared at the man, at the flat eyes with no black pupil, no highlight of white; they seemed odd compared to the other finely rendered brush strokes. With the tip of his knife, Jonathon scraped at one of the man's eyes. Chip by chip the brown paint flaked off until he saw black underneath and then...blue.

Blue.

Someone had painted over the eyes. When Jonathon had chipped away every trace of brown, the man in the painting seemed to spring out, his face suddenly alive, with something both resigned and desperate around the mouth. Jonathon stepped back.

It was the hooded man who had haunted his dreams, the man who had appeared to him on Kalivi—whose face was an older version of his own. In the painting though, the man looked only eighteen or nineteen. The white flower clasped in his hand was a pinnea, and Jonathon realized that the sweet, sharp smell that had always haunted the attic was the scent of the pinnea. The man's other hand was open, the palm up.

"But how?" Jonathon asked. "How?" He saw something jammed beneath the frame's inner edge and pulled out a gold, heart-shaped locket on a chain. It flashed, glittering. He remembered a sweep of scarlet against the night; remembered stately music and the gleam of candlelight on honey-colored hair; remembered the locket falling forward from Amberly's neck in his dream at the old Middlefield Inn.

He slipped his thumbnail into the clasp. The locket sprang open, and a twist of hair fell into his hand—dark red hair with stripes of gold. Jonathon clutched it, then bent toward the picture; Raymont's hair had been painted over too.

The attic seemed to spin, and for a moment Jonathon saw a shuttle dart across his grandmother's loom. Now he knew why Rhohar had chosen him: the blood of Dalriada kings ran in his veins. Athira's words echoed in his ears: A king's envoy journeyed to your great gathering place...the envoy fell in love with a Valley woman. They conceived a child and the dirt-dwellers killed him. No one remembers what became of the woman or their child....

Jonathon touched the picture. Raymont Brae was the child of that love, the child of Amberly and the Dalriada envoy, the taint of Greengarden that had become Greengard to guard its secret. Raymont had inherited the golden stripe, which made him a king...it isn't passed in a straight line, Athira had said. Was it he who started the search for the Firegolds, knowing they would make him whole?

"Jonathon?" his father cried from the doorway. His face was pinched, with a yellow tinge, and he stooped a little. The light from the window fell on his boots, illuminating the scrolls tooled on the leather. "I saw Rhohar, but I didn't believe....Why are you up here in the attic?"

Jonathon stared at his father—his father who loved trips to the Red Mountains, who had knowingly married a woman half Dalriada, who was descended from the blue-eyed king in the portrait. Then Jonathon's stomach cramped, and he didn't know whether to laugh or cry or shriek because his father was his father—and part Dalriada too.

"Look," Jonathon said, stepping away from the painting.

"This is Raymont Brae. Remind you of anybody?"

His father looked. His eyes moved from the picture to Jonathon, then back to the picture.

"Earth's Mercy," he said and walked up to the easel. Jonathon leaned Cahaud against the wall, unstrapped his quiver, and pulled off his tunic. He held out his knife, hilt first.

"Take it, Pa," he said. "Give me the O-Bredann."

"The what?" His father's eyes were still locked on the picture.

"The mark like Ma's—over her heart."

His father looked at him.

"I went to Kalivi Mountain," Jonathon said.

"You did?" His father took the knife, testing the edge with his thumb. "I have a mark too." He rubbed the scar above his eyebrow. "Karena gave me this."

"Ma did! Why?"

He sighed. "Two days after you were born, I took you from her side while she was asleep. I took you up Black Canyon and—"

"I know." Jonathon said, his voice hollow. "You left me to die."

"No!" His father's shoulders tensed, then sagged. "And yes," he added.

Jonathon started to turn away, then, in the sudden silence, thought he heard the ring of hooves on rock in the cavern on Kalivi. He turned back and looked straight at his father, waiting.

"The midwife had spread the word all over," his father said at last. "Curse her. Dakken tried to stir up trouble, said folks couldn't risk having another loony-blue around. There was talk, ugly talk about following the old law, the old ways. I was...afraid."

"You?" Jonathon asked, finding that hard to imagine.

His father nodded. "Those blue eyes meant you might grow up to be a full-fledged Dalriada—antler-mark and all. If anyone learned the truth, you and your ma would both be killed." He paused. "And I was furious—with your ma. I didn't understand how you could have been born with blue eyes unless she—unless you weren't my son—though I do now." He glanced at the portrait.

"What a nightmare," he continued. "I was out of my mind. So I took you and rode into the hills. There was a tree…" he closed his eyes. "A strange tree. I climbed way up and found a hollow, a kind of cradle in the wood. I put you in it."

Jonathon linked his hands behind his back to keep them from shaking.

"I left you there," his father said. "But as I rode I kept seeing you in my mind. You were so small and helpless. I remembered how your hand curled around my thumb. After maybe five miles, I rode back and got you."

"But Mr. Landers said you came back without me," Jonathon said.

His father nodded. "I rode up to the Wildcat Hills and left you with Old Man Craven."

"Craven!"

"Your ma had always been kind to him, so he agreed to hide you until I could get a dispensation from Middlefield. When I got home she came at me with a knife before I could tell her the plan. Lucky for me she was still weak from the birth, or I'd have ended up looking like Dakken—or worse."

Jonathon's father tapped the hilt, looking at the floor, then the ceiling. "But Jonathon, I came to…care for you. At first because you were hers. And later…well, for you. For yourself. I never understood how much until I thought I might lose you too."

A wave of warmth spread through Jonathon, flowing out to his fingers and toes until he was almost light-headed. "Give me the mark now, Pa," he said. He barely felt the sting as the knife cut his skin. When his father finished, Jonathon glanced down at the two shallow slashes with the long swirl beneath, all welling with blood.

"I'm glad you're home, son," his father said, handing him a handkerchief. "You've really grown up." Then his eyes, half pleased, half horrified, looked back at the portrait, and he picked up the hank of hair lying on the easel.

"I brought you something." Jonathon took out his pouch, unlaced it, and poured seven golden seeds into his father's hand.

"They look like apple seeds," his father said, "but gold? Did you paint them?" Suddenly his eyes lit up, and his hand snapped shut around the seeds. "No. They can't be—?"

Jonathon nodded. "Firegold seeds."

His father sat down abruptly on the old sofa. "With these we can—you've saved the orchard, saved us. But how? Where?"

"It's a long story," Jonathon said, dabbing at the blood on his chest. Sweating in the hot, still air, he walked over to the round window, where his reflection looked back, sharp and clear. He turned the latch and pushed, but nothing happened. Then, as he leaned into it, the hinges yielded, and the window swung open. Fresh air poured into the attic. Porter flew like a streak into the sky.

Jonathon looked out over the orchard rows; over the barn, shed and pasture beyond; over Coyote Road and the aspens snaking up the canyon between the sagebrush hills. White clouds spread across the horizon, softening the hard line between the land and the sky. All edges seemed soft, blending into one another—even the mix of light and dark in the leaves of the old oak creaking nearby. Over everything, binding it all together, was the distant roar of the Mirandin. Truly, he had Sol Faringen.

Like a gate opening, his heart flooded with joy. He knew he could ride between the Valley and the Red Mountains whenever he wished. The two couldn't be separated inside himself.

He would stay in the Valley and plant the Firegold seeds, use his gift of Making, as Tlell called it, to help the trees grow. Maybe their magic could make the world whole again, could close the rift between the Valley folk and the Dalriadas, as it had in him.

"Cheeky critter," a voice exclaimed. Down in the yard, Uncle Wilford was looking at Porter, who had landed on top of Rhohar's head.

"Uncle Wilford!" Jonathon shouted. "I'm home!"

The old man looked up. His dry, crinkled face lit.

"Rosamund said you were back, Jonathon," he called, pushing up his hat. "It's about time you came home. I thought I was going to have to go chasing after you and get another perfectly good hat ruined."

This book's text was set in 12/13 Adobe Garamond type,
a modern reinterpretation of Claude Garamond's
original old style text face.